The Quilt Left Behind

a novel by

Ann Hazelwood

American Quilter's Society

www.AmericanQuilter.com

Located in Paducah, Kentucky, the American Quilter's Society (AQS) is dedicated to promoting the accomplishments of today's quilters. Through its publications and events, AQS strives to honor today's quiltmakers and their work and to inspire future creativity and innovation in quiltmaking.

EXECUTIVE BOOK EDITOR: ELAINE BRELSFORD
COPY EDITOR: ANN HAMMEL
PROOFING: HANNAH ALTON
GRAPHIC DESIGN: LYNDA SMITH
COVER DESIGN: MICHAEL BUCKINGHAM

American Quilter's Society

PO Box 3290
Paducah, KY 42002-3290
americanquilter.com

Additional copies of this book may be ordered from the American Quilter's Society, PO Box 3290, Paducah, KY 42002-3290, or online at shopAQS.com

Library of Congress Control Number: 2020932379

Dedication

I'd like to dedicate this book to my youngest son, Jason Meyer Watkins. He lives in New York and is an editor for *Saturday Night Live*. His special interest in my career has been helpful and meaningful. He encourages me to think outside the box with my endeavors. I frequently call him my hero, and he knows why. Thank you!

Of course, my biggest fan is my husband, Keith Hazelwood. He is not only there for heavy lifting these days but is also my best promoter. Thank you, sweetie!

I'm lucky to have family, friends, and loyal readers to give me the courage to keep on writing. Thank you all so much!

Ann Hazelwood

Crazy Quilt Block

Chapter 1

"You what? Did you say that you've added twenty-two quilts to your quilt room in the shop?" Karen asked in disbelief.

I nodded and smiled.

"Now, there's got to be a story to that," Bonita responded. "I guess I'm going to learn a lot about these Dinner Detectives."

"Did I hear you say Dinner Detectives?" Randal asked as he brought our coffee order to our round table at Kate's Coffee.

We chuckled.

"That's right, Randal." I nodded. "I'd like to inform you of our other mission in life. You know Betty, Carrie Mae, and Karen, but we are more than just wine country folks!"

"Randal, this is Bonita," Karen said. "She's from Honduras and is learning about possible ways to help the unfortunate in the rural areas there. I wanted her to meet Lily, since she's in the quilting business."

"Welcome to Augusta," Randal said, shaking Bonita's hand. "I want to warn you that hanging out with these detectives may get you into trouble."

We laughed.

"Don't I know!" Bonita responded with a chuckle. "They've got me excited about more than quilting. I'm learning all about Doc and Rosie, too."

"Ah, nonsense, I say," Randal said, waving his hand as he went back to the kitchen.

We all loved meeting at Kate's Coffee, but at our last meeting, we'd gathered for dinner at my house. Our main mission was to figure out more about the ghostly Doc who seemed to haunt me. Betty and Carrie Mae were the brave ones who had helped me figure out some information about the doctor. Karen knew of the challenge and wanted to help. When Bonita first came to visit, she had also picked up on the feeling that others were in the house. She was quickly informed about Doc and Rosie, who had made their presence known. We happened to be meeting the same night that lightning hit Doc's office. Karen and Bonita had gone home before the lightning hit Doc's house in the early morning hours. You can imagine how shocked they were to hear what had happened.

"So, did you win a lottery ticket to be able to buy all these quilts?" Bonita asked in her warm Spanish accent. "That's a lot of money," she said, rolling her fingers. "Tell me more, if you don't mind sharing."

"This happened through the generosity of my friend, Butler," I explained. "Carrie Mae introduced me to him because he brokered high-end quilts around the world. To make a long story short, he moved on to marketing another product, and he asked if I would try to move some of his quilt inventory. It's a fabulous opportunity for me, because I can't afford to buy quilts of this caliber."

"You must see them, ladies," Carrie Mae chimed in. "Lily's red-and-white quilts are special, but Butler's quilts are the cream of the crop, you might say."

"We should try to do that before you leave town, Bonita," Karen responded with excitement. "Maybe I'll get some design ideas for my barn quilts."

"Did you say there is a wine country barn quilt tour coming up?" Bonita asked Karen.

Karen nodded. "In late summer, I think," she replied. "I'm leaving that all up to Buzz, my sweet husband. I think August would be a good time. It gets too busy around here in the fall."

"That would be really cool, Karen," I said. "It's also an excellent time to see the countryside."

"Do you have an artist for the Plein Air Art Festival this weekend?" Karen asked as she bit into her blueberry muffin.

"Yes," I answered. "I can't remember her name, but she painted a wonderful scene of Doc's house last year. I ended up buying it."

"Yup, that's what happens," Betty laughed. "Observers fall in love with a scene or place and buy the painting, sometimes even before it's done. The event is a win-win for everyone involved. I hear they have expanded to include more artists this year."

"Hopefully it will bring more people into the shops and restaurants," I said. "The winter was pretty brutal, so I'm hoping spring sales will make up for it."

"We have some artists who come to the streets on the weekend in my community, but no one can really afford to buy," Bonita added. "We have to depend on tourists, so when they aren't there, it's hopeless."

I was about to suggest some craft ideas to her when Randal showed up at our table and sat down.

"Did they finish the back of Doc's house yet?" he asked after he'd refilled our coffee.

"Almost," I said with hope in my voice. "It's really just an exterior project. Thank goodness the inside of his office just had smoke damage. I even picked up some of the smell in the house. I think I finally have it aired out."

"You will be eternally grateful to Snowshoes for seeing that bolt of lightning that hit Doc's office on his way to work," Randal assessed. "Calling the firemen early saved the office, and maybe even your house."

"So true!" I said, shaking my head as I recalled that dreadful stormy night.

"I'm surprised it didn't happen when we were still there," Bonita responded. "Some of that lightning seemed to come right into your house at one point. It scared me half to death."

"I thought it was Doc talking back to us," Karen joked. "If he heard our conversation, he may have wanted to react."

"I think I need to let Doc rest for a while," I suggested.

"And put us out of a job?" Betty teased.

"There's always Rosie!" I reminded her. "She would love some attention."

"She is your friend from the city that Karen told me about?" Bonita questioned.

"Yes. She came with the inventory I brought from her estate after she was killed," I explained. "She, like Doc, had a violent death, but she seems to be at peace, and I feel she is there to protect me. Oh, I miss her."

Chapter 2

"Hello, guys!" Judy greeted us as she came out of the kitchen. "Is anyone up for some rhubarb cobbler that just came out of the oven?"

"I'd love to taste it!" I responded quickly. "I've never had that before."

"It sounds delicious!" Bonita said.

"Oh, my mother made lots of things out of rhubarb," Betty recalled. "Some I could do without. Why don't you bring us one nice serving so we can all try it?"

"Sure," Judy agreed. "It's a treat from Randal, so if you want your own piece, just speak up. Lily, don't forget that we're going to the new knitting shop on Monday," she reminded me before she returned to the kitchen.

"Oh, I want to see it too," Karen said. "I used to knit, but I don't have time anymore."

"It's too hot for knitting where I come from," Bonita added.

"I sure wish we could have found that owner a place here in Augusta to open her shop," voiced Carrie Mae. "We need more specialty shops like that. I hope Gracie continues to do well with her quilt shop."

"I'm taking Bonita to meet Gracie tomorrow," Karen said. "Bonita will be impressed."

"Yes, I want to take some supplies back with me if I have room," Bonita said with excitement.

"Well, the quilt class certainly supports Gracie," I said. "She'll be happy to tell you what the basics are for beginners. In our quilt class, we're all making blocks to make a wine country quilt for ourselves. Susan said that if we like, we can make an extra one for a quilt to put in the library."

"That's a great idea," Karen said.

"I decided to do all of mine in redwork embroidery," I revealed. "I don't have much of a fabric stash, and I think it will be good to work on when I'm not busy with customers in the shop. It's an inexpensive craft which might be good for you and others to learn, Bonita."

"I see," Bonita responded, but she looked a bit unsure about the details of the conversation.

"It will certainly complement your red-and-white quilt collection," Betty said. "When I was young, I did all redwork blocks in different flowers. I liked not having to change colors as I worked."

"Oh, Betty, do you still have it?" I asked with interest.

"I really don't know what happened to it," Betty said after thinking for a moment. "I may have left it behind with some other things of Mom's on her farm years ago."

"If you ever find it again, I'd love to see it," I said.

"If it's still around, it's up in the attic," Betty replied.

"So redwork is an old craft?" Bonita asked innocently.

"Embroidery has been around forever, but when red

embroidery floss became dye fast in 1880, folks started just using red thread to outline images."

"Interesting!" Bonita responded.

"I embroidered when I was younger," Karen told us. "You have to practice on a regular basis to do nice stitches. I really can't handle any more stuff to store at our house. When I got Mom's things, I got her mother's things as well. We'll never use all those quilts or linens."

"What about the other members of your family, Karen?" I asked.

She gave a big sigh. "Trust me, they don't want them," she replied sadly.

"I don't own such things," Bonita revealed. "I guess that's odd, isn't it? My mother and grandmother were so poor. They did well to make us the clothing that we needed. I would cherish anything old like that."

"Well, there you go, Karen," Carrie Mae declared. "Give Bonita some of those treasures."

"That's a great idea," I agreed. "You can also sell them if you don't want to keep them. Judy has brought me some of her quilts to sell on consignment. It's pretty cool when you see something that was unwanted go to someone who appreciates it. Bonita, if you're successful at getting women to make some things, perhaps I could help you sell them in my shop."

Bonita's eyes brightened. "Oh, that is such good news," she said with a big smile. "You all are getting me excited."

"Bonita, you're welcome to go through some of my stuff if you like," Karen added.

"Gladly, my friend," Bonita said.

Judy brought out a large serving of the cobbler and

placed it in front of us. We each took our spoons and helped ourselves. There were good reactions.

"I don't know what I was expecting, but this is delicious," Karen said.

"I love any kind of cobbler, especially with good coffee," I mentioned.

"How do you like it, ladies?" Randal asked.

"I loved it," Bonita replied. "Thank you so much."

"I'm happy to have you detectives here any time," Randal joked. "I'm glad you liked it."

"Did Marge make this?" I asked.

He nodded and smiled.

"Please tell her how much we enjoyed it," I requested.

"I will. She's preparing soup for the lunch crowd right now."

"Yikes!" Karen shouted. "It's nearly lunchtime. We need to go, Bonita."

"Me too," I said, getting out of the chair.

"Well, I can lollygag since I have Korine to open the shop when I'm late or not there," Carrie Mae bragged.

"I told you that you'd love it," I responded. "You can also sleep in as long as you like."

"Oh, Korine loves it," Betty said. "I'm glad you pushed that notion of Carrie Mae hiring her, Lily."

"This was fun, ladies," Bonita said as she prepared to leave. "I look forward to seeing your quilts, Lily."

"I'll let you all know," I said. "Maybe Monday will work, after the visit to Washington."

"Sounds good," Betty said. "Let us know if we can bring something."

Chapter 3

It was an early spring day as I put Rosie's rocking chair on the porch. I chose a pink-and-aqua Dresden Plate quilt to drape across the back, showing one of the plates prominently. I always hoped that the quilt I displayed each day would go home with a customer. Occasionally, I got lucky.

When I walked back inside, I went to the quilt room in my shop that now housed the valuable quilts Butler had brought for me to sell. They were folded nicely in a large, wooden-walled glass case that Carrie Mae had loaned me. The massive case itself was for sale for just over five thousand dollars. I wasn't worried that it would sell at that price. I had placed a sign inside the locked case that instructed interested customers to ask permission to see the quilts. That request had only been made a few times. When customers saw the higher prices on the quilts, they generally lost interest rather quickly.

I knew it would take time for dealers and collectors to learn that I carried such an inventory. Butler had been nice enough to tell his former clients that I was the new keeper of his exquisite quilts; I cherished having them join my modest assortment of everyday quilts. I found myself checking on them regularly as if I were taking care of precious children.

"Good morning!" a voice called from the front door.

"Kitty!" I exclaimed. "How are you?"

"Just great!" she answered. "I'm here to ask another favor."

"Sure. Anything."

"Ray and I are going out east again, and we wondered if you could keep an eye on the guest house for us."

"Of course! I guess you still don't have any nibbles from anyone wanting to buy it?"

"No. We have a little interest from wannabe renters, but we don't want that responsibility. Once again, you're most welcome to use it for your niece if she comes to visit while we're gone. You'd have to turn the water back on, but otherwise, it should be okay. Johann said he would use his water and hose to keep our flowers alive outside."

"I don't think my niece will be visiting then, but thank you for the offer. She loved staying there as much as I did. If I had the money, I would just buy it from you."

"Now I think that is a great idea!"

"Oh, no. I have enough on my plate, thank you."

We laughed together.

"I heard about some dandy quilts you just received," Kitty said casually. "May I take a peek?"

"Absolutely! Let me get the key," I said, walking into the quilt room.

"How special they look. What a nice display! Oh, you have a Baltimore Album quilt. I rarely see them anymore."

"Yes, it's gorgeous. Would you like to see it opened? I'd love to show it to someone who really appreciates it."

"Could I?"

Luckily, the quilt was close to the top, so I pulled it off the shelf. When I opened it up, Kitty went crazy.

"Lily, this is amazing! What's the provenance of this one?"

"The tag says there is a signature date on the quilt from 1851, and the maker's name is Sarah Whitfield. Here it is inked on the fabric, but very lightly. She had to be very proud of this."

"Oh, it just gives me chills. Every time we go out east, I tell Ray I'm going to bring one home someday. He thinks I'm nuts, but there's something about this pattern that says so much about the maker. The tedious appliqué and quilting are beyond belief, not to mention all the embellishments. Ray thinks we must be able to resell everything we buy on our trips, but occasionally, I like to buy something for myself. I'm afraid to ask, but what is the price?"

"It's twelve thousand dollars," I said. "It's never been used, and when a quilt has documentation like this, that isn't a bad price. I've seen them sell for higher on the Internet."

"You're right," Kitty agreed. "I could stare at this forever. Thanks for letting me see it. Let me help you fold it. I'm going to tell Ray about it, but he'll give me the same lecture."

I smiled and understood. It was a lot of money. I said, "There are some other incredible appliqués in the case as well. I'm glad you appreciate such work."

"I'd best get going. I'll just give you the key now while I'm here, if that's okay. We should be back in a few weeks. We sure appreciate it."

"No problem. With the nicer weather coming, I can check more frequently."

"Oh, I forgot," Kitty said, stopping in her tracks. "The last guest we had there left a quilt behind. We called to tell her and offered to send it back to her, but she said not to bother. She said it was old and worn, and that she just used it for traveling. She told us that we could just throw it away. Horrible, right? Lily, if you want it, please help yourself when you stop by there. Maybe you could get a little something for it here in the shop."

"Well, that's an odd and sad story, isn't it?"

"You wouldn't believe what some folks leave behind. This woman also left some perfectly good makeup, which I know was expensive. She said to throw that away as well, so I did."

"Well, don't worry about the quilt. I'll look at it. I can always use some inexpensive quilts here in the shop."

"Great! Thanks again for everything. You have our contact numbers if you need us."

"Yes, not to worry. Have a wonderful time." I followed Kitty to the door and was happy to see a couple walking towards the shop. So far, my day had been penniless.

Chapter 4

The young couple said that they were staying at the Red Brick Inn of Augusta Bed & Breakfast to celebrate their wedding anniversary. They were pretty engaged in their own conversation. "Thanks for letting us look," the husband said as they left.

It made me wonder if there were any shops that charged to let folks look! Realistically, I knew it was part of doing business. You never knew when a later sale might result because of something someone had seen on a previous visit while they were just looking around.

While it was quiet, I turned on my laptop to see what my siblings were up to. I was surprised to hear from Ellen, our newly found sister. She was now a part of our emailing group and seemed to be very comfortable joining in on the conversations.

Ellen reminded us of her invitation to come see her in Paducah during the big quilt show taking place in April. She attached a flyer advertising the event. All of us were committed except Laurie. Laurie had made it clear that it was a busy time of year for her at her shop in Fish Creek, Wisconsin. Laurie was not a quilter and didn't have the interest that Loretta and I did. Lynn was an artist, so seeing the art quilts interested her. She had also heard about Paducah's art district and wanted to see it. Ellen said she lived in the district. Loretta was the only one to respond to Ellen in the email, saying she wanted exact dates so she could get off work at the hospital. I responded that I would follow the lead of Lynn and Loretta's schedule and that a vacation would be most welcomed.

Loretta then responded that her husband Bill was having some health issues related to his heart and that she was worried about him. Many years ago, he'd had a mild heart attack, but had been fine. Bill was a high school teacher and often got too involved in the students' problems. I responded by asking her to wish him well. Loretta and Bill were both in their sixties.

Laurie joined in as I was typing. She first responded to the issue of Bill's health and then went on to say that most of the shops in Fish Creek were opening early because the early spring was bringing such good weather. She said there weren't typically blooms or decent weather until May in Wisconsin.

Loretta commented that they still had a little snow on the ground in Green Bay, but that the nice weather was helping it melt.

I asked about Lucy and Sarah. Nothing had been said about them lately. I knew Sarah was brokenhearted from the breakup with Lucy's father.

Minutes later, Loretta said Sarah was looking for a better-paying job and that she was seeing the two of them more frequently on the weekends. That was good to hear.

I closed my laptop when a young man in a fireman's uniform stepped into the shop. "Hello, may I help you?"

"Hi, my name is Jim Martin. I was on my way to work and noticed you're repairing the building that was on fire recently."

"Oh, yes. Thank you so much for your quick response. That certainly kept it from spreading to my house."

"You're welcome. That's what we're trained to do. Lightning struck a lot of places that evening. You were lucky that someone saw it happen."

"I know. It was our wonderful mailman on his way to work."

"You've got a cute little shop here, and a mighty bright one, I might add," he teased.

"Yes, I'm the yellow house in town, and it has really grown on me. I'm easy to find!"

He grinned and nodded. "My grandmother quilted, and I have some of her quilts."

"That's nice."

"Well, I'm afraid to use them out of respect, so I just have them put away."

"Well, I'm sure she made them to be used, don't you think?"

"My girlfriend said they're too fragile, so I don't use them."

"I haven't seen them, but are they in poor condition?"

"Oh, no. They're like new. I don't think my grandmother ever used them."

"I think she would smile and approve if you used them."

"You have a point there." He blushed. "I guess I'd better

be on my way. I'd like to bring my girlfriend here sometime."

"That would be great. Thank you again for your help with the fire."

"Nice to meet you!" he said as he left.

Once again, I felt a deep sense of community in this little town where folks really cared about one another. Even the firefighter took the time to check on me. As I thought about it more, it gave me an idea for my column in *Spirit* magazine. I could call it "It Takes a Village." The column could demonstrate that when a little town like Augusta has a tragedy or problem, everyone experiences it. When they have something to celebrate or plan, the whole village gets on board. That's something that is potentially absent when one lives in a large city. A neighborhood or organization could embrace such a notion, but I knew that here in Augusta, I was blessed with a village.

Chapter 5

The next morning, before I opened, I made sure I went by Gracie's Quilt shop to get white fabric and plenty of red floss for my wine country quilt. My mind was spinning with ideas for the blocks, but I'd have to find designs to outline since I couldn't draw well. Susan had talked us all into buying light boxes a while back, so I was glad I had one to help me. I was about to leave for Gracie's shop when my landline rang.

"Is this Lily Rosenthal?" a female voice asked.

"Yes, it is. How can I help you?"

"My name is Jenny Jordon, and I now live in your old apartment on The Hill."

"Oh my goodness. It's nice to know who's living there. I've driven by on occasion, wondering."

"I tracked you down with the help of the current landlord. Evidently, he had records from the lady who previously owned the place when you were a tenant. I understand that she died here."

"Yes, sweet Bertie Maxwell. She was such a dear!"

"Well, I found something that belongs to you."

"Really? I thought I'd gotten everything out, and I worked so hard to leave it clean."

"Yes, the place was spotless, but when I recently went up to the attic, I found some things. Did you ever go up there?"

"No, not at all. That was where Bertie stored things. I only rented the second floor."

"Well, this landlord is letting me store some things up there because it's available. The guy downstairs is elderly and doesn't use it."

"Was it creepy up there?"

She chuckled. "It was dirty, that's for sure. The previous landlord had left some furniture up there, which surprised me. She also had a trunk with a few things inside. There was quilt top that had a note attached. It was addressed to you, like she meant to give it to you."

"Really?"

"I didn't think too much about it, but it did get my curiosity going as to what the story behind it might be. The quilt is nothing fancy. It appears to be made from scraps. There were unfinished crocheted pieces as well. I'll likely pitch most of what I found, but this quilt top had been assigned to someone. That's why I asked my landlord about who was here and when."

"Oh, Jenny, please hang on to that for me. Bertie knew I loved quilts, but I know she was upset with me when I told her I was leaving. She wouldn't even speak to me for a while. She said I was like a daughter to her, so it was hard for her to imagine me moving so far away."

"I see. Well, I'm glad I found you. You may want to see some of her other things before I remove them. I'll give you my number. I work at Concordia Publishing nearby, so I can quickly meet you here."

"Are you a writer?"

"I'm not sure what I am," she quipped. "I do a bit of everything, but I mostly edit. I get to write things on my own every now and then."

"That is so ironic! When I lived there, I was an editor for Dexter Publishing until I quit. I ended up in retail and living in Augusta, Missouri. I have my own column now with *Spirit* magazine, so you never know what's ahead."

"That is fascinating! I would love to meet you. Maybe we could go to lunch when you come."

"I would love to see my old apartment, if that would be okay with you."

"Of course, and I'll show you your landlady's things as well. We can have lunch right here in my apartment."

"Oh, I don't want to be any trouble. I'll give you a call. Thanks so much for contacting me."

I sat down to digest what I had just heard. Had Bertie made me a quilt? Was it supposed to have been a gift for me? Meeting Jenny would be exciting. Just imagine: two writers in the same apartment! I could think of so many questions to ask her.

Chapter 6

When I got to Gracie's shop, she was helping a customer with fabric choices. I looked for the floss and pulled off every skein of red she had on the rack. I remembered Holly telling me that in 1880, Turkey red floss became colorfast. This was a blessing for quilters who wanted to use red in their quilts. Redwork embroidery quilts became the rage between 1880 and 1930, and I was pleased to have some in my collection.

"Well, it appears that we're going to do a little embroidery," Gracie said as she took my floss to the checkout.

"Just a little." I smiled. "I also need you to cut five yards of this nice white cotton for my blocks. My wine country quilt is going to be done in all redwork. I just don't enjoy appliqué, and I don't have the fabric stash to work from."

"Lily, I can certainly help you with that problem," Gracie teased.

"I'm sure you can! I think this will be nice to pick up and work on between customers. When the weather gets warmer, I can sit on the porch and stitch."

"Great idea. Your quilt will be something different from

the others as well."

"I'm anxious to get started. Are you working alone today?"

"Yes, most days I can handle by myself, but Brenda sometimes helps me on the weekends. By the way, I heard through the grapevine that you've added some beautiful quilts to your inventory."

"Yes, I did. It's exciting and scary at the same time. Come by sometime and take a look."

"I will. Since we're alone, I want to remind you about what I asked about at Buzz and Karen's party."

"Refresh my memory," I said slowly, trying to recall.

"You were dancing with a rather handsome and assertive bearded man."

I smiled, remembering the evening. "Oh, that was Anthony."

"So, what's the deal? You said you didn't want to comment about him at the time."

"It's nothing. Karen had tried to fix us up, and I refused since I'm seeing Marc. Anthony asked Marc if he could dance with me, and he was being particularly flirtatious that evening. That's all."

"Forgive me, girlfriend, but you seemed to be eating it up."

I chuckled again. "It's one of my biggest problems, Gracie. I didn't want to offend anyone, so I tried to humor him. He's a friend of so many folks that I know."

"That doesn't sound like you. I think you're quite direct with your feelings. Is he single?"

"Yes, are you interested?"

Gracie blushed. "I doubt that he'd be interested in me,

but he sure is handsome."

"He's from Italy and has been in the wine business all his life. He's what they call a wine sommelier."

"That's exciting! I've never met one."

"Hello, ladies," Heidi greeted us as she came into the shop.

"Good to see you, Heidi," Gracie responded.

"I'm looking for fabric with a wine print," Heidi stated.

Gracie and I looked at one another and smiled.

"This must be for our class's wine country quilt," I guessed.

Heidi nodded and smiled.

I said, "Well, ladies, I need to get back to my shop. Good seeing you!"

"Thanks, Lily!" Gracie said.

As I exited, Marilyn was entering the quilt shop. I briefly said hello and decided to stop at Johann's for a few things.

"Well, if it isn't Lily," Johann greeted me. "I haven't seen you since your fire. According to Snowshoes, that bolt of lightning was huge."

"You're right! It was a scary evening. There were times when I felt that the lightning bolts were going to come into my house!"

"I'm surprised to see you're putting that back portion of the office back again. I think that was added later," he said, scratching his head.

"I really need to," I explained. "I don't want to change something from the past. I'm just replacing the exterior. The inside will be empty. I cleaned it all out some time back. Hey, are those fresh strawberries?"

"Yes, they are! They also delivered tomatoes and

cantaloupe from a hothouse near Marthasville. You want to try some?"

"I'll take some of everything!" I said as I picked up a cantaloupe. "I guess you've heard by now that Kitty and Ray are leaving town again. They asked me to keep watch on the guesthouse, so if you see me next door, you'll know why."

"Sure. I'll do the same and will try to keep things watered. It's nice that they can travel like they do."

"I need to stop over there and pick up something Kitty left for me. She said someone left a quilt behind and that I could have it."

"Lily to the rescue, huh?" Johann chuckled.

"I can't believe someone would just leave their quilt behind, but I'm happy to have it."

"Lands, girl! I've had a few rentals in my lifetime, and you wouldn't believe what folks leave behind."

"Like quilts?"

He nodded as he bagged my groceries. "They mostly leave things that are in terrible shape, of course. When I'd get my boys to clean up places, I'd have them trash it all unless they wanted anything."

"Oh my! That's kind of sad."

Chapter 7

I left Johann's feeling a bit down, then went next door to Kitty's guesthouse and unlocked the door. I picked up the scent of lavender, which was coming from a vase sitting on the kitchen table. As I glanced again at the adorable place, it brought back pleasant memories. It wouldn't have been big enough for Amy's knitting shop, I assessed. It was meant to be the small cozy nest that it was.

On the large bed was the quilt that Kitty wanted me to take. It was folded up and appeared to be faded. I unfolded the quilt and noticed an appliquéd circle in the center of a six-point star, which had a name embroidered in it. The stitching wasn't the neatest, and it had been washed many times. It read "Aunt Bessie 1936." The date matched the era of the tiny prints used for the star. There were some small holes, but the faded colors were the most significant detail. The quilt had been loved and had most likely been very pretty in its day.

I sat down on the bed and brushed my hand slowly across the quilting stitches. What was it that made the owner disconnect from this quilt? Why wasn't it important enough to have it sent back to her or even for her to come and get it? Perhaps it was because it was old and worn. I guessed that went for people as well, sometimes. I occasionally saw some of that attitude in my shop when I let customers know I only carried antique quilts. It was only the present and future that mattered to some. I refolded the quilt and gave another look around the room. I would take the quilt back to the shop, where it would be put on a shelf. If the price was right, it might get a customer's attention.

On the way back to the shop, I noticed more activity on the streets. Once home, I took time to nibble on some of Johann's strawberries before I put out Rosie's rocker. I decided to honor my newly acquired quilt, so I spread it across the back of the chair. Parts of the quilt were brighter than others. I placed a price of fifty dollars on it and hoped for the best.

I unpacked my quilt block supplies and took them to the upstairs porch, where I would likely work on the blocks. I could precut them so they would be ready to go as I needed them. I rushed back downstairs when I heard a couple of ladies come into the shop. They hardly knew I was there due to their lively conversation.

"What a cute little shop you have," one said.

"Thanks. Where are you ladies from?" I inquired.

"I'm from near Washington, but my friend is visiting from Pennsylvania."

"How nice! Welcome to Augusta," I said to the pair.

"The town is so cute," the woman continued. "We had lunch at one of the wineries and then decided to come here to look at your quilts."

"Please do," I responded as I led them to the quilt room. "They're all in here. If you'd like to see any of the quilts in the case, just let me know."

"My, you do have a lot of quilts," the woman from Pennsylvania said.

"Do you live near the Amish?" I asked. "Do they still sell a lot of Amish quilts there?"

"I suppose the tourists still buy them every now and then, but I don't like the patterns they're using now," she explained. "I like the traditional patterns they used to make a long time ago, not the flowery appliqués they're doing now."

I had to agree with what she said, but I said nothing. I left them to explore the items in the quilt room because I felt I had a good chance of a sale between the two of them. When I walked towards the counter, I saw a girl take the quilt off Rosie's rocker. A young man was with her and helped her look at it more closely. I opened the door and asked if I could be of some help.

"Is this quilt only fifty dollars, or is that a mistake?" the girl asked in disbelief.

"It's correct," I answered. "It's seen better days, but for the right owner, it still has a lot of love to give."

"It's so soft, and I love all those old-fashioned names stitched on it," she said, admiring the details in the handiwork.

"Well, get it," the man encouraged. "The price is right, that's for sure."

"I think I will," she said as she handed the quilt to me. "I'd like to see what else you have as well."

The other two ladies were now looking in the main room. One had a small shelf in her hand, and the other one carried a framed print of a woman from the 1800s. "I'm glad you found something," I said.

"I love your quilts," the woman from Pennsylvania said. "I just decided not to fool with such a purchase on this trip."

The two ladies engaged in a short conversation with the young couple, who were now purchasing the older quilt. The young girl bragged about her bargain, and the ladies cheered her on.

Chapter 8

When I brought in Rosie's rocker at the end of the day, I thought about the young girl giving life to the quilt that had been left behind. She'd seen something different in the quilt than what the previous owner had seen. I guessed it depended on whether one saw something as half-full or half-empty. She had admired it and the price had been affordable.

It had been a good day. I went upstairs for the evening, prepared a salad for dinner, and then got out my quilt fabric. Around nine in the evening, my phone rang. I was pleased to see that it was Marc.

"How was your day, sweetheart?" he asked.

"Not bad. How about yours?"

"I've been in meetings all day with a new client in town. We did take time for a lengthy lunch, so I got to walk outdoors just for a bit."

"I'm glad you got to get some fresh air."

"I was wondering if you'd have any interest in coming to the city this weekend. This new client has suggested going to dinner, which would include his wife, so I'd like to include you if you're available."

"That sounds lovely! If I close early on Saturday, I could make it in time for dinner."

"I'd like that a lot. By the way, I saw Carl and Lynn at Bristol's restaurant earlier this week, but I could only say hello."

We continued talking for another half hour before we convinced each other it was time to hang up. Seeing Marc on Saturday would be something to look forward to.

I put away my quilting project and went to bed thinking of Marc and his great smile. I then remembered that the next day would bring the arrival of my plein air artist. I wished I had purchased some of Johann's flowers to make the flower beds in the front of my shop look more inviting. Perhaps I could still do that early in the morning. The previous year, Korine had done all my planting for spring. I decided to plant flowers in my antique watering can. I could then place it on the porch by Rosie's rocker.

At one that morning, I looked at the clock in frustration as I added a few final things to the to-do list that I had begun. I placed my paper and pen on the bedside table, turned off the light, and yearned for sleep. I repositioned my pillow and started thinking of the phone call I'd had with Jenny Jordon. I still found it hard to believe that Bertie had made a quilt for me. When could I get there to see it? I moved the pillow again and eventually drifted off to sleep.

Because I had gotten little sleep, the start to the next day was slow. I got dressed and went downstairs to get some coffee. Ted was getting ready to mow the lawn. I grabbed my jacket and went out to say hello. "Good morning, Ted. I'm glad you're here. I have an artist setting up in the yard soon."

"It won't take me long. I'll get this front done first."

"I'm leaving to go to Johann's to get some flowers. There's coffee if you want some."

"I'm good. I have another place to cut when I leave here."

"Have a good day, then."

When I got to Johann's, I selected a few marigolds and red geraniums. I loved red and yellow together. Johann had topsoil on sale, so I grabbed some of that as well. As I drove down the street, I could see artists setting up here and there. By the time I got home, my artist had arrived and was already painting.

"Good morning!" I greeted her as I carried an armful of flowers to the house.

"What lovely flowers! Are those for me?" she asked jokingly.

"Sorry, it's my attempt to look more springlike. I should have done this sooner."

"Look at how I'm painting your house." She motioned to the canvas, which was already teeming with color. "I'm featuring that cute sign with your yellow house in the background."

"That is so sweet. I love my sign. The yellow house is so strong. I would like to purchase that when you're finished. I may end up being a collector of your work!"

"Are you sure? That would be grand!"

"There's hot coffee if you get chilly out here," I offered.

"You are too good to me, Lily!" she said, smiling.

Chapter 9

It was ten before I saw any activity in the area. I couldn't resist going outside every now and then to see how the painting was coming along. The artist had an eye for design and was able to capture the best angle of the house. When I saw a well-dressed man walk into the shop, I went back inside to see if I could help him.

"Hello, I'm Harold Carpenter from a newspaper called the *Daily Press.*"

"Nice to meet you," I responded. "How can I help you?"

"I've read your columns in *Spirit* magazine. We're looking for someone to write a weekly column for us. It would give you three times the exposure, and more income as well. Would that interest you?"

"Oh!" I said, surprised.

"I know that your column is very popular. We want the same type of content. We're interested in you because you are a local resident and a business owner."

"Mr. Carpenter, I'm flattered, but I barely have time to write my monthly column, much less a weekly one. I'm afraid that I have to decline."

"I didn't mean to put you on the spot," he apologized. "Would you think about it for a while? I'll leave my card in case you have any questions."

"I'll take your card, of course, but my answer will remain the same. *Spirit* magazine has been very good to me."

"It was nice to meet you," he said kindly. "After you've had some time to consider it, I think you'll realize that this is something that could be very good for your future."

I watched him as he left and couldn't help smiling to myself. What were the chances of this happening? I knew there was no way that I could take on any more responsibilities. I couldn't wait to tell Alex!

As more and more customers came into the shop, it took my mind off Mr. Carpenter. Every time I looked out the window, there was a crowd around the artist. I wondered if she'd had any other offers on her painting.

The next morning, I woke up realizing that I had my evening dinner date with Marc to look forward to. The dinner sounded somewhat dressy, so I would have to choose one of my many black outfits. Since I didn't know the other couple, I realized that I felt a bit nervous. As the day wore on, I informed my artist that I would be closing early, and she agreed to leave early as well. As I was thinking of closing, I got a call from Alex.

"Guess what, Lily Girl?" he asked.

I could tell that he was particularly excited about something. "What?"

"I decided to lease a car instead of buying one again."

"Okay, so what's the big deal about that?"

"It's a convertible! A red convertible! Jealous?"

"Good heavens, Alex! Are you going through some kind of midlife thing?"

"Maybe!" he said, chuckling. "The accident on New Year's Eve caused me to have to get a different vehicle. I put it off as long as I could, and now I've finally made a decision. I'm so excited about this car! I can't wait to drive out to Augusta and speed around those curves."

"Not funny, Alex," I warned. "I hope you don't plan to come this weekend, because I'm going in to meet Marc. He's taking a client and his wife to dinner, so I'm joining him."

"So much for that," Alex said, sounding deflated.

"I have a little excitement of my own to share, by the way. I recently received a job offer."

"Really?"

I told him about my visit from Mr. Carpenter. I could tell by Alex's silence that he was jealous and didn't quite know what to say. He paused before he responded.

"So, what did you decide, Lily Girl?"

"I turned him down, of course. The thought of adding more to my life right now is crazy. I couldn't take all that pressure. That's why I'm out here in Augusta."

"You know those offers don't come along every day, don't you?" Alex questioned.

"I know. I did take his card because that seemed to make him feel better."

Alex chuckled.

"I need to get going. Enjoy your new toy!"

Chapter 10

As I drove away from the house, a light mist fell on my windshield. I had a lot on my mind as I drove along the curvy roads. I followed a line of cars that were cautiously watching the slick pavement. There wasn't a time when I traveled these roads that I didn't think of that horrific accident near Sugar Creek Winery. I should never have agreed to go in the car with Nick when I knew he'd consumed a lot of wine. That collision took away someone's life. I tried to block it out of my mind and concentrate instead on seeing Marc. I arrived at his condo around six. I just needed to freshen up.

"You look great as always," Marc said sweetly, giving me a kiss. "We're going to meet up with them at a restaurant called Prasino. I think you'll like it."

"Where does this couple live?" I asked.

"New York. We're representing the husband's company in a case here in St. Louis. We won't talk business, I promise."

"Sweetie, you should know by now that I can talk about almost anything. Before I forget, I wanted to tell you that I got a phone call from the woman who lives in my old apartment."

"Really? Why?"

"She was up in the attic and found a quilt top that had my name on it. Evidently Bertie had made it for me. It's strange, but Jenny is a writer also and works for Concordia Publishing House. I'm meeting her next week. I can't wait to see what my old place looks like."

"I was in your neighborhood recently, and they did get that mess cleaned up from Rosie's burned shop."

"Good! I'll bet it looks so different with that building gone. I wonder what will happen in that space. I don't think I'd know anyone in that neighborhood anymore."

"Well, with mostly apartments around there, you know there will be turnover." Marc glanced at his watch and said, "We need to be on our way."

The restaurant was in a newly-developed section of town called Streets of St. Charles. When we walked in, I admired the contemporary design, which featured lots of windows. When Marc told the hostess that we had reservations, we learned that the other couple was already seated.

When we arrived at the table, Marc introduced me to a very attractive couple in their fifties named John and Sandra. Not a single smile was offered by either of them. They looked as though they were prepared for a business meeting.

"Nice to meet you," I said as I sat down.

A waiter immediately took our drink orders. I waited for Marc to start the conversation. He told the couple a little about the restaurant, which came highly recommended, and that it was his first time to try it out. They nodded.

"I must tell you a little bit about Lily," Marc said with a wide smile. "She lives about an hour from here in a little community called Augusta, Missouri. She has a clever antique and quilt shop in the center of town."

They looked at me curiously, like I was from another planet. "Oh, how cute," Sandra replied.

"It must be difficult being so far from life in the city," John added.

"Not really," I responded with confidence. "I lived in St. Louis for many years, in the Italian neighborhood called The Hill, but I find the wine country quite beautiful and satisfying."

"Are you referring to the neighborhood in St. Louis where they recently had a shooting reported on the news?" John asked. "Maybe it's where the St. Louis mafia resides."

Everyone laughed quietly—everyone except me. "Not that I'm aware of," I stated.

"I think John was just being a bit sarcastic, Lily," Marc explained. "I have to say, you will never find better Italian restaurants anywhere in the country. By the way, it's where I met this girl."

Marc grinned, but the couple did not. They couldn't have cared less.

"So, what do you do?" I asked Sandra.

"I'm currently the fashion editor of a magazine, a subsidiary of *Vogue*, in fact."

"Oh, how interesting!" I responded. I wanted to crawl under the table as I thought of my simple little black dress.

"Well, Lily has her own column in *Spirit* magazine," Marc stated proudly. "She recently turned down a weekly newspaper column."

"I've never heard of *Spirit* magazine," Sandra countered. "What do you write about?"

I took a generous swallow of merlot before answering. "I write about quilts, antiques, and community life in Augusta," I stated. "I can choose what I write about, which is nice."

"Really?" she asked in disbelief.

As we began to order our food, John and Sandra lamented that the menu did not offer them many choices. It seemed that they adhered to a rather restrictive diet. I could sense Marc beginning to become frustrated with them. To rescue the situation a bit, I heard myself filling them in on the history of St. Charles. Getting little response from that, I asked, "John, are you a baseball fan like Marc?"

John chuckled. "Baseball must be a Midwest thing. Some of the guys at work like the Mets, however."

"Marc and I took a trip to Cooperstown," I said.

"Cooperstown?" Sandra asked.

Marc graciously explained that Cooperstown is home to the National Baseball Hall of Fame and Museum, and John pretended to know what Marc was talking about. We managed to get through the meal, but I could tell that Sandra was bored to tears. Overall, Marc recovered from his earlier frustration and managed to converse with them better than I could, but he was probably used to this behavior from some of his clients. The good news of the night was that it ended early and Marc agreed to meet with John the next morning at the office. After they left the restaurant, Marc and I looked at each other and burst into laughter.

"I'm so sorry, Lily," Marc said. "I knew nothing about them personally."

"Well, they don't have to ruin the entire evening. I think there's still time to enjoy dessert!"

"You are my kind of girl, Lily," Marc said, squeezing my hand.

Chapter 11

On the drive home, I couldn't help but think about the experience with John and Sandra. There was no doubt that we lived in two different worlds, but wasn't it a shame that we couldn't have had a civil conversation? There were several opportunities for Sandra to talk about what she did and what drove the fashion world, but they passed without comment. Her reaction to my occupation and what I wrote about was disappointing. She could have learned something from me as well.

Did living in a bigger city or having an impressive title dictate the importance of an individual? It made me think of the saying that you can be a big fish in a little pond or a little fish in a big pond. How does one measure the success of each? That could be a good column topic. How Sandra and I felt about our jobs was likely the same. She probably felt like she was reaching the masses with her fashion opinions, and I felt like I was using my quilts to touch people, and at the same time, reconnect with history.

I hoped I hadn't embarrassed Marc in any way. Marc

was a high-profile lawyer in a big city, yet he seemed to be attracted to my charming lifestyle in a small town. We both respected and admired what the other brought to the table for their clients.

It was after lunch when I opened the shop. My plein air artist showed up shortly after that. I knew she had to be about finished with her painting, so I went out to visit with her. "How is the painting coming along?" I asked.

"Do you want to take a look?"

I smiled and nodded. "I love it! I don't know how you do it!"

"I still need to add a few finishing touches to it. I'll bring it in as soon as I'm done."

When I saw a woman go into the shop, I joined her. As I entered, she quickly exited. I hoped it wasn't a sign as to how the rest of the day would proceed. I found my redwork blocks and perched myself behind the counter, then was surprised to see Susan coming toward the shop.

"Wow, did you see that painting of your shop?" she asked with excitement.

"Yes, and it has my name on it," I bragged.

"I would hope so! Lily, would you mind if I tagged along with you and Judy tomorrow when you go to the knitting shop? You're going after class, right?"

"Right. Judy said the coffee shop near the store has great sandwiches for lunch."

"Perfect!"

"I can't stay too late because my Dinner Detectives are coming over."

Susan giggled. "I hope you solve some things here, Lily," she said, shaking her head. "When you do, I hope you'll share it with the rest of us. Is that your wine country quilt block that you're working on?"

I nodded. "It's slow going, but I like to pick it up when I'm not busy." ·

"Would you mind showing me those awesome quilts I've heard about?"

"Sure! If there are any that you want to see unfolded, I can unlock the case and show them to you."

"No, that's not necessary. I just want to see what everyone is talking about."

When we walked in the quilt room, Susan's eyes widened.

"The cabinet of Carrie Mae's is perfect for them, don't you think? I refold them frequently and keep the lights out in this room at night just to keep the exposure down."

"They are gorgeous! May I take a photo of the case?"

"I'd rather you not, Susan. These quilts don't belong to me, so I haven't allowed anyone to do that."

"Oh, I understand. During one of our classes, I hope you can tell us more about them."

"I'd be happy to. I'll see you tomorrow, then. I'm glad you're going with us."

Chapter 12

On Monday morning, I grabbed my quilt block and hurried to class. I never wanted to be late because I enjoyed visiting with the other members of the group. I was forever indebted to Susan for inviting me to join the class when I first moved to Augusta. Everyone was there except Edna. Marilyn said Edna had just had knee surgery and was having a tough time of it. When Susan got our attention, the first thing she showed us was a get-well card for Edna that she wanted each of us to sign.

"She's taking advantage of being at home by working on her quilt blocks," Marilyn reported. "I brought her first one with me for our show and tell." Marilyn held it up.

"Oh, it's beautiful," Susan said right away.

"It's a scene from the Plein Air Festival," Marilyn explained. "Can you believe the detail Mom embroidered?"

We applauded, inspired by the beautiful workmanship.

"Appliqué is right up her alley, and she'll do amazing things with this theme," I said.

"Mom and I are trying not to make the same kind of

block each month," Marilyn said. "She did say that she's not about to make an extra block every month, and she hopes you'll understand, Susan."

"Of course!" Susan agreed. "That is optional, and I know how long it takes for Edna to produce those intricate blocks."

"I'll be doing well to make one each month," Heidi joked.

"Mine is a simple wine bottle with a plate of cheese," Marilyn continued. "I had to get into Mom's fabric stash."

"Well, let's see what you brought, Heidi," Susan requested.

"I hope you can recognize the Augusta Winery sign," Heidi stated. "It's really just supposed to represent the wineries in general."

When we saw her work, we applauded.

"My blocks will all be done in redwork because I haven't perfected the other skills," I said. "My scene is simple, with the rolling hills and some grapevines growing in rows."

A nice response followed.

"Mine's not done," Judy admitted. "It's the big stone turtle that's on the patio at Kate's Coffee."

"I love that idea, Judy," I said. "That is so clever!"

"Candace, what about you?" Susan asked.

Candace looked down. "I'm sorry, guys. No block today," she said sadly. "My mom has been seriously ill, and it's taken up all my time and energy."

"We're sorry to hear that," Susan responded. "Don't give it a thought. We're glad you're here."

"Thanks," Candace said. "I just had to get away and think about something else for a little while."

Hearing Candace describe her situation was a reminder of how life changes course, especially as parents age. When that happens, priorities must shift very quickly.

"Today, ladies, I want to show you how to square up your blocks. This is important because as you create blocks using different techniques, they can vary in size," Susan instructed. "You can do this before you start and make sure you have extra fabric to cut off, or wait until you're done and then look for the smallest block to size them with. This is where your 12½" square template comes in handy."

That information was good to know for my redwork blocks. I did cut them larger than needed. For my purposes, I just wanted them to be ready to go, and I didn't want to go through the cutting process every time. When the class was nearly over, I told Judy that Susan would be going with us to see Amy's new knitting shop. As we were leaving, Susan asked Judy if it was alright for her to join us, and Judy didn't mind at all.

"I'm sure that Amy will love the extra customer," Judy assured Susan as we climbed into the car, ready for our afternoon adventure.

It didn't take us long to get to Washington. The Washington Coffee Shop was in the center of town and near Amy's shop. I could see right away that Amy would have more traffic here than she would have had if she had ended up in Augusta.

The large coffee shop was unique. Its décor was very eclectic. There were clusters of furniture for conversation, and the tables and chairs were chrome sets from the 1950s. We had to stand in line to order. The menu was surprisingly extensive for a coffee shop. Judy had heard that their scones were to die for. I settled on a BLT after I saw someone walk to their table with one on their plate. The place filled up quickly with what appeared to be the business lunch crowd.

"My, Randal's coffee shop is so different than this, isn't it?" Judy commented.

"It is, but in a good way," I answered. "I like the coziness of Kate's Coffee."

"I agree," Susan said. "I like the patio there. This place doesn't have one."

We continued to chat as we ate our delicious lunch. I told myself that I needed to do this more often!

Chapter 13

"Hello, ladies!" Amy said when we walked in the shop. "It's good to see you!"

"This is really cute, Amy," I said as I looked around at all the beautiful colors of yarn lining the white walls.

"Thanks!" she said with delight. "I don't have much room, but when the lease is up on the shop next door, I'll be expanding and will have more room for classes. There's a little side room back here that was a closet. I have my finished things for sale in there."

"How clever!" Judy replied. "It doesn't take long to realize that you don't have enough space."

"So, ladies, who knits?" Amy asked, teasing.

"Not me!" I responded. "I'm not interested enough to start, but I'll keep buying your wonderful finished items."

"That works for me," Amy laughed.

We took our time as we tried to look at every little thing. Susan bought a simple pattern and some pink yarn. I purchased a shawl that would be perfect for Carrie Mae as she sat in her shop. I also splurged and bought a crocheted afghan that I would give to Laurie for her birthday.

"Thanks so much, ladies!" Amy said as we were about to leave. "You've made my day, as you can imagine."

"Yes, I can relate, Amy," I said sincerely. We all left happy and were convinced that Amy would do just fine. I checked my watch on the way home to make sure I had enough time to get ready for my guests that night.

When I got home, I put frozen toasted ravioli in the oven on low heat so it would be ready to serve. It was from The Hill, and I wanted my guests to enjoy some of the treats I'd experienced there. I added a veggie tray to snack on as well. Of course, everything would go great with wine, which I knew we all enjoyed.

Betty and Carrie Mae arrived early and together, as was typical for the two of them. Betty brought chocolate cookies, which were always yummy and appreciated. The evening was chilly, so I turned on the fireplace, which delighted my friends. Bonita and Karen arrived fifteen minutes later. Karen brought a red wine that she insisted we drink, so I let her do the honors and pour it. When I brought out the platter of ravioli, the aroma brought smiles of delight to everyone's faces.

"Oh, what a treat, Lily," Bonita said. "Karen said this is a common regional Italian appetizer."

"I must be part Italian," I joked. "It was amazing to be around their wonderful markets and restaurants when I lived on The Hill. I didn't tell you all that I'm going back to visit the woman who lives in my old apartment there. She called to tell me she'd found a quilt top in the attic that my landlord, Bertie, had left behind. She said it has my name on it. I can hardly believe it. I knew Bertie really well, and I didn't know she did any handwork."

"I remember you talking about Bertie," Carrie Mae recalled.

"Yes, and I broke her heart when I told her I was moving to Augusta. She didn't speak to me for a while, so I guess she decided not to give the quilt to me after all."

"How sad," Bonita responded. "I'm glad you're ending up with it."

"A coincidence is that the person who lives in my apartment is also an editor like I was," I shared. "Isn't that strange?"

"Not really," Bonita said calmly. "There is a karma that comes with a house or building that attracts a certain type of person. How nice that you will be able to meet her."

"I can't wait!" I said with excitement. "More wine, anyone? I really like this, Karen."

"So back to why we're here," Carrie Mae reminded us. "Lily, do you still feel like Doc has been around since you had the fire?"

They all stared at me. "I have two spirits here, let's face it," I confessed. "Yes, I can still feel that they are here, but they've both been silent recently."

"Well, that's good to hear," Karen said with relief.

"I just can't believe that you were never afraid," Bonita said, shaking her head.

"I think Doc should feel good about Lily replacing the part of his office that was burned, don't you?" Betty asked. "It certainly wasn't Lily's fault that lightning struck the place."

"I wouldn't go so far as to claim that, Betty," Carrie Mae countered. "Angry spirits can cause all kinds of things to happen. I've lived long enough to know about a few things!"

"Oh, for heaven's sake!" Karen said, laughing at Carrie Mae's declaration.

Chapter 14

"I keep wondering if they're aware of one another's presence," Betty wondered aloud.

"Do you mean Doc and Rosie?" Karen asked.

"I'd say yes," I said. "But they're here for different reasons, so their paths shouldn't cross."

"Suppose Doc tries to hurt Lily. Would Rosie step in?" Karen asked, sounding concerned.

"I wouldn't discount that happening," Bonita said.

I broke up the conversation by taking them into the small quilt room upstairs, where I kept my red-and-white quilt collection. I knew Bonita was anxious to see them. She was shocked and short on words. I explained what attracted me to red-and-white quilts and then showed her the first quilt I ever bought. The others were interested as well. My first purchase had been a redwork summer quilt that had hand tatting in each corner to secure the layers. It was still in perfect condition.

"I would like to try redwork sometime," Bonita shared.

"It doesn't take a lot of supplies," I said. "I'll bet Gracie would donate some of the floss if you asked her."

"Great idea," Karen agreed. "We'll ask her."

"You are a very lucky lady, Lily," Bonita said with sincerity. "Women love the color red, so you may have an idea there."

Our lively conversation continued into the night, from the latest gossip to answering questions Bonita had about Doc and Rosie.

"Oh, ladies, it's getting late," Betty eventually said. "That wine is knocking this old lady out!"

"I'm ready to go as well," Carrie Mae chimed in. "Thanks for showing us the quilts, Lily. I had forgotten about some of the ones you'd purchased from me."

"I guess we have to leave you now with Doc and Rosie," Karen joked as we walked down the stairs. "How you sleep at night beats me!"

"Goodnight, and thanks for the wine, Karen," I said as they went to their cars.

After they left, I got ready for bed. Our conversation had been a bit exhausting. I wasn't sure it had been healthy to have the constant reminder of Doc and Rosie. Finishing the evening by visiting my red-and-white friends had been helpful. It was good to admire them again.

It was ten by then, and my thoughts turned to Marc. I wished that he would communicate with me more, but he had a lot on his plate. Perhaps the start of baseball season would cause him to make time for some fun.

I was about to crawl into bed when I remembered that I hadn't set the alarm downstairs. I could see flashing lights coming from Doc's office. It was a strange time for his activity. I looked out the door to make sure no one was parked outside. All seemed well until, out of the corner of my eye, I saw a light coming from the quilt room. I remembered turning it off, as I had every night since I'd had the new quilts. I wanted the quilts spared from as much light as possible. I turned the light out again and headed up the stairs.

Feeling a bit lonely, I got my laptop out to see if there was conversation going on between my siblings. There was nothing except a few comments from my column readers. I put the laptop aside with disappointment. I turned out the lights, which brought sleep, but my dreams became more and more disturbing. I kept seeing women go in and out of Doc's office with my red quilts. However, when I'd go outside to open the door, there would be no one there. I could hear them talking and laughing, but there wasn't a soul around.

I woke up in a cold sweat, so I got up to get a drink of water. Perhaps if I went out onto the porch and picked up my embroidery, that would make me sleepy. The embroidery helped me get my mind off my dream as I stitched another hill on my block. I leaned my head back to rest my eyes for a bit and fell asleep. The next thing I knew, it was morning. I jumped up to get my day going. When I got out of the shower, the phone was ringing. It was Alex.

"Hey, it's supposed to be a beautiful day. I thought I'd take my red lady out for a drive over your way. Are you free for lunch?"

"I'll make time! I'm anxious to meet the red lady. Do you think she's ready to take the hills?"

"She's a spunky sort—just how I like my ladies!"

I chuckled. "Okay, I'll see you around noon."

I knew I shouldn't be closing the shop, but it had been quite a while since I'd seen Alex. Of course, I was curious to know if Mindy was making progress with him. I suspected that not much was moving forward in their relationship, since Alex had had so much to say about his red lady recently! I decided to open the shop for a couple of hours. Before I did, however, I hung the new painting above my couch on the porch upstairs. I hoped I'd remember to show Alex.

Chapter 15

I was talking to a customer's husband on the porch of my shop when Alex drove up in his flashy convertible.

"Your boyfriend?" the husband asked, eager to tease me.

"No, just a friend," I said with a smile. "We have a lunch date."

The flashy red car captured the customer's interest as well.

"Alex, it is beautiful," I praised as he got out of the car. "I love the tan interior!"

"Honey, I'm going to buy this Windsor chair to put by my desk upstairs," the customer announced.

That was good to hear! We all went inside the shop, and the husband agreed that the chair would be perfect.

"Sorry we delayed your date," he said to Alex.

"Not to worry," Alex responded. "You just made my friend's day with this purchase. Nothing makes her happier!"

The husband laughed.

After they left, I locked the door and told Alex to check out my new painting upstairs. He, too, thought it was exceptional. On the way to the winery, he asked me a serious question.

"You're really content with the way things are in your life right now, aren't you?"

"Boy, that question came out of the blue," I replied as I attempted to protect my hair from the wind.

"I can't believe you turned down that offer from the *Daily Press*. They pay very well, from what I hear."

"The extra money isn't important at this point in time, Alex. It isn't like it was when you got me the gig with *Spirit*. Richard's happy with what I do, and it's manageable. Why don't you inquire about writing for the *Daily Press*?"

"I have to admit that I've thought about it. On the other hand, *Spirit* keeps me pretty busy, so I really can't complain."

After we ordered our food and got settled at a table that had a magnificent view, we finally got around to discussing Mindy. I could tell Alex was uncomfortable with the topic.

"Mindy is using all the tools in her toolbox," he said slowly. "She's even dangling job opportunities that her daddy can offer me."

"Seriously?"

He nodded.

"For heaven's sake, Alex. What are you telling her that leads her to think she still has a chance of a permanent commitment with you?"

He grinned. "Are you jealous?"

"Oh, please! You gripe to me about her aggressiveness, but she keeps it up, despite what you're telling me. Do you love her and don't want to admit it?"

"Love? That's a very big word. No, I'm not in love, if that's what you want to hear."

"It's not about what I want to hear. It should be about what makes you happy. You know I support however you feel about her. You obviously can't say no to her. Is it her looks? The sex?"

"I guess I just want someone like you."

"What?"

"You know what I mean."

"No, I don't."

"We've got this great friendship with absolutely no pressure."

"Listen to yourself! We are buddies. Mindy wants more than that. She adores you and wants to know that you are committed to her."

"They say you should marry your best friend."

I looked at him and started to giggle. "Don't look at me!" I said, trying to stifle my laughter. "You shouldn't have to marry anyone. Haven't you told her that you don't want to get married?"

"Sort of. Any other woman would certainly take the hint, but she hasn't seemed to get it."

"She thinks you're going to change, that's why."

"So what should I do?"

"For the moment, why don't you go pay the bill while I think about your situation?"

He smiled and got up to do just that. I took a deep breath and used his absence to collect my thoughts. Poor Alex. He must have thought that all women think like me, and they don't. He really didn't love Mindy, but he continued to be dazzled by other things she could offer. When Alex came back, we didn't return to the subject of Mindy. After a while, I realized that I needed to get back to work.

"Are you okay to drive back to the city?" I asked as we got in the car to leave.

"Is that an offer for one of your sleepovers?" he teased.

Alex had spent the night at my place before, comfortably situated on the sofa. I shook my head and laughed. "Come back to the house and I'll make some coffee. We haven't had a visit in a long time. We can continue to catch up."

"Sounds like a plan," he said as he pulled up the top of the convertible.

Chapter 16

When Alex and I returned to the house, lights were flashing in Doc's office.

"I'll be! I finally get to see this for myself," Alex marveled.

"I told you! It was a green light when Santa was occupying the office."

When we walked in the shop, I again saw a light coming from the quilt room. I was certain that I had turned them off for the day. I strode to the quilt room and looked around before turning them off. As I made coffee, Alex turned on the news. There was something on about a robbery that had taken place on The Hill. That reminded me to tell him about Jenny Jordon living in my apartment and how she'd found a quilt for me in the attic. When I told him about her background, it got his attention. "I really want to go see her soon," I said.

"It's pretty weird having another editor live there, don't you think?"

"It is. I'm also curious to see what the place looks like. She said there were other things left in the attic as well, like furniture. She found the quilt with my name on it inside a trunk."

"You really have some luck with folks leaving you things! Rosie leaves you first option on her store and then some cash in a cookie jar. Carrie Mae offers you a location where you can open your business and live as well, which is really something! Butler gives you a valuable quilt for Christmas, and now leaves you his fortune in quilts, you might say."

"I know, I know. I've been very fortunate. You forgot about my best friend getting me a writing job with a wonderful magazine," I teased.

He chuckled. "Aw, shucks. It scored points with my boss, who was looking for someone like you."

"More coffee?"

"I'm good, but I really need to get home."

"Are you sure? It's not that late. But you do need to be careful in that new car of yours."

"You're sounding like a wife."

"You don't know anything about having a wife. You know how much you mean to me."

"Now don't get goofy! I've got to go." Before he left, he turned to look at the painting again.

"I like this painting better than the one of Doc's house," he mentioned.

"I think I do, too! Text me when you get home, okay?"

"I will," he said, giving me a hug. "I hope Doc gives you some peace tonight."

"I think the lights are out now. Don't worry."

Alex waved as he got in his car. I sighed. Alex was a gem of a friend. It was only nine by now, so while it was still rather early, I decided to give Jenny Jordan a call. "I hope I'm not calling too late," I said when she answered.

"No, not at all! I'm just enjoying sitting on the porch."

"Oh, I remember those nights. How I loved that porch."

"Have you figured out when you can come?"

"When are you free?"

"I'm off Friday, if that will work for you. I'll fix a simple Italian lunch to make you homesick, okay?"

"I would love that," I said.

Talking to Jenny did make me feel a bit homesick, but I also felt I'd met a new friend. What could I give Jenny for inviting me and even telling me about the quilt?

That night, sleep came easy. The visit with Alex and my happy thoughts of The Hill gave me peace.

Chapter 17

The next morning, when I put out Rosie's rocker, I saw a man pull up in a pickup truck. He carried a large trash bag filled with something.

"Good morning," he said as he approached me. "Are you the quilt lady?"

"I suppose you could call me that," I responded, smiling.

"Well, have I got a deal for you today," he claimed as he followed me into the shop.

Without hesitation, he emptied the bag on the counter, revealing a pile of old quilts. I wanted to instruct him to stop, but it was too late. The mess that accompanied the bagful of quilts was not something I wanted in my shop. I took a deep breath. "I'm guessing that you want to sell these?"

"You betcha. When my wife left me, she left all this old stuff. She took anything that was good, of course! It's quite a story!"

I looked at the quilts long enough to know that I didn't want them. They smelled strongly of smoke. "I'm sorry, but I'm not in the market to buy any more quilts right now."

"Don't you even want to look at them? I'll give you a real good price! What else am I going to do with them? My neighbor said that you're the lady who sells things like this in town."

"I understand, but let me give you a little advice. You need to air these quilts out to get rid of the odor. If you decide to try to sell them, that would help a lot."

I could tell that I'd insulted him. "Well, thanks a lot!" he said angrily as he pushed the quilts back into the bag.

"Good luck," I said weakly as he marched out.

The smell remained, so I decided to keep the door open for a bit to allow some fresh air to come indoors. It was sad to think of those quilts being left behind. That man had no attachment to them, and even worse, disliked where they came from. They had become unwanted objects instead of a labor of love that provided warmth. I could only hope that there were no pets or children left behind in that situation.

Then there were cases where quilts could be caught up in a dispute. In a divorce, both parties sometimes felt they were deserving of a specific quilt. After a death, remaining family members may believe they were promised a quilt or had the rights to it. I was reminded of the story of Solomon in the Bible. When faced with two women who each claimed that a baby belonged to them, Solomon suggested that the infant be cut in half to satisfy the conflict. Of course, he knew that the true mother would be the one who vehemently disagreed with that suggestion! Hopefully, no one would end up cutting a quilt in half just to have a portion of it!

My morning's start had an impact on me for the remainder of the day. I decided to call Carrie Mae to see if the same man had made a stop at her place.

Carrie Mae responded, "Lands, Lily! He first approached Korine as he dumped them all on the counter. Korine said she felt like holding her nose. I got him out of here fast and didn't send him to anyone else. For all we know, he could have stolen those quilts. I think I may know the family he's from. What a darned shame."

"I doubt he'll have any luck giving them away, much less selling them. Sad, isn't it?"

"It is." She then continued, "Hey, I got a call from Butler this morning."

"You did?"

"He was checking on me, he said. He was going to give you a call as well. I think he's curious about how you're doing with the quilts."

"Oh! He will certainly be the first one I call when I sell one of them."

"He wants to have lunch with us soon."

"Of course! That would be nice. I have someone coming in, so I need to go." A clean-cut man entered the shop.

"I take it that you might be Lily?"

"I am. How can I help you?"

Chapter 18

"I'm Ray's brother, Ed," the man announced.

"I'm glad to meet you. I guess you know Ray and Kitty are out of town."

"Yes, I do. I think that they were in Connecticut the last time I talked with them."

"So, what can I do for you, Ed?"

"Well, Kitty has a birthday coming up, and Ray asked me to take care of getting a birthday present for her."

"Here?"

"Evidently, Kitty fell in love with a pricey Baltimore Album quilt that you have in your shop."

"Yes, she did."

"Well, he asked me to give you a deposit on the quilt. He'll settle up with you on the balance when he returns."

"Are you kidding me? He's willing to pay the asking price?"

"That's what he told me. He said Kitty couldn't stop talking about it. I don't need to see it, but here's a check for a thousand dollars, if that will do for a deposit."

"My goodness! I can't believe it. Sure, that will do nicely."

"It does sound like a generous gift, but that's the way Ray is." He chuckled. "You'll give me a receipt, I suppose?"

"I think I can manage that! Let me remove the ticket and do this properly." Feeling light on my feet, I walked into the quilt room with the key to unlock the cabinet. I found the tag and checked the price before locking the quilt itself back up in the cabinet, then took the tag to the counter and began writing up the sales slip while Ed casually looked around the room.

"Are you into antiques like your brother and sister-in-law?" I asked.

"Not really. I appreciate them, but I prefer more contemporary pieces."

I handed him the receipt and thanked him for putting down the deposit for Ray. "Kitty sure will be pleased!"

"They'll still be gone during her birthday, but Ray is going to tell her about the quilt on the day. It was nice to meet you, Lily."

"It was really nice meeting you, too. You sure made my day!"

He grinned.

After he'd left, I was too overwhelmed to even do my happy dance. I thought of Butler right away. I had told Carrie Mae that he would be the first to know if I sold one of his quilts. I nervously found his number in my phone.

"Butler?"

"Yes, Lily. How are you?"

"I'm in disbelief! I just sold the Baltimore Album quilt!"

"Good job! Tell me about it."

I knew my voice was shaky as I told him about my relationship with Kitty and Ray. I told him how she'd always wanted to buy a Baltimore Album quilt when they went out east and that Kitty's birthday had been the perfect time for Ray to act on her desire for the quilt that she'd seen in my shop.

Butler replied, "That's great, but wait to send my portion of the money when he comes back to pay for it in full. See how your relationships are starting to pay off? It took me years to establish that."

"I told Carrie Mae this morning that you would be the first to know when I sold one of the quilts."

"Well, we need to celebrate."

"Sure. Carrie Mae said we should all do lunch."

"Very well. I'll arrange it."

When I hung up, I had to tend to some folks looking around the shop. When I got a break, I called Carrie Mae to tell her about my sale and that the quilt would be going to our friend Kitty.

"Well, they can afford it!" Carrie Mae revealed. "Kitty will be thrilled, and she'll take great care of it."

"I know she will. I think she may call me when Ray tells her."

"You never know who your next buyer might be. You can't judge a book by its cover, either. Don't hesitate to unlock that cabinet if someone shows interest. It's the only way to sell. They have to touch the product."

"You are so wise, my friend. By the way, I'm going to The Hill tomorrow to meet up with the person living in my old apartment."

"That should be interesting. Don't get too emotional and want to move back."

I chuckled. "I won't. Oh, yes, Butler said he'd set up a lunch soon to celebrate my sale."

"Great idea."

Chapter 19

My adventure back to The Hill made me feel a bit anxious. As I planned my day, I decided to take Jenny a bottle of wine as a thank you. It appeared to be a beautiful day, so I was feeling a bit guilty about closing the shop. Perhaps I should have asked Judy to work for me that day. I certainly didn't want to rush my visit. I had so many questions to ask Jenny. As I showered and dressed, I thought of Bertie and Rosie. They had been such good friends to me during the many years I'd lived in that area. I left Augusta curious about what the day would bring.

As I drove closer to the neighborhood, I recalled making this trip many times when I would drive out to wine country for some peace and quiet. I had spent many Sunday afternoons at Wine Country Gardens, eating, reading, or writing.

As soon as I arrived in the neighborhood, my eyes searched for the empty spot where Rosie's shop had burned down. I slowed down. There was an empty space that still contained some ashes. Her shop had been just a couple of blocks from my apartment, so most Saturdays I'd drop by to say hello or to take a look at her latest items. She'd always taken time to visit with me. She had been the first to know how bored I was with my job and how I wished I had something different planned for my life, and she was so good about devoting her attention to her customers. Her wealth of knowledge regarding antiques was amazing. She had many repeat customers, which was something I was beginning to see in my own business. Unfortunately, she dealt mostly in cash, and her young helpers had noticed and started taking advantage of her in many ways. It seemed strange at times to think that she was still with me. So many things—like her rocker—were just great reminders of her.

I looked at my watch to make sure I wasn't too early or late. I was able to park right across the street from my old apartment. On the exterior, it looked pretty much the same. The spring daffodils in Bertie's yard were blooming in the same places. The only things missing were her stone flower pots that had contained fresh ferns every year. I looked up to the second floor, where I'd spent time observing folks like Harry, who had walked the street every day. He would always stop to tease Bertie, who would be sitting on the porch. I knew how much she'd looked forward to it, despite her complaining about it. I went up the stairs and knocked, and then heard someone approaching the door.

"Lily?" Jenny confirmed as she opened the door.

She looked just as I had imagined her. She had light brown hair that was long enough to put up in a messy ponytail. Her penetrating brown eyes glistened. She looked to be in her late thirties or early forties. Her baggy t-shirt and jeans with holes told me she was a person who felt most comfortable in casual clothes. She was pretty close to looking adorable. "Jenny, thanks so much for calling me."

"Come in! Come in!"

My eyes quickly wandered as we headed towards a cozy grouping of furniture in her living room.

"It feels so strange to be here," I said, taking a deep breath.

"Well, I love it here! I've always loved The Hill, and it's so close to my work. I think my landlord said the sign had only been in the window a couple of days when I applied."

"Does he live in the building?"

"No, but he knows the man who lives downstairs pretty well. They're both really nice."

"I'd love to have a little tour, if you don't mind, but I don't want to be nosy."

She chuckled. "Sure! I'm not the neatest housekeeper, so beware."

"Neither am I!"

"I have a simple lunch for us. I picked up some things from Tony's I thought you might enjoy. What would you like to drink?"

"Tea or water will be fine. I brought you a bottle of wine from wine country."

"How sweet! Thank you! Let's go in the kitchen."

"Oh, you kept a touch of red like I had," I said with admiration.

"For some reason, I thought it might have been your favorite color," she said with a grin.

"When I saw the white cabinets, I just had to paint the knobs red," I shared.

"I love it."

Jenny's small kitchen table had a floral vintage tablecloth

on top, like the ones I sold in my shop. She filled 1950s striped glasses with our iced tea.

"Lily, tell me more about why you moved from here. Going from The Hill to the wine country is pretty extreme."

It was hard to simplify my story, but when I got to the part about being bored with my editing job, I could tell she really related.

"You just quit your job cold?" she asked in disbelief.

"I know. I couldn't believe it myself. One day I realized that I just couldn't do it anymore. My friend Alex had quit before I did and had started out as a writer on his own. I was so jealous, but then I told myself that anything would be better than going to work there another day. Also, I had a small amount of savings that I knew would help me for a while."

We started eating our lunch, and Jenny's questions kept coming. When I told her that I'd purchased Rosie's inventory from her shop and explained that it had been the building that had just burned in her neighborhood, she was blown away and wanted to hear more.

Chapter 20

"I've heard folks mention Rosie's shop."

"We'd become close. She was so worried about how I was going to make a living. When she put the shop up for sale, she suggested that I buy the place and take it over. Of course, I wanted to get away. I needed a bigger change than that. After she was killed, it was noted in her will that I had first right of refusal to buy her inventory."

Jenny's eyes got as big as saucers.

I continued by explaining, "I didn't know what to do. I talked to my friend Carrie Mae, an antique shop owner in Augusta, about it. She said that if I decided to buy it, I could store the inventory in an extra house that she had just purchased. I decided it was meant to be and used the last of my savings to do it. When we did an inventory, Carrie Mae said that if I changed my mind, she would buy it. She said the price had been a good deal."

"Oh, that had to be so scary for you!"

"Tell me about it! Alex kept cheering me on. When I looked at the house Carrie Mae was referring to, it was a bright yellow charmer. We stored the things downstairs, and then when I saw that the upstairs had once been an apartment, I thought it made sense for me to move there and open a little shop."

"Wow, what a story!"

"I felt Rosie with me the whole time, and I believe she came with me to Augusta."

"Like a ghost?" Jenny asked.

I nodded. "It's kind of cool. I feel that she protects me, which is crazy. She had this rocking chair that I put on the front porch every morning. It's a wonderful reminder of her. There have been times when the rocker seemingly rocks on its own, which scares the wits out of some folks."

Jenny was listening intently. "That's interesting, because I have strange things happen here. Did you have a ghost when you lived here?"

"No, I can't say that I did. Bertie, however, would refer to a ghost she called Walter."

Jenny giggled. "I know this will sound crazy, but I hear a cat meow every now and then. It's like the cat is right here in the kitchen, especially when I'm eating my breakfast. I'm kind of used to it now."

"Oh my! Perhaps you know that Bertie had a cat named Sugar. That cat was her most prized possession. Bertie would always give her honey because that cat loved it so. I kept telling her it wasn't good for the cat, but she didn't listen."

"Honey?"

I nodded.

"I eat honey on my toast every morning."

We burst into laughter.

"Well, Jenny, now you know who is joining you!"

"I guess I'll have to start talking to her and calling her Sugar. I don't know how supernatural things work, but it doesn't frighten me."

"That's good. Now I have another spirit in my house. I'm pretty sure it's the doctor who once lived there and had an office on the same property. He can get scary occasionally."

"Oh my! Would you like more tea?"

"Please! This visit is so interesting. Tell me more about your job at Concordia Publishing."

"I like the company a lot, and I really like the people I work with, but I'm so frustrated about not being able to do my own writing. When I get home at night, I'm drained and don't feel like it."

"I understand. I felt the same way. Editing takes such concentration."

She nodded. "My friends all work there, so it's not easy to think about leaving."

"Alex was the only one that I really got close to."

"Is it a romantic relationship?"

"No, not at all! I have a significant other that I met in front of Ambrose Church here in the neighborhood. He asked for directions to Joe Garagiola's house, and then we ran into each other at my sister's gallery."

"You've got to be kidding me! I should be paying more attention, I guess. I hardly date at all, but that's fine with me. I frankly don't have the energy that it takes."

"I understand. I felt the same way. I really wish you would drive out to see me and the little town of Augusta sometime."

"Oh, I'd love that! Maybe I'll discover a new mission in life like you did. How did you get your writing job with the magazine? That's pretty cool!"

"Alex does freelance work for them. He knew they were looking for someone to write a human interest column, and he thought of me. I needed the extra income, so it's worked out nicely. I get to choose what I want to write about, which really pleases me."

"What a dream that would be! Hey, we'd better get around to why you came to see me. Let me get the quilt top."

She went towards the bedroom, and I looked around the darling kitchen. I looked above the cabinets where I'd kept a cookie jar that I'd found money in when I'd purchased the inventory from Rosie. If I told that story to Jenny, she'd never believe it in a million years.

"Here's what I found," she said as she returned and pulled the quilt top out of a bag.

"Jenny, this is a Log Cabin pattern. The way you described it, I thought it would just be some blocks sewn together."

Jenny shrugged her shoulders.

Chapter 21

I unfolded the colorful top. It had a musty smell. It was truly scrappy despite Bertie's attempt to make a dark and light side to the Log pieces. I looked closer and saw pieces of fabric that matched some of the aprons that Bertie had frequently worn. It made me smile as I saw her inaccurate attempt at piecing the pattern. God bless her.

"Did you notice that there's a lot of red in this quilt?" Jenny asked.

"She used to tease me quite a bit about my obsession with red-and-white quilts. It's strange that she never talked about having any interest in making one."

"Here's the note that was attached. It was definitely for you."

The simple message said, "For Lily." It was Bertie's handwriting. There was no doubt. Had she put the quilt away with a note so she would remember who it was for, or had she put it away in anger when I'd told her I was moving away? I would never know.

"There were other things, but I left them in her trunk,"

Jenny went on. "I'm personally not interested in anything else that I saw. There were some linens and a baby cap."

"Interesting. I guess one day we'll all leave things behind that won't have an explanation."

Jenny nodded. "Well, let me show you around the place," she offered as we got up from the table. "The second bedroom is serving as a catchall place for me. It's nice having an extra bed, but no one usually sees this room."

"It was my quilt room," I said proudly. "I had a large table in the center so it would be under the light. When I'd get a new quilt, I would spread it out and examine its condition before storing it. Sometimes there were surprises and sometimes there were disappointments."

"Like what?" Her face wrinkled in question.

"With antique quilts, you never know what you're getting. I would look for stains or damage that needed attention. Sometimes I'd wash them before putting them away. I tried to buy quilts that had never been washed. The sizing on the fabric can keep them clean longer." I looked around the room. "I see you removed the shelving that I left."

"Yes. Since I planned for this to be another bedroom, the shelves had to go. Did you store your quilts on them?"

I nodded and smiled.

"I really like my master bedroom," Jenny said as we entered it. "These old houses have large rooms, which I love."

"I agree. You have very good taste."

"I should probably give my mom the credit. She loves to decorate and has a say in my world most of the time."

"Does she live close by?"

"Yes. She lives in Hampton Gardens apartments."

"Those are still maintained nicely and are in a good

location."

She nodded in agreement. "Let's go out to the porch."

"Oh, Jenny, I loved this porch! I wish you could have known some of the neighborhood characters that I got to know through the years. Harry from down the street and Bertie had a love-hate relationship. After Bertie died, Harry took her cat and Sugar lived with him."

Jenny smiled and said, "Oh, how sweet!"

"Then sometime later, Harry called to tell me that Sugar had passed away from a lonely heart. The next thing I knew, Harry had passed on as well."

"How sad. I'm so glad you told me about Sugar. She will now be my invisible pet cat."

We chuckled, then sat on the porch for another half hour drinking tea. Jenny shared some of her observations regarding the neighborhood, but it didn't appear that she had engaged with the community.

"Well, Jenny, I don't want to wear out my welcome. I'd better take my quilt top and go home. I really appreciate the lunch and your letting me see the place. I hope you'll come out to Augusta sometime soon."

"I'll do that when time allows. Enjoy your keepsake from Bertie. I hope in some way she knows you now have it."

I left Jenny's apartment feeling pretty good. I had no regrets about moving from The Hill like I'd thought I might. Jenny was certainly younger than me, but she was a lot like me. Her world didn't include quilts, but from the inventory of books she'd had around the place, I'd surmised that she must be an avid reader. Her earth-toned décor was nicely done, and I liked that she'd kept the touch of red in the kitchen.

I made a quick stop at Tony's to stock up on some of my favorite things and then visited the corner market that had locally-made goodies. Going by St. Ambrose Church made me think of my sweet Marc.

When I arrived back at the yellow house in Augusta, I took Bertie's quilt top out of the bag. I wanted to air it out after I looked at it again by myself. It looked like some of my work, where there were some good stitching days and some bad ones. I remembered Bertie complaining about her eyesight in those later years. I wished I could hug her and thank her for thinking of me. I could still hear her footsteps coming up the stairs as soon as she heard me get up in the morning. Sometimes she had food to share—and sometimes she was just lonely for a little gossip.

Chapter 22

The next day, I made a point of emailing my siblings about the experience of being in my previous apartment once again. The email was longer than I had planned, but I wanted them to know how much I liked Jenny. I couldn't wait for any responses because by the time I completed my email, it was time to open the shop.

After I put Rosie's chair on the porch, I made my daily walk through the shop to do any straightening that was needed. I walked into the quilt room, and everything seemed fine. When I got to the counter, something made me go back into the quilt room. I walked to the quilt cabinet and my heart sank. A quilt was missing! Kitty's Baltimore Album quilt was still there. Which one was gone? I rushed to get the inventory list that Butler had left with me. Fortunately, next to the description was a photo of each quilt.

It didn't take long to figure out which one was missing through the glass cabinet doors. It was a crazy quilt that had an unusual appliqué of a gloved hand holding a silk scarf. I remembered that I'd had to be careful about how I'd folded it so the folds wouldn't affect the motif. Butler's stock number was 13300. The description read, "Crazy quilt made by Florence E. McKinney in 1886. It is pieced, appliquéd, embroidered, and embellished. There are approximately one hundred different animals depicted on the quilt in assorted sizes. Black velvet border with ribbon flowers. 80" x 76". Made in Brooklyn Heights, New York. Excellent condition. $18,000.00."

The quilt wasn't there. It wasn't anywhere! The cabinet was still locked. With no windows in the room and an activated alarm system, how could this have happened? To be certain that it was indeed missing, I unlocked the cabinet and counted all the quilts. When Butler had delivered them to me, there had been twenty-five quilts. Now there were only twenty-four.

"Oh, dear Lord in heaven," I said aloud. "Please don't let this be happening."

I looked at the list again. The loss of eighteen thousand dollars was sickening. I couldn't possibly tell Butler that a quilt was missing. He would come out immediately and take all the quilts back. However, I wouldn't dare report this to the police without talking to Butler first.

I went to get a drink of water because I had begun to feel faint. I turned my sign to indicate that the shop was closed and locked the door. I then remembered a night or two ago, when I'd seen the light on in the quilt room after I was pretty sure I had turned it off. Had someone been in the room?

I drank the whole glass of water and went back to the quilt room. I tried to think of who had been in the room recently. I could count on my fingers the few times I'd unlocked the cabinet for anyone. As soon as folks saw one of the price tags, their interest waned.

Beginning to feel nauseous, I went upstairs to rest for a few minutes. I could hear someone trying to open the shop door, but I was too sick to answer. I wished I hadn't left Rosie's rocker outside, but right then, I didn't care. It had a 1930s quilt on the back, which could easily be gone when I got back to the rocker, but I had to concentrate on the missing crazy quilt.

I wanted to ask for help, but who could I confide in? I sure didn't want to upset Carrie Mae and let her think I had been careless. Even she would never understand how this could happen. My stomach churned, and soon I was in the bathroom retching horribly. I wanted to die right then and there. The sound of someone trying to get me to answer the door continued. They tried the door and then proceeded to knock. Why didn't they just go away? After a bit, there was silence.

I stared out of the back windows on the porch, trying to clear my head. I started to consider that I had two spirits in the house and thought perhaps one had moved things around. However, the things moved previously had belonged to Doc, who'd had a reason. Rosie was harmless. Truly, there was no reason for either one of them to move that quilt. How long could I put this off without telling Butler? Perhaps if a little time went by, I would discover that there had been some kind of mix-up.

At four, I returned downstairs. When I could tell that no one was near the shop, I decided to go out and bring in the rocker and quilt. I walked back to the quilt room and got on my knees to ask the Almighty for some help.

Chapter 23

The next morning, I paced from the kitchen to the quilt room and back again. I couldn't think of one good possibility for where the quilt could be. Not one. Was Doc trying to terrify me? I still felt that I needed a little more time before I alerted Butler. The phone rang, and it was Carrie Mae. It didn't take her long to mention that Betty had tried to visit me yesterday to drop off some garden lettuce, but my shop was closed, and the door was locked.

"She was concerned about you leaving your rocker outside with such a lovely quilt on it."

I paused. I really didn't want to lie to Carrie Mae. "I wasn't feeling well. I locked the door and forgot all about the rocker and quilt."

"Well, honey, what's the matter?" she asked in a motherly tone.

"Something very bad happened, and it made me ill."

"What, child? What?"

I paused again. "I'm afraid to tell you."

"Me? You're afraid to tell me?"

"It's not good. I should probably be telling the police, not you."

"Are you hurt? Did someone hurt or threaten you?"

"Worse."

"Worse?"

"I'm not trying to be a drama queen here, honestly!" I began to cry.

"I'll be right over. Don't open the shop until I get there."

"Okay," I said, sniffling. "I'll watch for you." When I hung up, I already felt a little better. I told myself that two minds were better than one, and I trusted Carrie Mae. Maybe she could think of something I hadn't yet.

It didn't take long before Carrie Mae was knocking at the door. She took one look at me and wrapped me in her arms. "It's going to be okay, whatever it is. Let's go out on the porch and talk about it."

We walked onto the back porch, where I had some wicker furniture and plants. We sat on the loveseat. I asked Carrie Mae if she wanted some tea, and she declined.

"I was up early and have already had my tea. Now let's hear what's on your mind."

"Well, I've really failed. I'm totally baffled by something that's taken place."

"Go ahead. What took place?"

I took a deep breath. "One of Butler's quilts is missing!" I blurted out. "I've only had that case open a few times. I'm always there with anyone who's looking at quilts. I have an alarm system and everything! I went over the records, and I know which one is missing."

"That's the really terrible thing that's upsetting you this much?"

"Of course! Butler will be furious and will never trust me again. Some caretaker and business owner I turned out to be. I can't bring myself to tell him yet. I just have to find that quilt!"

"Thank goodness that's all it is, Lily. I was worried that someone had tried to harm you. It's only a quilt. We'll get to the bottom of it." She patted my hand gently.

"It's an eighteen-thousand-dollar quilt, not just any quilt! What about Butler?"

"Never mind about Butler right now. He'll understand when we know more. Relax, honey. There's always an explanation. Remember what we went through with his nephew?"

I nodded and explained, "There were twenty-five quilts brought in, and now there are only twenty-four. Ray has a down payment on one for Kitty, but that one is still here."

"Well, aren't we glad that it wasn't Kitty's quilt that was taken?" Carrie Mae smiled. "See? There's always a bright side."

I got up and paced the floor. I was starting to feel sick again just talking about it.

"Look at you! This is all part of doing business. There are scary moments from time to time. I know it feels like a personal attack, but these things happen."

"Eighteen thousand dollars is not a minor business mistake! I'll never be able to pay Butler back."

"I know, I know. Look at me, Lily. You've had strange things go on here ever since you've moved in. You brought Rosie here, and you obviously got Doc all riled up trying to find out about his past. I say we all put our heads together and get you through this."

"Are you referring to the Dinner Detectives?"

"Why not?"

"Oh, Carrie Mae, I can't let this get out!"

"I agree, but I don't think you have to worry about any of them. They'll know how serious this is."

"I'll have to do something soon. I can't let this go. Maybe I should just go ahead and call the sheriff's department."

"That's up to you, sweetie, but they won't take kindly to you blaming ghosts for what might be going on. They'll notify Butler first thing. Let's see if the Dinner Detectives can come up with something. Let's call an emergency meeting right now and see if we can get them here tonight."

"Seriously?"

"The sooner, the better!"

Chapter 24

We made calls to the Dinner Detectives. Karen said she might be late but would be there at some point. Bonita seemed the most concerned and wanted to know more than I wanted to share over the phone. Carrie Mae suggested that we order carryout from Kate's Coffee to keep it simple. I agreed to pick it up, and Betty said she'd come with Carrie Mae as always.

Feeling a bit better about having their support, I opened the shop for the afternoon, but kept a close eye on the quilt room. I wasn't in the mood for customer chatter, so I opened my laptop to check my emails. My siblings remained silent. Marc called in the afternoon to check on my availability for a Cardinals game he wanted to go to. I checked my calendar, but evidently my mood was noticed.

"Are you okay?"

"Oh, sure. I'm a little distracted. I have folks in the shop right now."

"Sorry. I'll let you get back to work. I'm leaving for a two-day meeting in Kansas City, but when I return, I'll be out to see my sweetheart."

"Your sweetheart would like that very much." For a moment, I forgot about the crazy quilt. If only Marc knew how I was struggling right now. After we hung up, I went to help a customer who was heading toward the quilt room.

"Can I help you?" I asked.

"I'm curious about your quilts," she said. "I've always had a fondness for quilts, but I didn't grow up with them like most people."

"Oh, that's too bad," I responded.

"We had store-bought blankets growing up. My mother never liked handmade things. She said it was a sign of being poor."

"She probably wanted the very best for you. Maybe she didn't have the nicest things when she was growing up."

"Exactly! You have some very pretty ones here. Do you quilt?"

"I'm learning. We have an ongoing quilt class here at our local library. Right now, we're all working on a wine country quilt."

"That sounds wonderful. I don't know how these quilters do all that handiwork."

"It takes practice. I'm finding that out."

"I see that you have some very nice ones in that cabinet. Are they more expensive?"

"Yes, they are. I'd be happy to show any of them to you if you're interested."

She smiled.

"What kind of quilt would you be interested in?"

"I think I'll know it when I see it. I see that some displayed here are around five hundred dollars. How much do the quilts in the cabinet cost?"

"Quite a bit more."

"How much more?"

"Hundreds and thousands more."

Her eyes widened. "Now I see why they're under lock and key. Do people pay that kind of money for quilts?"

I nodded. Now she seemed even more intrigued. I said, "People invest in quilts and collect them. They're always looking to better their collections or investments."

"Then they don't put them on their beds?"

"Some might. Some move them on to other dealers around the world."

"How very interesting! If it's not too much trouble, could I see that pretty all-white one?" She pointed directly to a wholecloth quilt on the top shelf in the cabinet.

"I'll get the key and show it to you."

"I see that you have an all-white one here on this chair, but it doesn't seem as detailed."

I left her and went to get the key. I was grateful that no one else was in the shop at the time. I returned, nervously unlocked the cabinet, and pulled out the wholecloth quilt. We remained silent as the customer helped me open the impressive white quilt. It was a beauty.

"Look at this center design," she said in awe. "It's all pineapples, isn't it? How did they make this?"

"It was made in 1850. This was made for a four-poster bed. See how the bottom corners are cut out? It's rather large because the beds were higher at that time. During that period, people used bed steps to get onto their beds."

"I've heard of bed steps before."

"The fringe on the edge was used around that time, too.

It's starting to show some deterioration. You don't see this combination every day. I can only imagine the household it came from."

"My, you know so much about quilts."

I smiled. "I've always loved pineapples. You probably know that they're a sign of hospitality."

"Yes, I know. Did you notice that the pineapple crown is the design the quilter used around the border?"

I picked up the tag and read aloud that the quilt was made in South Carolina, but the maker was unknown.

"What a shame, since she put so much work into this."

"It is a shame that this beautiful quilt is out here being admired and we can't give recognition to whoever made it. That happens frequently," I lamented.

"Do I dare ask the price?"

"It's nine thousand dollars. I'm actually surprised it's not more." The look on the customer's face was expressionless. Had she not heard me?

"I saw that the white one over here on the rack is six hundred dollars."

"Yes, but you can surely see the difference, can't you?"

"Yes, indeed! May I see the back?"

We turned the quilt over. It was spotless. The intricate quilting designs showed even better. "I have a feeling that this was never used. It was likely put away for a very special occasion," I said. We began to fold up the quilt.

"Thank you for showing this to me. If you can do a tad bit better on the price, I'd like to purchase it."

"You would?" I asked, feeling lightheaded once again.

"If I'm going to own a quilt, I want the best, and I want it to be fabulous!" she exclaimed.

"I'm selling these quilts for a friend, but I can certainly give you ten percent off."

"Excellent. I'm excited."

My legs were weak, but I nodded and smiled like this was an everyday occurrence. I locked the cabinet and took the quilt to the counter. I wrapped it carefully in acid-free tissue paper and put it in a shopping bag.

Chapter 25

There weren't enough words to express my gratitude to this woman for making such a big purchase. She obviously had deep pockets to be able to afford the very best. I was proud of myself for taking the time to educate her without feeling like it was a sales tactic. I hadn't thought for one moment that she would actually buy a quilt!

I wanted to get on the phone and call Butler, but then I'd have to tell him about the quilt that was missing. I decided to wait and see what the Dinner Detectives had to say. I made a note in my records that I had sold the wholecloth quilt from South Carolina. Now there were twenty-three quilts in the cabinet. An hour later, I closed the shop and went to pick up my deli order from Kate's Coffee.

"How was your day?" Randal asked.

"Very good, I have to say," I said, smiling.

"Terrific! Are you having a little celebration tonight?" he asked as he looked at my order.

"It's just the Dinner Detectives." I blushed.

"You know that your group is always welcome to meet

here," Randal mentioned.

"Well, these ladies like their wine, so what can I say?"

He chuckled and nodded. "Of course. You all enjoy! I appreciate the order."

As I got in my car, I was reminded once again that I lived in a very small town. When I lived on The Hill, no one had ever asked any questions or noticed very much about my personal life. Bertie had been an exception. I'd learned to appreciate her concern and her desire to be neighborly.

I prepared the upstairs porch for our meeting. The spring air encouraged me to open some of the windows so we could feel the breeze. I got out the wine and arranged our little deli sandwiches on a tiered platter to make them look more festive. For a moment I felt excited about our get-together—until I remembered the reason for the meeting. The pangs of sickness came back as I heard a knock at the door. Carrie Mae and Betty were the first to arrive.

"Are you feeling okay, sweetie?" Carrie Mae asked as they came in.

"Now that the two of you are here, I feel much better," I replied. "Oh, here come Karen and Bonita, so we'll just go upstairs together. Welcome, ladies!"

Bonita had a very concerned look on her face. She touched my hand as we started up the stairs. She probably thought I was stressed over the spirits acting up.

"I brought the wine again," Karen said as she presented a bottle to me. "It's not fair for you to always provide everything, and you all seemed to enjoy this wine last time."

"We did!" Carrie Mae replied as she seated herself by one of the windows. "I love this weather! It's so nice to leave the windows open at night. I remember the breezes from when

Art and I lived up here. Of course, it wasn't all gussied up like Lily has it."

We chuckled.

"I'm helping myself to these sandwiches," Betty stated. "I'm hungry, and they look delicious."

Karen poured wine for everyone. We chose the same seats we'd occupied the last time we'd met. Suddenly, everyone became quiet and looked to me for an explanation for the night's meeting.

"Okay, here's the deal," I began. "I shared with Carrie Mae this morning what I discovered yesterday." I took a deep breath. "I'm totally sick with worry about what has happened, and Carrie Mae assured me there would be an explanation and that it would be best to include you all."

"What's happened?" Karen asked.

"You have to promise me that what is discussed in this room tonight remains in this room," I stated.

"Of course, Lily," Betty responded. "That goes without saying."

I began telling them every little detail about looking in the cabinet and discovering that there was a quilt missing. Then I explained that there had been a time or two when the light had been on in the quilt room when I had remembered turning it off. They gasped, but didn't say anything. I was pleased not to be interrupted as I continued. After I had shared the situation with them, I brought my explanation to a close.

"Oh, how awful for you," Karen was the first to say. "I've had things stolen, but nothing of this magnitude."

Chapter 26

"So, the cabinet was locked?" Bonita wanted to confirm. "Are you very certain about that?"

"Yes, most certain," I said. "I take this responsibility quite seriously. I have the alarm as well, which didn't go off. No glass was broken to get into the cabinet, and I still had my key."

"I hate to add salt here, Lily, but there are lockpickers that can get in any door," Karen offered.

"I have thought of that," I said, feeling forlorn.

"Lordy, ladies, you know how Doc has moved things around here before," Carrie Mae said.

"But Carrie Mae, those were his things," I argued. "This quilt doesn't belong to him, and he's never bothered my quilts before."

"I think we can rule Doc out if we don't find the quilt in his office or in the basement," Betty suggested. "Have you looked in those two places?"

"No," I said quietly.

"Then there's no time like the present, Lily," Carrie Mae

said firmly. "I'll go with you if you like. There's no point in discussing this any further until we rule that out."

Bonita remained silent. She looked deep in thought.

"You all stay here," Carrie Mae instructed. "Let's go, Lily."

She took my hand, and off we went. I grabbed the keys to the basement and to Doc's office. Carrie Mae reminded me that we would each need a flashlight. We headed to Doc's office first.

The office door creaked as I slowly opened it. We stood there with our flashlights, half-hoping that Doc would flash his own lights to help us see better! The front of the office was as I had left it from Christmas, and the back part was the newly-built replacement due to the fire. The place was pretty empty.

"It's good enough for me. How about you?" Carrie Mae asked.

"Me too!" I said, locking the door. I happened to glance up toward the house and saw the ladies looking out the window to see if we had discovered anything.

We carefully walked to the side of the house, where the basement door was located. I always kept the light on above the door so I could see to unlock it. From there, it was pitch-black. "Carrie Mae, hold on to me," I instructed. "These steps are narrow and steep. Hold on to the rail, and I'll shine the light ahead."

"Okay, okay," she agreed as she slowly took one step at a time. "Just don't rush me."

"This is so creepy!" I whispered. "Can you imagine coming down here with the doctor in those days?"

"Shine your flashlight on one side, and I'll do the other side," Carrie Mae advised. "Lord, it smells old and moldy. Do you get any of this smell upstairs?"

"No, I can't say that I do," I responded. "What's that? What was that noise?"

"I don't know."

"It sounded like women laughing," I said.

"My hearing isn't so good, you know," Carrie Mae replied.

"There it is again. Did you hear it this time?"

She slowly nodded her head. "Maybe, but never mind. Do you see anything?"

"No. I don't see anything different, but I don't like that creepy sound."

"Okay, let's go."

"Did you lock the door, Carrie Mae?" I asked with the jitters. "I thought it was open."

"What? Does it open now?"

"Yes," I said with relief. "Let's go!"

We exited much faster than we had entered!

Chapter 27

"Whew!" Carrie Mae said, taking a deep breath. "Good to be in fresh air. Guess we can rule out Doc as a suspect."

"But Carrie Mae, remember that sound we heard?" I reminded her.

"I suppose I did hear something, but I was mostly looking. Your assessment of women giggling is fair, but let's forget that for now and get inside!"

When we returned upstairs and joined the others, the looks on their faces were almost comical.

"Any luck?" Karen asked.

Carrie Mae and I looked at each other and paused.

"You saw nothing?" Betty asked with her hands on her hips.

"We didn't find a quilt, but we heard something," I reported.

"What did you hear?" Bonita asked.

"I wasn't sure what it sounded like until I heard it the second time," I said.

"And?" Bonita questioned.

"It was a constant sound of women laughing," I confessed. "I don't know how else to describe it."

They were puzzled as well.

"Did you hear it, Carrie Mae?" Betty asked.

She nodded. "Now you all know that I don't hear so well," Carrie Mae said. "It wasn't you all, was it?"

Everyone then broke into laughter.

"Now, stop, ladies, and think about what you just heard," Betty urged. "Doc was affiliated with lots of women, remember?"

"Oh, Betty, that's pretty farfetched thinking," Karen voiced.

"Have you ever heard that noise before tonight?" Bonita asked.

Everyone stared at me. "No, but I want to hear what each of you are thinking right now," I said in frustration. "That's why you're here tonight. Forget the noise. My real concern is Butler, not me. He may or may not want me to call the police. I really worry about what Butler will think."

"I have a feeling that Butler won't want the police involved," Carrie Mae said. "I know him pretty well. He knows that if it gets out that you have high-dollar quilts, it will risk their security."

"She's right," Betty agreed.

"What about Rosie?" Karen asked. "What makes her the innocent party here?"

"Rosie has been my protector," I explained. "Rosie would understand how hurtful this is. She had two employees steal from her before she died."

"Ladies, I think this is God's way of informing you that He is in charge, not these silly spirits," Bonita suggested.

"Perhaps we should all pray together, yes?"

"Oh, Bonita, I have prayed and prayed," I lamented.

"Have you seen anyone lurking around the neighborhood that you've wondered about?" Karen asked.

"I don't know about the neighborhood, but I do get some interesting people in the shop trying to sell me quilts, and it doesn't always go well," I replied.

"Did you ever get the sense that they might come back to harm you?"

I began to feel uncomfortable.

"Maybe they think you're too hoity-toity to want their quilts," Karen continued. "We have folks tell us that their husbands can make barn quilts, and they question us as to why ours cost so much. They never like my answer."

"I could see some of them wanting to slash my tires or key my car, but taking a quilt is a little beyond my imagination," I said.

Bonita said, "I'm still thinking about the voices you just heard, Lily. Do you really feel safe? You must ask God for protection and trust Him."

"Thank you, Bonita," Carrie Mae agreed.

"If Lily was in any danger, she would know by now," Betty said. "Right, everyone?"

"Ladies, let's not make Lily feel worse," Karen warned.

"Lily, can't you ask Rosie to protect you from Doc?" Betty asked with a teasing smile on her face.

"Don't count on that," Bonita stated. "Remember, I told you who is in charge here."

"She's right, Lily," Carrie Mae said. Then, turning her attention to her food, she said, "My, these sandwiches are delicious."

"I'm sorry I don't have any dessert," I said apologetically. "I don't know what I was thinking."

"Well, next time, come to my house. We need to make that happen before Bonita leaves," Karen suggested.

"That is very gracious, Karen, but with all that Lily has going on here, we should meet here," Carrie Mae insisted. "Lily, the next time you hear those voices, listen very carefully."

"I will."

"I'm sorry, Lily, but I'm trying very hard to keep my eyes open," Carrie Mae stated. "Are you ready to go home, Betty?"

"I am," Betty agreed. "After all this talk, I need to rest."

"We should all go," Bonita said. "I will pray for you tonight, Lily. You must have some peace here."

"Thank you, Bonita," I said with a smile. "I appreciate you reminding us of God's protection. I truly believe in that."

She smiled and gave me a warm embrace. How nice it felt to be in the company of such good friends, especially when my heart was so heavy.

Chapter 28

Once again, the Dinner Detectives left my house without solving anything, but I felt better. It was too bad I couldn't share my good news about selling the wholecloth quilt with them, but it would have changed the reason behind them coming to my home. Their comments had helped me to think outside the box. I was mentally drained, but I liked how Bonita had reminded me to turn my concerns over to God. I put away the rest of the sandwiches and went down to turn on the alarm. My mind was weary. I wanted to forget the noises I'd heard. I said my prayers and crawled into bed, knowing that sleep would come soon.

It didn't take long for me to dream about Doc and his hundreds of women laughing at me. They were everywhere I went. When I opened the closets, they popped out. I was screaming Rosie's name, pleading with her to help me. That was when I woke up. I got up and tried to think of something else. I turned on the TV. When I couldn't pay attention to that, I got my laptop and took it to bed. I decided to check my emails.

It was good to read a pleasant message from Ellen. She was getting excited about our upcoming visit. She'd decided to get a little painting done on her house and was trying to organize her thoughts about what we should do during our visit. I had to admit that I was really excited about this trip, and I would be glad to get away from the drama in my own home.

Loretta responded that she needed new clothes for the trip because she hadn't been shopping for herself in ages. She said it was always a bad idea to take Sarah shopping with her because she would end up just buying items for Sarah and Lucy. There had been no response from Laurie, which didn't surprise me. It did make me wonder how she was doing. Lynn finally chimed in, saying that the number one place she wanted to visit was The National Quilt Museum that she'd heard so much about. I, too, was curious to see the latest and greatest quilts from around the world.

I was beginning to feel calmer, so I tried again to get some sleep. I turned out the lights and attempted to picture myself in Paducah, Kentucky. I'd have to remember to ask Judy to fill in for me while I'd be gone like I had so many times before. I'd heard that Paducah was also called Quilt City USA. Nice!

In a few hours, the morning sunshine came directly through my window. It forced me to get up and start the day. I remembered that it was quilt class day. The class would be a nice distraction from thoughts about my missing quilt.

As soon as I got coffee, I walked into the quilt room, hoping that the crazy quilt would have reappeared. I stood there staring at the cabinet. Once again, I heard women's voices laughing. It scared me, so I went back to the counter, and the noise went away. Why was I hearing that? Maybe it was just my imagination.

I tried to concentrate on going to class, so I got out my quilt block supplies and put them in my travel quilt bag to take with me. I wasn't quite finished with the first one, but the class would be expecting me to announce my next design. I remembered taking photos around Augusta near Christmastime. One photo was of Ebenezer United Church of Christ, which played quite a role in the Christmas Walk. The photo showed most of the steeple. That would make a great redwork block.

Hoping we would have pastries at class, I took a last sip of coffee and hurried out the door. Once there, I was surprised to see Gracie walk in. Was she going to participate?

"Hi, Gracie," I greeted. "Good of you to join us!"

"Thanks. I have Brenda watching the shop today, so I thought I would drop in."

"Look who's here!" Susan said when we walked in. "Help yourselves to some coffee and muffins that Judy brought from the coffee shop, and then we'll get started. Edna, good to see you back! How is that new knee working for you?"

"It was a tough process, but I'm doing better."

"Good to hear!" Susan responded. "We want to welcome Gracie today," she mentioned.

"Glad to be here," Gracie replied. "I'm just amazed at what you all do."

Chapter 29

"Today, besides showing our blocks, we should announce our next one," Susan said. "I will also help you identify your block, which is necessary for this kind of quilt. People will want to know what the name of a building is, for instance."

"Susan said that if we made a pattern for any of our designs, she would copy them for sharing, which I think is very nice of her," Heidi said.

"Thank you, Susan," Marilyn said. "We really do have some talented people in this class."

It was fun and interesting hearing about how each person chose the blocks they did for their quilt. When I told them that I had chosen Ebenezer Church for my next block, it got a great response.

"That's my church," Heidi bragged. "I may have to do that one also."

"Good idea!" I agreed. I then realized that I was enjoying myself, even though my mind had constantly been on my missing quilt.

"Lily, before you go, I want a word with you," Gracie

whispered.

When Gracie and I walked out together, she said something that totally caught me off guard.

"Congratulations on selling that wonderful wholecloth quilt," she said, giving me a knowing smile.

"How did you know?"

"The owner came in the shop to show it to me."

"Oh!"

"It was amazing! I was pleased that she showed it to me. She was just thrilled about it."

"That she was, but I guess I feel like I don't want the word to get out about Butler's quilts."

"Well, if it makes you feel any better, she didn't say what she paid for it."

"That's good. I'm a little paranoid about security, I guess."

"You should feel proud! You have a wonderful business there. You probably make more off of one quilt than I do selling fabric all month."

"I never thought of it that way. Thanks for not saying anything in front of the other folks today."

"Sure! Hey, do you have time for lunch? I have the entire day since Brenda's at the shop, so I'm going to take advantage of it. I'm hungry for some clam chowder at Ashley Rose. How about it?"

"You know, that sounds good. I think I will join you."

"Okay, I'll meet you there."

I felt comfortable going back to Ashley Rose. Anthony might not even hang out there anymore for all I knew. When I walked in, Gracie wasn't there. She'd probably gone by to check on Brenda.

"Well, am I dreaming or what?" Sally joked from behind

the counter. "Long time, no see!"

"I know, it's been a while. I'm meeting my friend for lunch, so we'll take that booth over there."

"And miss my good company?" Anthony's voice said from behind me.

I jumped. "Oh! Hello, Anthony!" I said, unable to hide my surprise. "How are you?"

"Good. Yourself?" he asked flirtatiously.

"Pretty good," I replied. "I'm meeting Gracie here for lunch. I think you met at her at Karen's New Year's Eve party. She should be here anytime."

"Well, I'd better not start flirting with you, then." He winked.

I laughed.

"Shucks, I thought I'd have my two favorite people here for lunch today," Sally quipped.

Anthony smoothly slipped his arm around me. "Maybe next week you'll get lucky, Sally," he teased.

"Oh, here you are!" Gracie said, joining us. "Hello, Anthony."

"How nice that you remembered my name," he said, giving Gracie a very friendly smile.

"I have a booth for us," I said as I moved closer to it.

"Anthony, you can join us if you'd like," Gracie said.

"I would absolutely be honored, but Miss Sally and I have some things to discuss in private," he joked.

I smiled and walked to the booth. The whole situation felt awkward.

"I truly meant what I suggested, Lily," Gracie repeated. "I know you like him."

I looked at her and could feel my eyes widen. "Well, it's

not okay with me, so let's get this clam chowder ordered," I said, hoping to move on.

"You are something, Lily Girl," Gracie giggled. "You sure don't have any problem getting men around here. I could use a lesson or two from you."

"I've told you, Marc is my significant other and has been for some time."

"Okay, okay! I think he's a keeper too," Gracie said, smiling.

"If you have any interest in Anthony, Sally would be happy to drop a hint for you," I informed her.

"I think Anthony would be too much for me to handle," she laughed.

The chowder finally arrived, and it was delicious. Gracie was chatty and always had business questions for me. Thankfully, my back was facing the counter, so I didn't have to see Anthony. I was sure that he kept his eye on us.

"We should do this more often, Lily," Gracie suggested. "There are times when I feel pretty lonely since I've moved to Augusta. Did you ever feel that way?"

"Sure. I got used to it and now really enjoy the quiet compared to the noise I heard in the city every day."

"I try to stay busy sewing in my free time. We always need samples for the shop. I try not to think about my former friend, but it's hard sometimes."

I nodded. "I'm proud of you for breaking that off. Did Brenda ever suspect anyone?"

"She never suspected me, let's put it that way. Her marriage is in trouble, but she doesn't do much to try and save it."

When I told the waitress to bring our ticket, she said

that the gentleman at the counter had taken care of it. That must have been Anthony. Gracie and I smiled at one another. When we got up to leave, Gracie was the first to go over and thank him. Despite her protests, maybe she had some interest in him after all.

"It was a pleasure to see you ladies," Anthony said as he stood up to say goodbye.

I quickly walked away so he wouldn't try to kiss me or expertly slip that arm around me again!

Chapter 30

When I got back to the shop, my landline was ringing.

"Lily Rosenthal?" the man on the phone asked.

"Yes, speaking."

"My name is Henry Walters, and I live in South St. Louis. I got your name from someone who told me that you buy quilts."

"I see. Do you want to sell some?"

"Yes, I've been a collector of a variety of quilts through the years. I'm a truck driver, so I've accumulated quilts from all over the country."

"Oh."

"I need to sell some of them, and I could use advice on a few that I need some help with. Is there any way you would make a house call on a day when your business is closed? I'll pay you for your time."

"Perhaps," I said.

"I live in the Tower Grove Park area."

"I see. I'm familiar with it."

"How soon could you come?"

"Maybe Monday at about one, but don't hold me to it right now."

"Oh, that would be great!"

We exchanged contact information. Butler was the only quilt collector I knew. I was sure this guy's quilts would be nothing fancy, but if his prices were right, I might benefit. In time, he might be able to buy from me.

I went out to water the flowers before settling in for the evening with my quilt blocks. I tried not to think about the missing quilt, but it resurfaced in my mind every time I had a still moment. The ten o'clock news was coming on when my cell phone rang. It was Gracie.

"Lily, you won't believe who just called me!"

"I guess you'd better tell me."

"Anthony!"

My heart sank. "Really? How did that happen?"

"He said he got my personal information from Sally. What do you make of it?"

"Well, you're both single and are two nice people. Did he ask you out?"

"Yes, he asked me out to dinner."

"You'll certainly learn about wine, and he's quite charming."

"I feel rather strange about it all because I know he'd rather be with you. I'll let you know how it goes. I hope you don't mind me going."

"Absolutely not," I said before hanging up.

Well, there it was. Anthony was moving on right in front of me. Was it an attempt to make me jealous or to just get my attention? What if Gracie really fell for him? I should be happy for her. It might also help her get over her last relationship. I went to bed thinking about my conversation with Gracie. Feeling frustrated, I decided to turn my thoughts to Marc. Marc, the baseball guy, the man who was indeed my heartthrob, and who I would be seeing soon.

The next morning, as I was paying a bill, I was surprised to see a call come in from Holly. "Hello, stranger!" I said. "I've been missing you!"

"I know. I miss you, too!"

"What's keeping you so busy?"

"I've had the painters here, and I continue to pitch things to make room for new pieces. I bought a new living room rug that's to die for. I'm also moving my sewing room into what was the den, so I have more room."

"Holy cow! I'm so happy for you. It has to be exciting."

She giggled. "I've also been meeting up with Clete about once a week, which is really something I look forward to. Don't make too much of it. He's not perfect, but it's so nice to go out to eat with someone every now and then. Clete said he'd like to meet you at some point."

"I'll try to come see you soon when I get to the city."

"How is Marc?"

"He's great! I hope to see him this weekend. I'm anxious for you to come out and see the amazing quilts I'm trying to sell for Butler. By the way, they're for sale, and I only know of one person who can actually afford them."

She laughed.

"I don't think I'll need another quilt. I'm trying to get rid of things, remember?"

"We never need another quilt, but these are amazing. I sold one for nine thousand dollars and am holding another one with an even higher price."

"Get out! You have got to be kidding!"

"No! I'm serious!"

"Okay. I may get Clete to come out there sooner rather than later."

"I'll try not to sell out!" I teased.

She burst into laughter.

"I can't wait to tell you about the woman who lives in my old apartment."

"Well, it can't be now. UPS is at my door."

"Okay, come out soon. I love you, girlfriend!"

"I love you, too!"

What a change it was to have this kind of conversation with Holly. Her late husband would never let her do anything to update the house, so she was really enjoying it for the first time. I got another cup of coffee and checked the quilt room. I stood there staring at the cabinet as if the crazy quilt was going to reappear.

Chapter 31

"Anyone here?" I heard a man's voice call out. I went to see who it was. It was Chuck Waller, the quilt buyer from Kentucky.

"Hi, Chuck!" I greeted him.

"How is the Augusta quilt lady?" he asked. "What do you want to get rid of today? Is there anything I can take off your hands for a good price?"

"Not for what you're willing to offer," I said teasingly.

"Let me take a look," he said, walking toward the quilt room. I followed behind him.

"Well, I'll be, a new cabinet of quilts under glass! Looks like you came into some dough!"

"I'm helping out another dealer. Those are not your kind of quilts."

"You're out of my league, alright. How much do you want for this Double Wedding Ring and Irish Chain here on this shelf?"

"I'll give you twenty percent off. That's it."

"Can't do it. Sorry!" he said, throwing up his hands.

"Just where do you pass on these bargain quilts, Chuck?"

"That's for me to know, little lady," he said with a wink.

"I guess you're out of luck this time."

"I guess so. I'll stop by Carrie Mae's and take a look over there."

Out the door he went. He was creepy in some ways. When I'd first opened the shop, I'd been desperate for any sale, which I'd often regretted. Over time, I'd learned to not give in to Chuck's pressure over the quilt prices.

The day drug on, and by four, my sales had come to just under fifty dollars. For just a moment, I thought of Chuck Waller's potential offer. After I locked the door, I poured myself a drink, went upstairs, and opened the windows on the porch. It felt refreshing. I picked up my embroidery, hoping to make some progress. Marc called around seven and confirmed that he would be out the next night to take me to dinner. He sounded like he was in a good mood.

"Did I tell you that we had your friend Anthony come to our law partner dinner last week?"

The question caught me off guard. "No. How did it go?"

"He was fantastic! Everyone enjoyed his presentation. He told me your favorite wine was Vintage Rose. You've never mentioned that."

"It's very good. I've had it at Ashley Rose a time or two." Now I was getting nervous. What else had Anthony told Marc? I decided to change the subject. "What time should I expect you?"

"I may not get there until seven. Is that okay?"

"It sounds perfect. I can't wait to see you."

"Ditto, my love," he said, ending the call.

My night was now complete after talking to Marc. Now I had the next night to look forward to.

Chapter 32

Getting to see Marc was on my mind all day, and my thoughts were sometimes interrupted by quick thoughts of Anthony. I wondered if Gracie would keep me informed about her date with Anthony. I also wondered what more Marc would tell me about his time spent with him.

It was a cloudy, rainy day, which meant there were very few people walking about in Augusta. At four, I eagerly brought in my rocker and closed the shop for the day. Since I didn't know where we were going for dinner, I wasn't sure what to wear. Did Marc ever get tired of seeing me in only black outfits? In the end, I dressed casually and planned to take a light jacket in case we sat outdoors. I nursed a glass of merlot while I waited for Marc to arrive. Finally, I had a text from him that said he was on his way. While I waited, I got out my laptop to check my mail. I was surprised to see an email from Sarah.

It read, "I found a new job doing reception work in a doctor's office. Mom knew the doctor, which helped. I am also happy to say that I've started dating a nice guy named

Lance Becker. He's quite handsome and works for his dad. He's an accountant, but not boring in the least. He met Lucy for the first time last week, and he seems to be quite taken with her. Mom has been great about babysitting, of course. I hope she doesn't start pushing marriage. How are Marc and Alex? I wish we could make a quick trip to Augusta, but it doesn't look possible right now. I told Mom that I wanted to be the one to give you an update. Love, Sarah and Lucy."

What good news for a change. I was so glad that Sarah had moved on. I heard Marc at the door, so I closed the computer and ran down to let him in. He was holding a lovely bouquet of roses and baby's breath. It caught me by surprise. "Oh my! What's the occasion?"

"Just because," he said as he kissed my cheek.

"Thanks, sweetheart! Hmmm, they smell divine! Let me put them in water before we go."

"I went ahead and made reservations at Chandler Hill Vineyards. I hope that will suit you. They have music tonight, so I thought that would be nice."

"It sounds wonderful! Am I dressed okay?"

"You would look appropriate in a dish towel," he teased.

"I'm not too sure about that! Do we have time for a drink, or should we leave?"

"We'd better go. This weather is causing traffic to move slowly. I passed an accident or two coming out here."

"Oh, don't say that!" I cringed at the thought of my accident.

Marc held the umbrella over me as we ran to the car. I kept looking at this wonderful man, who continually put me at ease in every situation. Had he gotten even more handsome than when I'd seen him last?

Going inside Chandler Hill reminded me so much of my time there with Carrie Mae and Butler. I was taken aback when Marc asked the waiter if they carried my favorite wine, Vintage Rose.

"Sorry, sir. We don't carry it," he replied. "I'll bring back a tasting of something similar."

"Great. Thank you," Marc responded.

I had so much to tell Marc, and he seemed to have plenty of news himself. He said that his sister Meg wanted to fly in to see him for his birthday in May. I added that it would be fun to have a little party for him. That suggestion didn't go over very well, judging from the look on his face.

I told him about getting a recent email from Sarah and added that even Holly was getting her life on the right track. Marc tried to listen intently, but we kept getting interrupted by the waiter and a few folks saying hello. We both chose salmon as our entrée. Our wine was similar to Vintage Rose and was called Forever. Just as we were beginning to enjoy the main course, Marc looked over my shoulder. Something had definitely caught his attention.

Chapter 33

"Lily, is that Anthony?" Marc asked, straining his neck.

I said a short prayer that it wouldn't be him.

"I think he's with that shop owner you introduced me to at Kitty's New Year's Eve party."

I turned around, and Anthony and Gracie were entering the dining room as if they were having a jolly old time. It was so odd seeing them together. Thankfully, they were seated at the other end of the dining room and didn't see us.

"Did you know they were an item?" Anthony asked.

"I don't think I'd refer to them as an item, but Gracie told me he had called her. They met at Kitty's party."

"That's great! I think I'll tell the waiter to send over a complimentary drink."

I smiled and nodded like I approved. Marc then instructed the waiter to suggest that Gracie and Anthony try the Forever wine as his treat.

"I sure will, sir," the waiter eagerly replied. "I'm so glad you like it."

Marc took pleasure in watching the reactions from

Anthony and Gracie when the waiter approached them. I couldn't look. I continued eating my meal. I was mostly waiting for the moment to pass. As we chatted throughout the remainder of our meal, I knew it would be just a matter of time before the two of them joined us. I could feel knots forming in my stomach.

The music started. For the first few songs, there were only a few couples on the dance floor. At the first slow song, Marc took my hand and was eager to dance. I followed, wanting to be in the moment, but I felt completely distracted by the presence of Anthony and Gracie. Out of the corner of my eye, I could see them also approaching the dance floor. Anthony was very affectionate towards Gracie. I knew Gracie well enough to know that she would fall hard for him. As they danced closer to us, Anthony tapped Marc on the shoulder.

"Nice choice for a California wine," Anthony said with a friendly smile. "Thanks so much for the suggestion."

"You're very welcome," Marc replied.

In that moment, Marc swept me off my feet in another direction. Even though I was taken aback, his moves were as smooth as glass.

"You seem distracted. Are you okay?" Marc asked when we sat down.

"I think the Forever wine has given me a slight headache, but it's no big deal," I said with a smile.

"Would you like to leave or have some dessert?"

"I'll pass on dessert, but please finish your wine," I suggested. "I'll take some black coffee instead."

"Stay put. I'll take care of it," he said as he got up and kissed me on the forehead.

As soon as Marc left the table, I saw Gracie approaching.

"Thanks for the wine," Gracie said. "How was your dinner?"

"Great! How's the date going?"

She blushed. "He's a charmer, alright, just like you said. It feels so odd to be out and about with a man like him. Can you believe I've never been to this place?" She seemed almost breathless. "I'd better get back. Enjoy the rest of your evening."

"Enjoy your evening, too," I said as she returned to Anthony.

"Sorry for the delay, sweetie," Marc said as he handed me the coffee. "I was bringing it back to you, but then I ran into Anthony."

I smiled.

"Anthony knows the owner, so he introduced me to him."

"Yes, I think Anthony knows everyone around here."

"Is Gracie having a good time?"

"Yes, it seems so."

We stayed another fifteen minutes, and then Marc suggested that we leave. He remained in a good mood, but there was no question that I was affected by Gracie and Anthony being there in the same room.

When we got back, the rain had finally stopped, and the air smelled refreshing. On the porch upstairs, we lit several candles and turned on soft music. Marc had enjoyed more wine than I had, and it showed. He leaned his head back on the couch and closed his eyes. He had an innocence about him that I loved. We both fell asleep in each other's arms. Marc was the first to totally doze off. I rested there wondering what it would be like to have a man like him near me every night.

Chapter 34

The next morning, Marc was anxious to be on his way. He kept checking his phone, which was typical.

"You know I'll be leaving next week for Paducah with Loretta and Lynn," I reminded him.

"Yes, the big trip to see Ellen. You should have a wonderful time. I hear good things about Paducah."

"I'm excited. I wish Laurie would go."

"I think you'll have a better experience without her since she has no particular interest in quilts. She's probably pleased that she didn't keep you all from going just because she didn't want to."

"I hope so."

"I don't know when we'll meet up again, but let's stay in touch. I'm off, sweetheart." I got a hug and a kiss. I whispered a sweet message in his ear and then watched him leave. As I closed the door, I wondered how we'd managed to sustain our relationship. Was it because we were separated by distance and doing our own things? It certainly made our visits more special. It was a pleasant Sunday afternoon, so I prepared to open in a few hours. When it was time to open the shop, my cell phone rang. It was Gracie. Did I really want to hear from her?

"Are you busy?" she asked right away.

"No, I just opened."

"I just had to call and tell you how much I appreciate your introducing me to Anthony. We had such a great evening."

"I'm glad. We had a lovely evening as well."

"Isn't it cool the way Anthony and Marc get along? Perhaps the four of us can do something together sometime."

I paused, thinking of how uncomfortable that might feel. "We'll have to think about that. Do you have another date set?"

"No, but he said he'd give me a call."

I grinned to myself. I couldn't resist saying, "Oh, I remember that line from high school."

We laughed together.

"Well, I'd better get back to work. I hope you have a busy day," I said.

"I hope you have a good one, too!" Gracie replied.

Of course Gracie had had a wonderful time. Who wouldn't like being wined and dined by a handsome, sexy man? Who wouldn't like that accent? I hoped Anthony wouldn't lead Gracie on with his actions. She was rather naïve in her business and personal affairs, it seemed to me. Also, she was vulnerable at the moment since she'd recently ended her affair.

I took my laptop to the front porch to check for emails from my siblings. There was one from Laurie, which surprised me. It was not in the group email. It read, "So, does your trip to Paducah mean that you won't be coming to Fish Creek for our joint birthday?"

That was a good question. I certainly couldn't afford another trip so soon after Paducah. I hated the thought of not celebrating with her. We had never missed celebrating our birthdays together. I had to be honest with her, though, just as she had been honest with me about not going to Paducah.

I replied that as much as I hated to break our tradition, I wouldn't be able to make another trip. I also understood if she couldn't leave either. We'd both known that would happen someday. I then changed the subject to ask how her business was going this season. After I responded, I went back inside for more coffee. I decided to call Judy to see if she could fill in for me while I was gone.

"Hey, good morning," she answered. "I was just thinking about you."

"I hope it was good," I responded. "I may have mentioned to you that I'm going to Paducah, so I wondered if you could fill in for me for a few days."

"Yes, in quilt class, you mentioned that you were going to see your sister there. I'll check with Randal about my schedule. I think I can go in early to help him bake before you open your shop."

"That would be great. Can you come by and pick up the shop key?"

"Oh, I have one. The last time I watched the shop, you told me to hang onto it."

"I did? I don't remember. It's been a while since you've worked here. Would you also mind checking on Kitty's guest house for me? She and Ray won't be back for a while. They keep a key under the back doormat, but don't tell anyone."

"Of course. Please don't worry, and just have a good time. If there's any problem, I'll let you know."

Chapter 35

Two women walked in and officially started my retail day. One was carrying a bag. I assumed that there was a quilt inside.

"Lily Rosenthal?" she asked, looking at me.

"Yes, that's me," I acknowledged. "How can I help you?"

"Well, I hear you know about quilts, so I wanted to share my unusual find with you and get your opinion."

I smiled at her.

"My sister Rosemary and I go to a lot of auctions, and we get some pretty good bargains, like what I'm about to show you." She opened her bag and pulled out two old quilts.

I could tell right away that they were from the early 1800s just from looking at the fabric. Along with the quilts was a plastic bag full of very old fabric. "Oh my! You did discover a treasure," I said.

"Ms. Rosenthal, you wouldn't believe this sale," the lady bragged. "This is just a sample of what we got!"

"Tell her where it was!" the other woman encouraged her.

"Well, it went like this," she began. "While the auctioneer was selling off farm equipment, we started to wander around the place to see what else might come up for auction. We went into an old barn where we knew some things would be auctioned. We saw an old trunk, so we thought we'd stick around to see that sold."

"You found these things in a trunk?" I asked.

They giggled.

"No, siree! When we were in the barn, which was huge and very old, I looked up in the rafters and saw some bales of hay and two boxes."

"And?" I prodded.

"You'll never guess what was written in big black letters on those boxes!" one of the women said with excitement.

"What?" I asked in anticipation.

"The word 'fabric' was written on one, and 'quilts' was written on the second," she stated. "I told my sister to run out and ask the auctioneer if those boxes would be auctioned off. I just couldn't believe what I was seeing!"

"What did he say?"

"He said that everything had to go, and that he'd be getting to those boxes eventually," she explained.

"Then you knew you had to stay?"

"We sure did!" She nodded. "Not many folks were left by that time, but we weren't about to leave. When he got the stuff out of the boxes, we couldn't believe the good condition of everything. We knew the quilts were old. Not only were the quilts rolled up, but when we got to the old fabric, every scrap was rolled tightly and tied with matching fabric. When we untied one roll, the condition was perfect! There wasn't any evidence of mice or any kind of varmints. None of the fabric had been washed, so the sizing probably helped to preserve it. The auctioneer thought that because the boxes were sitting on the rafters away from the hay bales, that may have kept the mice away. Even though we got excited, the auctioneer couldn't believe we wanted this old stuff. We got everything for hardly anything!"

"You really did get a rare find!" I exclaimed. "What about family? Did anyone show any interest?"

"There wasn't family around that we noticed," one of the women claimed. "Everything went very cheaply at the end. How old do you think these quilts are, Ms. Rosenthal?"

I unfolded them, and there was no doubt that they were simple patchwork quilts from the early 1800s. To see this much fabric of this age in one quilt was rare indeed. The quilts didn't appear to have any wear to them. When I unfolded some of the fabric, it was just as the women had described in that it was totally untouched. I figured the boxes had been surrounded by air, and if the fabric hadn't touched the cardboard, it shouldn't have had acid markings.

"You really have a wonderful find here," I repeated. "Do you want to sell any of it?"

"Absolutely not!" one of the women stated firmly. "We love every piece. I wish the owner could know how much we appreciate all of this and how well we will take care of it. We just wonder how and why the boxes were put up there in the first place."

"Well, as people move, things get packed away, and some boxes never get opened again," I said. "At least someone didn't come along and decide to throw it all away."

"I guess they kept thinking that someone someday would take an interest, and they were right!" the new owner said.

Chapter 36

As we continued to admire the fabric and the quilts, the items remained on the counter as other customers came and went. The two women were soaking up any information I could give them. I thought of Holly and how excited she would be to see what they had purchased.

"We sure thank you for taking the time to look at all of this," one of the women said. "Now we need to get this back in the bag properly."

"It was a pleasure, ladies," I said, helping them fold the quilts. "It's so nice to see that you appreciate what you have." They wanted to keep talking, but I needed to get them on their way so I could attend to some of the other folks coming in the shop.

After they said their final goodbyes to me, I thought about how crazy their story was. The quilts and fabric that were left behind had had a happy ending for a change. They had been discovered in a different era. It was encouraging to me that the owners cared about what they had rather than how much everything was worth. For once, it wasn't about the money. As the day went along, I couldn't get the sisters off my mind. Those two could write an article about their exciting findings! When I closed the shop, I decided to check on Kitty's guesthouse and then pick something up for dinner at Johann's store.

I parked in front of Johann's since he was right next door to the guesthouse. The flowers at the guesthouse were looking beautiful. I remembered how much I'd enjoyed them when I'd stayed there. I had a quick look around, and everything seemed fine. I peeked at Kitty's guestbook, and the notes made me smile. It made me sad that there was no one using this little gem. I locked it up and went next door to get some fresh produce. Johann's was a busy place after work, with people stopping by to pick up needed dinner items. Also, if you didn't get groceries, you always could find out a little gossip!

"I just got those hothouse tomatoes in today, Lily," Johann let me know. "I had a pretty good BLT sandwich for lunch, and they were delicious!"

"Oh, that sounds so good," I responded. "I may have to do the same."

"Hey, Lily!"

It was Karen with an armload of things.

"Anything new with you?"

"Now, Karen, if anything was new with me, I would let you guys know right away," I joked. "I'm leaving next week to go out of town, so I hope when I return, a miracle will happen."

She smiled and nodded. "That would be a huge miracle! Are we going to meet when you return?"

"Absolutely!" I assured her. "We have something big to

solve. Judy will cover for me in the shop while I'm gone."

"Make sure she doesn't show those quilts to just anyone," Karen warned. "She would feel terrible if anything happened on her watch."

"I know." I nodded. "I haven't told her about the missing quilt."

Karen nodded. "Where are the diet things?" she asked, looking around.

"I don't think he carries anything like that, except some sugar-free ice cream," I replied. "You don't need to diet!"

We parted ways, and I went home thinking about making a delicious BLT sandwich. I also needed to make a list for my upcoming trip and pay some bills. Before I could get inside, Carrie Mae called on my cell phone.

"I'm just warning you that Butler will be calling to arrange our lunch."

"Oh dear. Okay."

"I put him off a bit by saying you were leaving on a trip to see your sister."

"Thanks for doing that, but I know that when we do get together, he'll want to see his quilts."

"You're probably right. Try not to worry about that now. If I don't see you before you leave, have a good time."

"I'll try. I really will!"

Chapter 37

Sure enough, ten minutes later, my phone rang. It was Butler.

"How are you doing, Lily? How was your day?"

"Great! It was interesting. I had a wonderful experience seeing some really old fabric and quilts from the early 1800s."

"Well, if you aren't becoming the great authority on quilts!"

I chuckled. "I just happened to be lucky enough to see what two sisters bought at an auction. They just wanted me to see them. They weren't looking to sell anything."

"Too bad. It sounds like that would have been a unique opportunity for you."

"It's all in good hands, which makes me happy."

"Seeing things like what you described is one of the perks of the business, wouldn't you say?"

"Absolutely!" I agreed. "I'll bet you're calling about setting up lunch."

"You read my mind."

"I'm leaving for Paducah, Kentucky to take in the quilt show and quilt museum, so I'm pretty busy now. My sister lives in the art district there, so two of my siblings are going with me."

"It sounds like a great trip, but pencil me in when you return, okay? How are the quilts doing?"

I swallowed hard. "I was going to wait and tell you when I saw you, but I sold the wholecloth quilt, too!"

"That's great, Lily!"

"I was shocked when the woman bought the wholecloth. She didn't even own a quilt, and when she admired that one, she didn't bat an eye at the price. It was like she was just buying a new watch or something minor."

He chuckled. "Well, I happen to know that you are a good salesperson, so you should take credit. There are two quilts now that have gone to happy homes."

The missing crazy quilt popped into my mind. "How's the art world going?" I asked to change the subject.

"It's feast or famine."

"Well, nice of you to call, Butler."

"You know I would call more often if you would let me," he flirted.

"I'll look forward to lunch," I said, ignoring that comment.

"So will I. Have a great trip."

I heaved a sigh of relief when the call was done. At least I'd had something good to tell him about his quilts. I had to figure out what happened to that crazy quilt. Where could it be?

That night, I wanted to retire early, but my cell phone rang. It was late—nearly midnight. Who would be calling at this hour? It was Alex.

"Hey, what's going on?" I asked.

"Sorry. Were you in bed?"

"In bed, but not asleep. Are you okay?"

"I just wanted to talk," he said, his words somewhat slurred.

"Okay. What's on your mind?"

"I'm confused again."

"About what?"

"Mindy wants me to attend an out-of-town family reunion with her in Florida. She makes it sound like an amazing paradise, and she really wants me to go. There's no doubt that she's getting pressure from her parents to get me to commit to our relationship. That family is used to getting what it wants."

"For heaven's sake, big boy! Are you seeing her so much that they expect that from you?"

"I don't know. I just see her every now and then, I guess," he stammered.

"Well, there you go! If you don't speak up, Mindy and her family will decide your future. You need to stand up to them."

"I don't trust myself. I'll be outnumbered."

"Man up! What did you think I was going to tell you?"

"I hear you, Lily."

"Have you been drinking a lot tonight?"

He didn't answer.

"You know you'll never find your answer in a bottle."

"Are you lecturing me?"

"Isn't it why you called?"

"Is this where I hang up?"

"Yes. Call me in the morning." The click I heard told me he had done just that. I puffed my pillow and went to sleep.

Chapter 38

The next day, I focused on packing for my trip. I flagged down Snowshoes and told him I'd be gone, but Judy would be watching the shop.

"You have a grand time, Lily," Snowshoes said cheerfully. "Here's your mail. You are getting quite a fan club. I guess you've noticed."

I smiled. "Some are fans, and some are not," I laughed as he headed back down the sidewalk.

I finished packing before I put Rosie's rocker on the porch. The weather was chilly one minute and warm the next. April in Missouri was certainly unpredictable.

I received a text from Alex.

. . .Sorry about last night. You were right as always. Have a great trip.

I didn't want to respond. It was hard to tell what he had decided about the trip now that he was sober. It was good to hear from him, at least. I knew he truly cared about my opinions.

I put my luggage aside and sent Lynn a text that I'd be there by nine the next morning. Loretta was flying in tonight, so I would see her at Lynn's first thing in the morning.

"Good morning, Lily," Korine said as she came in.

"Hey, girl! Are you on your way to work?"

"I am, but Carrie Mae doesn't like me coming too early. I thought I'd stop by to say hello."

"How about some coffee?"

"No thanks. Hey, I heard you got in some really cool old quilts."

"I did! Take a look. I keep them locked in a cabinet that I'm borrowing from Carrie Mae."

"Locked up, huh? They must be valuable," she said, walking to the quilt room.

I followed her to the room as she admired the quilts from a distance. I knew that Korine knew very little about quilts. I was hoping that Carrie Mae hadn't told her about the missing one.

"So, have you sold any?"

I nodded.

"Do you still have those spirits around?"

"Now, Korine, just know that all is well here," I assured her.

"That's because they like you better than me."

I chuckled.

"Well, I'd better get to work. Good to see you," Korine said.

"Judy will be here while I'm gone, just so you know."

"Oh, yeah. Have a good time."

The day was quiet. It seemed that there was a different feeling than when the town was abuzz with an upcoming festival or holiday. I decided to take my laptop to the counter to see if there had been any word from my siblings.

Loretta had sent Lynn her flight information. Ellen's email had directions for our road trip. It looked like it would be nearly a four-hour drive from Lynn's house by the time we stopped for a break along the way. I wrote a simple reply to all of my sisters, saying that I was really looking forward to the trip. When I closed my laptop, I remembered that I wanted to put aside four bottles of wine to take to Ellen's house. Living in wine country gave me this responsibility, it seemed.

My landline rang. It was a call from the truck driver, who was anxious about having me visit him. I explained why I was busy and told him that my coming to see his quilts would have to wait until I returned from Paducah. He was pretty good about accepting my excuse. At the end of the day, I was less than two hundred dollars richer. How pathetic was that? It was a good thing I had a check from the magazine coming soon!

I needed to get to bed early so I'd be ready for the trip in the morning. I put my luggage downstairs by the door, made sure the quilt room lights were off, and set the alarm. Would those preparations be assuring enough for me to get a good night's sleep?

Chapter 39

Laughter, hugs, and excitement were in the air when I arrived at Lynn's the next morning. Loretta and Lynn were in good moods, and they talked me into enjoying a cup of coffee while Carl packed our luggage in Lynn's SUV.

"Did you get the instructions to Ellen's place?" I asked, feeling a bit anxious.

"Yes, it's quite easy," Lynn claimed. "I've driven the route before when going to Nashville. I got a text from Ellen this morning. She said she would have a late lunch prepared for us when we arrive, so we'd better get going."

"Is everyone ready for the sister train that's about to leave for Paducah, Kentucky?" Carl called when he came inside. "There's not much room for any purchases, so keep that in mind."

We laughed at his warning. We each gave Carl a hug, and then he took a picture of us outside of the SUV. I sat in the back seat. I knew the rules when we got together. I was the youngest and was used to following my sisters. Loretta was used to being in charge, and since Lynn was the driver, I had no role to play other than to try to chime in every now and then.

We drove through downtown St. Louis, and as always, I got chills when I saw the St. Louis Arch. Traffic was congested at times, so we tried not to talk so Lynn could concentrate on driving through it.

"I don't know how folks drive this every day," Loretta stated. "From where I live, I'm just blocks from the hospital."

"And I just have to go downstairs to get to work," I bragged. That gave them a chuckle.

When we finally got on the interstate, the tension eased, and Loretta and Lynn became chattier. I could hear some of their conversations, but not everything. Since their faces couldn't be seen and their backs were turned, it wasn't always clear what they were talking about. I immersed myself in looking out the window so I could enjoy every aspect of the experience.

The scenery was quite beautiful. April in Missouri offered every shade of green as the foliage came alive for the summer months ahead. Redbud trees in bloom popped up in the scenery every now and then, which was stunning. It was every bit as beautiful as the rolling hills of wine country. After a stop or two, I was quite pleased about how quickly the time had passed.

Seeing billboards for The National Quilt Museum along the way increased our excitement for what was ahead. Downtown Paducah was a few miles from the interstate, where most of the hotels were located. Signs welcoming quilters were everywhere. Paducah really tried to welcome the thousands of people pouring into town for the quilt show!

Ellen's directions were simple and clear. We knew right

away that we were in the art district when we entered a neighborhood of historic homes and creative galleries. When we arrived at Ellen's address, we discovered a charming, narrow row-like house that was painted pale yellow and had green shutters. The atmosphere was right out of a storybook! The neighboring houses were different shapes and sizes. Some were still under renovation. Next door to Ellen was a gallery with an apartment upstairs. We got out and stretched as we admired the diverse surroundings.

"Welcome to Paducah!" Ellen called as she came out of the house.

We hugged as if we were long-lost relatives. As I observed Ellen, I could see that this had to be terribly exciting for her.

"We'll get your luggage later," Ellen suggested. "Please come inside and relax. I know you must be tired and hungry."

"We did have some munchies in the car, but I'm starved," Loretta confessed. "I'm so used to eating on the early shift at the hospital."

"Oh, Ellen, your house is simply adorable," I said. "I can see that you've made good use of your work on the walls."

"Actually, Lily, very little is my work," she replied. "The local artists support each other by purchasing one another's artwork."

"That's awesome!" Lynn said. "Our art association tries to do the same thing. I can't wait to see your studio."

"It's on my basement level," Ellen explained. "I use paint and various things that can be messy. Plus, I don't want any of the fumes up here. It's always a mess, but I'll be happy to show you after lunch."

Chapter 40

Lunch was served in a small addition to Ellen's kitchen, formerly a back porch. The antique windows remained and provided a fantastic view of the scenic backyard. The place settings were all pottery, and each one was a different pattern.

"How clever!" Loretta exclaimed. "We have a restaurant in Green Bay that sets their tables like this. These goblets are so unique."

"Yes, I like all this pottery too," Ellen agreed. "I recently purchased the goblets from a fairly new potter in town. I've planned a hot chicken sandwich and a nice little salad for you. I hope you'll like it. We have a quite famous bakery in town called Kirchhoff's, where I purchased the delicious bread."

"Ellen, you've outdone yourself," I said as I took a seat.

While Ellen poured iced tea, she talked about how she'd had to renovate the property to use it as a studio.

"I have some of my small quilts in the gallery next door for sale, and I try to participate in any fundraising efforts that benefit the artists," she explained.

"Some people think that artists can't get along because

they're too independent," I shared. "Do you find that to be the case here?"

"There's no question that we're diverse," she answered. "For the most part, however, we really support one another. We all love living here and have a lot of fun. I'm sure you'll be meeting some of these folks as the days go by."

"Wonderful!" Lynn responded.

"This is delicious, Ellen," I said between bites. "Do you like to cook?"

"I like to entertain," she said. "When it comes to cooking for me, I'm happy with a salad or a bowl of cereal."

We laughed and agreed.

"We have a lot of potluck dinners here in the neighborhood. It makes it easier for everyone to entertain."

"How fun!" Loretta responded. "Bill and I lead such a boring life. Sometimes I think all we do is get up, go to work, and come home to sleep. All of you girls lead such creative lifestyles. How did I get left out?"

We laughed at her exasperation.

"You were the oldest, and the first child gets all the pressures of having new parents," I laughed. "If I remember, our dad always wanted a boy. He had to be pleased with your career, but the rest of us were probably a disappointment to him. I don't think he ever understood art as an actual livelihood."

"Well, I'm beginning to feel more and more like I fit in," Ellen joked, wearing a smile.

"Of course you fit in," I said. "It took me quite a few years to find a creative career."

"Now, little sister, all those years of editing prepared you for the writing career that you have now," Loretta reminded me. "God has a plan for us, remember?"

"You have to feel so special about what you're doing, Loretta," Ellen stated. "You truly make a difference in people's lives regarding their health. I don't think the rest of us can say that."

"It's not always pretty," Loretta said as she shook her head. "When I'm the head nurse on the night shift, it's a challenge. Keeping up with the medical information continues to be a struggle as I get a little older."

"How is Sarah?" Ellen asked as she cleared our plates.

"She has a decent job as a receptionist in a medical building, and she's dating a normal guy who is an accountant," Loretta reported, and we all chuckled at her using the word "normal." "We're keeping our fingers crossed that she keeps both. You all may know more than me. She keeps things pretty close."

"Well, I just loved being around little Lucy at Christmastime," Ellen said. "She has to be such a joy for all of you."

We agreed.

"Now she's into everything since she's walking," Loretta complained.

"But since you're the grandmother, it's okay, right?" Ellen teased.

We laughed.

"So, Ellen, how is your mother?" Loretta asked.

"Frankly, it's been a while since I've heard from her," Ellen responded. "I called last week and left a message. She rarely calls back. For all I know, she's traveling. I didn't tell her that you were coming. I wasn't up to hearing any kind of reaction from her."

"I'm sorry," I said, not knowing what else to say.

"Now, who's up for some chocolate mousse with whipped cream and raspberries?" Ellen asked.

Chapter 41

We were all stuffed and exhausted by the time we left Ellen's comfortable table.

"Before it gets dark, would you like to walk around the neighborhood to get a little exercise?" Ellen suggested. "Let's get you settled in your rooms, and then you can decide. Tomorrow, the quilt show opens. It will be a full day, so you'll want to get your rest."

"When do we visit the quilt museum?" Lynn asked with anticipation.

"Anytime," Ellen replied. "Would you like to go there first thing in the morning?"

"Whatever you suggest," I chimed in.

"Let's do," Lynn confirmed. "I want to spend a fair amount of time there, if you all don't mind."

"Sounds like a plan," Loretta agreed.

As usual, whatever my siblings decided was fine by me. After all, I'd come in on the scene a lot later than they did! As Lynn and Loretta proceeded to unpack their luggage, Ellen stopped me in the hallway.

"How did Laurie respond to you all coming here?" she asked, concerned.

"Pretty well," I said. "It's really hard for her to get away after being closed for the winter. Tourist season has just started."

"Absolutely!" Ellen nodded. Then she asked, "Do you think she has fully accepted me?"

I paused. "Ellen, Laurie is a hard person to read sometimes," I explained. "She has a different view on life than the rest of us. She's very disappointed that I won't be coming to see her to share our birthdays together. This will be the first year that we'll be separated."

"And the reason is that you chose to come here instead, right?" Ellen surmised.

"Well, I'm a business owner, too!" I replied. "I can't just take off anytime I want. I've really looked forward to this trip, Ellen. There's the additional bonus that since I'm in the quilt business, this trip can be a tax write-off for me."

"That's right!" Ellen laughed.

We took our time and managed to walk the neighborhood during cocktail time. It was a beautiful night. Some of the houses had outdoor lighting with beautiful patios. It didn't take long for some of the neighbors to stop us just to say hello. Ellen's introductions were interesting. She referred to us as her family and beamed with pride while doing so. Back at Ellen's, we set an early bedtime because we anticipated a very full day ahead. I was worried that I wouldn't be able to turn my mind off the day's events, but I did exactly that. In the morning, there was a light knock at my door that reminded me that it was time to get up.

"Coffee awaits you, Lily," Ellen announced softly.

From my bed, I studied a lovely painting on the opposite

wall. It was a scene of a very young woman walking through a field of sunflowers. The title was Finding My Way. I loved the whole scene, but it reminded me that I needed to have an article done after I returned home. "Finding Your Way" would be a good title. I could elaborate on changes, challenges, and detours that complicate one's journey. Finding your way in a new job, community, or relationship could be complicated. I thought of Ellen finding her way back to her family after feeling lost and unwanted. Perhaps that was why she'd bought this painting. I finally joined the others, and they started to give me some grief for taking so long. I ignored them, and off we went.

Located close by was The National Quilt Museum. The building was contemporary in style and featured the theme "Honoring Today's Quilter." The word "museum" is often interpreted to mean a place where old stuff is kept and displayed. This museum was different in that it collected and featured the latest and greatest quilts from around the world.

When we walked in, the first thing I noticed was that there were attendees from all over the world. As we stood in the lobby, the crowd got thicker. Ellen pointed out Frank, the executive director of the museum. He was busy greeting people and entertaining some who were standing in line to purchase items from the gift shop. I was impressed that he took the time to mingle with the crowd.

Ellen had a "Friend" membership card and had arranged for our tickets ahead of time. Just as we were about to enter the main gallery, Frank came close enough for Ellen to introduce us to him. I would have predicted that the director of the museum would be an elderly woman, but Frank was a young, handsome man and someone I wouldn't have envisioned as the museum's executive director.

Chapter 42

"Welcome to Paducah, ladies," Frank said. "I understand that this is your first visit."

"It is, but we've certainly heard so much about the city and its great quilt museum," Lynn responded.

After the introductions, Frank said he had been trying to convince Ellen to become one of the museum's volunteers.

"Oh, Ellen, that would be so awesome," I said.

"I know, but it's one more day that I won't get any of my work done," she explained. "There may be times that I can help out during specific events."

"I wish I could do it," Loretta said.

"Well, I'm going to make sure that my sisters get signed up to become Friends of the Museum," Ellen promised.

"Absolutely." I nodded.

"We have white-gloved docents inside the galleries to answer any questions you may have," Frank offered. "You can't take photographs or touch anything, of course. I hope that when you're finished, you'll stop by our gift shop. We have an extensive book inventory and lots of lovely gifts for you to take home."

"No question about that," Loretta laughed, looking in the direction of the crowded shop. "Thanks for taking time to say hello. I'm sure we're going to enjoy this experience."

The main gallery was quite impressive. The center area showcased the recent best-of-show quilts. Ellen said this year's best of show would be displayed in the show's main venue. Off the main gallery were two more large galleries. Ellen explained that at least one of them would have an antique quilt exhibit.

"Lily, you would have the loved the exhibit we recently had called 'The Story of Red and White.' It was a red-and-white quilt collection. I couldn't believe there were so many unique patterns in red and white. Most of them were from 1880 to 1930."

"Yes, I would have loved it!" I confirmed. "My collection is rather hodgepodge. It's mostly just what I like in red and white."

"Seriously?" Lynn responded. "Trust me, Ellen. Lily's collection is amazing. Next time you get to Augusta, ask her to show you."

"I certainly will!" Ellen laughed.

The next forty-five minutes were spent examining the beautiful quilts. The new quilts had techniques and embellishments that I'd never thought possible. Ellen was nice enough to explain some of them to me.

I was more at home with the antique quilts. I was able to separate from the others so I could spend more time looking at them. It was amazing to see so many in such good condition. To curate one of these exhibits had to be such an honor. Ellen said the museum's quilts traveled around the world, and one exhibit had recently been booked in Japan.

The descriptions of each quilt exhibited were helpful and quite fascinating. As I was about to leave the gallery, a docent reminded me to sign the guestbook. There were signatures from around the world, and many had penned amazing things regarding their visit to the museum. When my sisters and I all came together at the exit, we were ready for the gift shop. Just then, I got a text from Alex.

. . .Having fun yet? Let me know how it goes.

I shrugged it off, knowing I could respond later.

The gift shop had two rooms that were devilishly tempting in many ways. Clever gift items were in abundance. In the first room alone, I knew I could find things for Marc, Alex, Holly, Judy, my quilt class, and even the Dinner Detectives. I saw jewelry, wall quilts, pottery, and stationery. One shelf had tempting precut fabrics, which I loved. It was hard to concentrate!

Chapter 43

The second room of the gift shop carried a lovely variety of books. They seemed to be the latest releases from quilt publishers, and there was a healthy supply of quilt fiction novels. Loretta was totally enthralled. She said she rarely got to go to places that sold quilting books and supplies. Lynn was more interested in the glass and wooden art. I chose to purchase some of their unique stationery and fabric precuts, which would be perfect for my fellow quilt class members. As a retailer, it was fun to watch other quilters and my siblings make their selections.

When we had finished checking out, Ellen said we needed to see the wooden quilt that was displayed in the museum's boardroom. It did indeed pique my interest as we followed her. After I saw the wooden quilt and touched it, I agreed that it was truly unique. It was amazing how much the wood looked like fabric! It took a great amount of talent to make such a piece of art.

We spent the rest of the afternoon at the quilt show in the Expo Center, where the winning quilts and hundreds more were displayed. At times, we were shoulder to shoulder with others in attendance. It felt a little claustrophobic at times. Some of the retail booths were crowded with quilters. There was no question in my mind that the quilting industry was alive and well. To make certain that each of us got to see specific things we were interested in, we split up again.

When I ran into Lynn, she went on and on about the beautiful displays in the booths. I had to admit that I was truly impressed as well. Loretta was found observing a longarm quilting machine. She was totally amazed at everything it could do. None of the rest of us had any interest in seeing them. I think she might have purchased one if we hadn't been with her.

"Do you think Bill would let me buy one of these instead of getting me a new car?" Loretta asked, laughing. "They run about the same price. I would love to have one of these in my basement."

Rather than discouraging Loretta, I suggested that we keep searching for one in her price range that would be the right size. As a hand quilter, I didn't have much advice to give. It was all part of the latest technology that was keeping the industry alive, and I was certainly grateful for that.

By six, we were dragging and looking to sit down almost anywhere. Ellen said she'd made reservations at a restaurant called Max's for seven o'clock. We decided to go back to Ellen's to rest and freshen up. I honestly thought we would have preferred to have stayed at Ellen's and crash with a glass of wine. However, Ellen's description of Max's made it sound like an interesting place to have dinner.

Max's was indeed a popular place to eat in downtown Paducah. The brick walls led to a large fireplace where pizza and other dishes were prepared. White tablecloths gave the dining area an upscale appearance in the historic building. Despite the tempting entrées, we decided to order salad and pizza. As we waited for our order, Ellen continued to share the history and local gossip of Paducah.

We retired early that evening, knowing we would be heading to the Pavilion in the morning. The Pavilion, locally known as the Bubble, was once a temporary structure but had become a permanent part of the quilt show. Quilts were exhibited there, and it also housed more retail booths. The day had flown by, and we'd ended another successful day at the quilt show.

When I sat up in bed the next morning, I was pleased to see a text from Laurie.

. . .I hope you are all having a good time. Love from Fish Creek.

It was obvious that she was thinking about us and perhaps felt a bit left out. When we gathered at Ellen's breakfast table, we were a quiet bunch as we savored our first cup of coffee.

"How do the locals accept the intrusion of quilters into their town?" Lynn asked.

"That's a good question, Lynn. It's a double-edged sword. It's fantastic for business, of course, but extra traffic and other inconveniences certainly come with it. Locals sometimes avoid restaurants and going downtown when the quilt show is in town."

Chapter 44

Before we ventured off for another day, I sent Holly and Alex a photo of us at the quilt show. I knew Holly would have a blast here. Perhaps there would be a year when we could make the trip together.

I was surprised when we walked into the Pavilion. It looked like we were in half of a white balloon! It was very well lit, and all the colors popped wherever we looked. We agreed to separate once again, as the number of booths and quilts was much greater than I had expected.

As I browsed the aisles, I thought of Susan and my quilt class. Seeing so much redwork inspired me and gave me new ideas for other blocks. I was surprised that there were so many red-and-white fabrics. I would have to bring some of it home!

The vendors were accommodating, despite the long lines and occasional impatient customers. I was also pleased to see some of the vendors doing demonstrations and using new techniques with their products. In one corner of the Pavilion, there was a pop-up lecture taking place. Chairs were arranged so that the crowd could listen to the quilt experts, which was tempting because it provided a short rest and an opportunity to get off your feet.

Every now and then as I shopped and looked around, I had the opportunity to chat with other quilters from across the country. No one had heard of Augusta, Missouri, but it was nice to meet people from Green Bay and Door County. Of course, I took the opportunity to tell them about Laurie and her shop.

I was starving, and it was time for lunch. Ellen suggested that we go to the outdoor food court, where the best BBQ in the land was supposed to be available. We spotted an empty picnic table and took turns acquiring our lunch from the many food vendors. We all had to try the BBQ, and Ellen encouraged us to save room for strawberry shortcake sold by the Boy Scouts. My mouth watered as I anticipated the shortcake dessert. As I took a picture of everyone eating strawberry shortcake, I realized how we had truly embraced Ellen as one of us. We liked her world here in Paducah very much.

After much discussion, we decided that the rest of the day would be spent shopping downtown. Ellen assured us that we could walk to downtown from where we were. She wanted us to see the painted murals by American artist Robert Dafford, which were located along the river wall. Once we reached the murals, Ellen explained that the concrete wall was built from 1939 to 1949 to protect the town from flooding. The beautiful murals were painted from 1996 to 2007.

"They all look freshly-painted," Lynn, the painter, observed.

"Yes, I know," Ellen agreed. "Every year, the artist's assistant returns to touch them up if they need it."

"That's wonderful," Loretta responded. "Does the river ever get up to the walls?"

"Oh, yes." Ellen nodded. "Spring can really bring high water.

One year—during the quilt show—city workers had to close the floodgates to protect the city. The whole town helped with the effort to relocate exhibits, booths, and events, and everything went on without a hitch."

When we arrived at the shop-lined streets, we sat down to rest at a corner restaurant that had outdoor seating. It was right across from Max's, where we'd had dinner. Their iced tea hit the spot as we planned the rest of the day from there.

"My feet are killing me," Loretta mentioned. "I'm used to having my comfortable shoes on at work."

"I can pick you up from here when you're finished," Ellen offered. "The walk was longer than you had thought it would be when I suggested it."

"Thank you, sister," Loretta said with gratitude. "That sounds like a wonderful plan."

"Well, I saw a dress shop that I simply have to visit," Lynn said.

"I can't wait to check out some of the antique shops," I said with excitement. "I'm curious about their retail prices, especially on antique quilts."

"How were the prices on the quilts in the vendor booths?" Ellen asked.

"They were high, but that didn't surprise me," I answered. "They have a lot of overhead at this show. I was fascinated watching a group of Japanese women as they purchased some quilts. I'm sure they felt like they were getting a bargain."

"Is your shop closed now, Lily?" Ellen asked.

"No, I have a friend filling in for me," I replied. "As a matter of fact, I'd better check on her to see how she's doing."

Chapter 45

I called Judy. She said that business was slow, but that everything was fine. I had been hoping that she would report an exciting sale she'd made. She urged me not to worry and to have a good time, which was easier said than done. We hung up, and I was satisfied that Judy was taking care of things while I was gone as she had several times before.

The three of us who wanted to shop went our separate ways and headed to shops that personally interested us. Ellen said she would pick us up at four. As I browsed through some of the antique shops, I was amazed at how dirty and cluttered some of them were. Most of the merchandise looked as if it had been there a long time. The few quilts I found were run-of-the-mill patterns in worn condition. I wasn't tempted to take any of them home to Augusta.

I did find some small collectables that I knew I could resell at a better price. I purchased some toothpick holders and butter pats. I typically had very good luck selling those types of things. One shop had stacks of linens. I managed to find a redwork splasher, which wasn't easy to find. The red embroidery read "Clean Hands, Clean Heart." I didn't think the shop owner knew what she had, as the price was very affordable.

I did stop at the dress shop that Lynn had mentioned. The prices were outrageous, but the clothes were very nice, and the selection was good. I tried on a striking black-and-white top that I could wear on a date with Marc. I swallowed the expensive price and added some silver drop earrings at the counter when I paid. It was so fun to look at other merchandise and to see what was trendy. I wished that there was a boutique in Augusta, but so far, there was no sign of such a thing.

At four, Ellen met us just as we had arranged. Back at Ellen's home, we felt revived and shared our purchases with one another as we laughed about our experiences throughout the afternoon. To our delight, Ellen had prepared some appetizers ahead of time, knowing that we would be ready for some nourishment. I went for the large platter of shrimp cocktail, which was one of my favorites.

Ellen's phone rang, and she took the call into the bedroom. The rest of us continued our conversation, sometimes erupting into loud laughter. As more time went by, we were beginning to wonder what was keeping Ellen. Lynn was about to go in and check on her when she came out of the bedroom. She had been crying.

"Ellen, what's wrong?" Loretta asked, concerned.

Ellen sat on the couch and took a deep breath. "Mother has had a heart attack and is in the hospital," she said quietly.

"How is she?" Lynn asked.

"She's okay for now," Ellen said, shaking her head. "They don't know how much damage has been done."

"Ellen, if you need to get there right away, we can handle things from here," I assured her. "We can leave tonight or first thing in the morning."

Ellen didn't react.

"Had she complained about her heart recently?" Loretta inquired.

"I can't answer that question," Ellen said. "We really don't talk about things. Important things, that is. I know she hasn't been in good health, but she always likes to make me think everything is okay."

"When did you see her last?" I asked.

"I went home for a couple days at Christmas so she wouldn't be alone," Ellen replied. "I had to make it short or it would go bad, if you know what I mean."

"Did she seem okay then?" Lynn asked.

"I suppose so." Ellen nodded. "She had asked her next-door neighbor to join us on Christmas afternoon. Everything seemed fine then."

Chapter 46

"What would you like to do, Ellen?" Loretta asked gently.

"I don't know how serious this is," Ellen said slowly.

"I would say that any kind of heart attack is serious," Loretta assured her. "You need to go see her."

We were all in total agreement about that.

"I'm sorry this has spoiled your trip," Ellen said, looking overwhelmed with sadness.

"Nothing has been spoiled," I replied. "I'm glad we could be here with you. Aunt Mary always meant a lot to us. Why don't you check on some flights out of Nashville? We'll be fine."

"Thanks," Ellen said. "I know you think I'm a cold person towards my mother, but I certainly never wished that anything bad would happen to her."

"My goodness, we know that," Loretta replied.

While Ellen made plans to go to Florida to see her mother, we decided we would get a good night's sleep and head home in the morning. After some time on the computer, Ellen announced that she could get on a midnight flight, which was good news. Within the next few minutes, she got another call. We knew instantly by the look on her face that it wasn't good news. Ellen dropped her cell phone on the floor and collapsed on the chair behind her.

"What is it?" Loretta asked, moving to be closer to Ellen. She scooped up Ellen's phone and began to converse with the person who had called. Loretta listened intently and then asked, "What time was it, exactly?" She paused. "Thank you," she said as she ended the call and looked at us. "Aunt Mary passed at five this afternoon. She had another heart attack."

It was a long, long night as each of us tried to process what had happened. Aunt Mary had died. Her passing left us with mixed feelings. Her telling us about having an affair with my dad had not been pleasant, especially since we had grown up feeling quite fond of her. We knew that Ellen had conflicting feelings about her mother as well. After a time, Ellen went into her bedroom, leaving each of us to our own thoughts.

Around one in the morning, Loretta made some coffee. We were too tired to sleep or to do much else. We talked quietly about what might happen. Would there even be a funeral? How would Ellen handle all of this? None of us changed our clothes. We stayed in the living room, consoling one another and hoping Ellen was getting some rest. Around six the next morning, Ellen came out of her room. She sat down to have coffee as she shared her plans.

"I knew Mother wanted to be cremated and didn't want a funeral," Ellen said simply.

"You know that for sure?" I questioned.

Ellen nodded. "She told me that several times," she confirmed. "If any of her friends feel there should be a memorial service, I'll let you know. Hopefully her estate will be simple to settle. She had downsized through the years, which will make things simpler."

"Oh, Ellen, we are so sorry that you have to go through this," I said, touching her hand.

"You all have gone through it, and I knew it would happen to me one day," she said calmly. "I was worried that she would have another heart attack, and sure enough, she did."

"Well, let's be glad that she didn't have to suffer long before she died," Lynn said softly.

Chapter 47

Seeing Ellen off was challenging and sad, but overall, she was holding up very well. Surprisingly, Lynn offered to go with her, but Ellen wouldn't hear of it. The trip back to Lynn's house felt the exact opposite from the excitement we'd felt on our way to Ellen's. On the way to Lynn's house, I called Marc to tell him what had happened. He felt bad for all of us and asked if there was anything he could do.

When we arrived at Lynn's, Carl had just gotten home. He could tell we had experienced something sad. We said goodbye to each other and agreed that even with the sadness, the trip was meant to be. We'd had a great time, had a lot of laughs, and enjoyed great shopping. Most of all, we had been able to be there for Ellen when she needed us most.

I would have liked to have picked up some treats from The Hill before going back to Augusta, but I wasn't in the mood. I had to admit that it had been nice to have had a break from worrying about the missing quilt. I could only pray for a miracle to happen. If Doc had anything to do with it being missing, it would eventually show up.

Getting back to Augusta always put a smile on my face. I walked in the shop door and scanned the place. Judy had left a note on the counter that read "Welcome home." I quickly checked the cash drawer and sales slips. We'd had some sales, so I was glad that the shop had remained open. I walked into the quilt room and turned on the lights. Nothing seemed different, so I took my suitcase and headed upstairs. I would add my new purchases to the shop inventory the next day. My thoughts kept returning to Aunt Mary. Then thoughts of my dad and Aunt Mary would enter my mind, causing me to feel stressed and conflicted about them. Deciding to go to bed, I was thankful for the familiar surroundings of my upstairs apartment. It was good to be home. I finally went to sleep that night from pure exhaustion.

The next morning, I slept an hour later than usual. I had to start getting excited about becoming a retailer again. While I was drinking a cup of coffee, I checked my laptop. I wondered who had told Laurie about Aunt Mary. I found out when I saw an email from Loretta that she had sent at six that morning. It read, "I decided to give Laurie a call from the airport. She was as upset as the rest of us. She asked about what kind of memorial we should have, if any. I hope you made it back safely to Augusta. Love, Loretta." A memorial wasn't something I had thought of. What would Aunt Mary have wanted? Perhaps there would be something in her will that would provide some direction.

After I put Rosie's rocker on the porch to start the business day, I decided to call Carrie Mae to let her know I was back. Korine answered and said that Carrie Mae had gone to Johann's. I asked her to have Carrie Mae call me when she returned.

"Did you have a good time, Lily?" Korine asked.

"I did, but we got some sad news as well. Be sure to tell Carrie Mae to call me." Korine didn't need to hear my report.

"I sure will," Korine agreed.

At ten that morning, when I couldn't get Ellen off my mind, I called her. She picked up after a while.

"I'm okay, Lily. I'm actually at the mortuary now and am waiting to speak to someone about the cremation."

"Did you get some sleep?"

"Not really, but I will once some decisions are made. I've talked to Mom's lawyer, which was difficult. I should have asked more questions, but then I wasn't thinking as clearly as I might have liked."

"You'll get through this one step at a time. We didn't really get a chance to properly thank you for such a wonderful stay at your house. We will never forget it. We loved Paducah."

"You'll never know how much it meant to me that you came. By the way, I did get a call from Laurie, who expressed her sympathy. I thought that was so nice of her."

"Oh, I'm glad. She has a very big heart."

When I hung up, I continued to feel sad for Ellen, who had a lot on her plate.

Chapter 48

Carrie Mae called back, and I had a lot to tell her. She was very sorry to hear about Aunt Mary and suggested giving a donation to the American Heart Association since Mary had died from a heart attack. She reminded me about Butler wanting to have lunch, but I told her to let a little time go by first. I also shared with her that I'd met a truck driver who supposedly had hundreds of quilts. That was interesting to her.

"Would you like some company when you go to see him?" Carrie Mae suggested.

"Are you serious?"

"You know there's a story there, Lily. Now that I have Korine here every day, I don't mind getting away and seeing something different. Remember when I sized up your inventory before you bought it from Rosie?"

"I do, and you were a big help. I'd love to have you join me. I'll give him a call and set it up. I told Karen I'd like to have the Detectives over to dinner soon, but I'm just too busy."

"There's always time to get together for just a short visit. I think Bonita will be going back to Honduras soon, if I recall. However, you have other things to think about now."

"Good point."

"Lily, I don't know how much longer you can put Butler off before he suspects something."

"I know, I know."

When I hung up, I saw that I had received a text from Alex.

. . .**Are you still mad at me?**

. . .***No. How did Mindy react?***

. . .**Mindy who?**

. . .***Oh boy!***

. . .**It's cool. Not to worry.**

I didn't reply any further. I was sure he'd call soon.

I made a few sales that consisted of three of my new toothpick holders and a white linen tablecloth that was from Rosie's inventory. It wasn't great, but I was grateful. I decided to give the truck driver a call once I'd closed the shop.

He answered right away and was delighted to hear from me. He gave me easy directions since I was familiar with the area. He was only going to be free the next day, so I told him I would come and would also bring another antique dealer with me who might be interested in his quilts. He was delighted. I called Carrie Mae back and told her I would pick her up first thing in the morning with the hopes that I could open the shop in the afternoon. The plan sounded fine to her.

I hung up and went upstairs to open my laptop. I was hoping there would be an update from Ellen. Loretta had emailed first and said that Bill had missed her. She also repeated how good it had been to get away. She, too, wondered what we could do for Ellen.

Lynn said she had called Ellen and asked what memorial her mother might have preferred. Ellen's email was the last message, saying that was the day that Aunt Mary had been cremated. Ellen said she'd called a few people that she knew her mother had kept in contact with to let them know of Aunt Mary's passing, and she'd also had an obituary put in the paper. She said there wouldn't be a memorial service and that we should each give to our own chosen charity, then went on to say that she hoped the estate would be settled soon. Other than the condo, Mary had no longer owned any other real estate. The condo's organization had said there was a waiting list for potential buyers, and Ellen had been pleased to hear that. Since Aunt Mary had continued to do alterations and sewing through the years, Ellen gave her leftover supplies to someone else still in the business. I was sure that some of Aunt Mary's clients would like to know what had happened to her, so I hoped they'd see the obituary when it was printed in the newspaper or online.

I finally responded that unless anyone else had a better idea, I was going to donate to the American Heart Association. I was also thinking of my own parents, who had both died from heart attacks. I didn't stay online to read any responses to my idea. Glancing outside, I realized that the weather was nice and decided to get a cold drink and sit out on the front porch. I had just sat down when Ted pulled in front of the house in his brand-new truck.

"Taking it easy, Ms. Lily?" he joked.

"Yes. The hot weather will start soon, and then it won't be pleasant out here."

"You're right about that! With all the rain we've been having, I guess I'll be by here tomorrow to mow your grass."

"Great. You do such a nice job. Ted, you'll be a senior in high school this fall, right?"

He nodded and smiled.

Chapter 49

"What do you want to do after you graduate?"

"That's a hot topic around my house. I'm considering college, but I know I can get a pretty well-paying job at Andy's Garage in Washington."

"Oh, Ted. You must get more education first."

"Don't you start on me too! I've got to go. See you tomorrow!"

"I'm going into the city, so do you want me to pay you now?"

"Later is fine."

It was so easy for a small-town kid to get stuck and feel comfortable near his hometown instead of going away. If Ted didn't leave for college after graduation, I knew he would never leave.

I went inside and turned out the lights in the quilt room. I stood there and stared at the cabinet.

"Whoever is listening, please bring Butler's quilt back," I said out loud. The request made me feel better, at least. As I left the quilt room, I heard the laughing sound again. Was I crazy? It only lasted a few seconds, but why?

I got out my cell phone and contributed to the American Heart Association. It was a small step to help me deal with my grief and bring some closure. Ellen must have been having many highs and lows throughout this situation. Feeling rather sad, I decided to call Marc. It took him a while to answer.

"Lily, I just got home from the office. How are you and your sisters doing?"

"We're each dealing with this in our own way. It seems strange not to have a funeral for Aunt Mary."

"I'm sure."

"I guess this makes me think more about my dad than it does her."

"Well, move on and embrace the present and future. That's my advice, sweetie."

"Are you staying home for the night?"

"Yes, I need to do some reading for tomorrow's court case. My dinner will be leftover spaghetti from last night."

"That sounds better than the cheese and crackers that I'm thinking about. By the way, I'm coming into the city tomorrow to see someone who wants to sell some of their quilt collection. I'm bringing Carrie Mae with me. Anyway, I'll let you get back to your work."

"Hearing from you has put a kick in my step. You're a gem to call. Hope tomorrow goes well. Love you, Lily Girl."

"I love you, too!"

Suddenly, a gust of wind came in from the opened windows on my porch. I suspected that a storm was coming. As soon as I closed the windows, rain began to fall. It seemed that every day there were spring showers. As a big burst of thunder and a streak of lightening came, I thought about Doc's office again. Surely lightning wouldn't strike twice in the same place. I prepared for bed and turned on a movie to get my mind off the storm. As the rain softened to a nice rhythm, I was able to drop off to sleep.

Early the next morning, I felt groggy. I couldn't get to that first cup of coffee fast enough. I looked out the window and saw that storm damage was evident. There were tree branches everywhere. Hopefully Ted would take care of them for me.

I had my trip to think about. I drove to Carrie Mae's to pick her up. Since she didn't come out, I had to go in and get her. She was downstairs, thankfully. Carrie Mae and Korine were sitting together having coffee.

"Good morning, ladies!" I greeted them. From the looks on their faces, they were feeling the same grogginess that I was experiencing. Carrie Mae got up and retrieved her purse.

"Now, don't hurry back," Korine encouraged.

"Just don't forget that the window washer comes today," Carrie Mae reminded her. "His money is in the drawer."

"Oh, sure!" Korine replied.

"Now, don't go moving any of the merchandise on that table," Carrie Mae added. "I haven't priced that yet. There's mail on the counter for Snowshoes, too."

"Okay, Carrie Mae," I said, taking her arm. "Korine will be fine. We need to get going."

Chapter 50

The trip into the city took longer than expected. Everyone was rushing to go to work, but it gave Carrie Mae and me a chance to visit. When Carrie Mae had a chance to be alone with me, she never missed the opportunity to ask me about my love life or someone else's.

"So, what do you think of Gracie stepping out with that wine guy?"

I chuckled. "Boy, you don't miss a thing, do you?" I teased. "The wine guy's name is Anthony, and I think it's great. They're both single, after all."

"I know everyone thinks that guy is great, including you, but there's something about him that I don't trust."

"Why do you say that?"

"He came in the shop once looking for old tin signs for advertising wine. He's well-spoken. It didn't take him long to ask about you, by the way. It was a while back, but I think he had his eye on you."

"What did he want to know about me?"

"He wanted to know if I had seen you lately and was asking

about how you were doing. Has he asked you out?"

"No. He knows I'm seeing someone."

Carrie Mae chuckled. "Now, do you think that guy is going to be discouraged by that?"

"You let me worry about it, okay? Help me look for house number 1284."

There it was, a large and stately Victorian home that sat on a well-manicured lawn. It wasn't what I had been expecting.

"Would you look at that?" Carrie Mae exclaimed. "Truck drivers must make more money than I thought."

"This has to be it. Oh, there he is, coming out of the house."

"Good heavens, look at the two Dobermans coming out, too. We'd best be careful!"

We waited in the car until Henry called the barking dogs off. They were reluctant, but they went to the back of the house.

"Hannah and Harvey are harmless, ladies. Welcome! Come on in," he said.

"Henry, this is my friend Carrie Mae Wilson that I told you about," I said as we closed the car doors.

"Nice to meet you," Henry said, shaking her hand.

When we walked in the front door, we were quite taken with the beauty of his home. It was filled with the very finest antiques. I watched Carrie Mae swoon over the place as if she had arrived in heaven.

"Your place is quite beautiful," I said.

"The house and contents have been in the family for generations," Henry explained. "Please have a seat. Will you have some tea or coffee?"

"I'd love some tea," Carrie Mae replied quickly. She was never bashful.

"Nothing for me, thank you," I added. My eyes were taking

in amazing things throughout the room.

"Franny is my housekeeper," Henry said as a woman peeked in the room. "She'll bring you some tea in a bit."

"So, you're an avid collector of antiques," I said, trying to get the conversation started.

"Yes, my whole family has that vice, I'm afraid, but my passion is quilts," he explained. "I have a lot of them that I've collected through the years. They aren't all pretty ones, but at the time, I felt I needed to acquire them. I keep them stored in the attic."

"The attic?" I questioned, suddenly fearful of the condition of the quilts we had driven this far to see.

He nodded. "Yes. I rolled them on PVC piping so they wouldn't get fold lines," he explained. "I just keep on stacking them. I'll take you up to see them first, and then I'll bring them down a couple at a time for you to look at. If you want any of them, just name your price. I must let them go. My passion has gotten a little out of hand, I'm afraid."

"So none of these were made by family?" I asked.

"No. I was never made aware of any quilters in our family."

"Then how did you acquire your love for quilts?" Carrie Mae asked.

"They speak to me," Henry said with a grin. "They're waiting to be loved and admired. They want to wrap themselves around you. I wouldn't think of sleeping with a blanket when I could have a quilt."

Carrie Mae and I looked at each other in disbelief.

"I've never heard anyone speak about quilts like that before," I marveled. "That was beautifully said."

Chapter 51

"How many years have you been collecting?" Carrie Mae asked.

"Hmm. I bought my first quilt in Waco, Texas, when I was in my early twenties," Henry said with a grin. "I'm fifty-five now, so you do the math."

Franny brought us tea. We made small talk for a few minutes, and then I sensed that Henry was eager to get started. I followed him up the spiral staircase from the second floor. The heat increased as we proceeded. When he opened the door to the attic, I couldn't believe my eyes. There stood a large pyramid of rolled quilts in the center! I couldn't imagine how any of the quilts at the bottom of the pile could survive both the heat and the weight forced upon them.

"Oh! I wasn't prepared for this," I gasped.

Henry chuckled. "I told you I had a lot of them," he boasted. "I'll have to bring two or three down at a time. That will give you time to look at them. The most recently-purchased ones will be at the top, of course. I brought them up this way, so it should be easier to get them down."

I was speechless. I wasn't sure how his plan would work. Nonetheless, I went down ahead of him while he carried the first two quilts. I couldn't get to air conditioning fast enough.

"Carrie Mae! You won't believe what I just saw up there," I said, huffing and puffing.

"I don't think Lily believed me," Henry joked as he turned to Carrie Mae. "I'll get you started here."

"This will take forever, I'm afraid," I said, suddenly feeling overwhelmed.

"Franny, come here and help us," Henry called towards the kitchen.

"Sure will," she said eagerly. "I know the routine. I help Mr. Henry roll these when he brings them home."

"That's quite a job!" I replied. "There must be hundreds up there!"

Carrie Mae shot me a questioning look.

As we began the process, the first thing that struck me was that the quilts were very warm from the heat as Franny helped us unroll them. Henry asked us to set the ones that we were interested in aside. I could quickly tell that we were not going to find any great quilts, but I told myself that there could be some surprises.

As it got closer to noon, we had made very little progress. Franny said she had prepared a light lunch for us on the patio, knowing that looking at the quilts would take most of the day. Carrie Mae went with the flow as she helped us go through the quilts as quickly as we could.

There were quilts with outrageous color schemes. We put some of those aside to consider. Some of the patterns were unique, too. It was hard to find a quilt that had all good qualities, however. By lunchtime, our favorite quilt was a pieced Tin Man quilt in red and white. I knew I would have to purchase it, despite its poor condition. Carrie Mae mostly sat in a comfortable chair with her tea as she nodded yes or no to each quilt.

Finally, at around one that afternoon, Henry insisted that we take a break and move to the patio. The simple sandwiches with cold iced tea hit the spot, and breathing fresh air felt good.

"You have a fair amount of property here," I commented.

"I have eight acres, which is mostly wooded behind the house," he described. "That's unusual in this part of town."

"What's in that large building over there?" I pointed.

He grinned. "It's where I put my 'gotta fix' projects and my worn quilts."

"Worn quilts?" Carrie Mae asked in disbelief. "I think I already saw those. No offense intended."

Henry laughed heartily. "You haven't seen worn until you've seen these," he teased.

"Well, then, may we take a look?" I asked, curious.

"If you must!" Henry said, shaking his head. "We still have a lot of quilts to go through."

"Not before you have some of my German chocolate cake," Franny said with her hands on her hips. She placed dessert plates in front of me and Carrie Mae.

"You didn't have to go to all that trouble," I responded. "However, I won't pass it up."

"Henry said you were coming from a distance away, and I wanted you to feel welcome," Franny said with a friendly smile.

"Thank you both so much!" I said, taking my last bite. "It's been a real treat seeing your place and your quilt collection."

Before we went back inside, Carrie Mae and I walked over to the large building to see the worn quilts Henry had talked about. Carrie Mae was the first to look in one of the large windows.

"Well, would you look at that!" she said in amazement. "That workbench must be the graveyard of quilts!" She giggled. "It looks like stacks of folded batting."

"It does indeed!" I said with disbelief. "It appears that Henry still has a use for them. Look at those on the furniture and the one wrapped around a quilt frame. It's not a bad idea. It sure beats throwing a quilt away!"

"Absolutely!" Carrie Mae agreed. "We'd better get back inside, or we'll have to spend the night here in order to finish up."

Chapter 52

An entire day had passed. Henry looked exhausted from climbing stairs in the horrible heat. The quilts closer to the bottom of the stack were getting worse and worse in condition. The oil from the plastic PVC piping tubes had left yellow and orange stains on them that had ruined their value. It was such a shame. I remained silent as Henry's growing disappointment showed on his face with each subsequent quilt. I tried to give Henry and Franny some advice as to how to clean some of them. They had their work cut out for them. Henry needed to devise a different method of storage, and I went over some options for him regarding that as well.

When it was time to leave, Henry wanted to pay me for my time and trouble. I asked him instead for reasonable prices on the six quilts I was interested in taking home. Carrie Mae had four that she wanted to purchase. Those ten quilts were the lucky ones. We still had our work cut out for us after they were purchased. They all needed some repair and attention. Henry had probably thought we would buy more, but we'd helped him with a very big task that he was going to have to tackle at some point in time anyway. It was five that evening when we left his house. We were anxious to get home and get cleaned up.

"Well, if that wasn't a strange experience!" Carrie Mae exclaimed as she yawned.

"Are you sorry you came along? I had no idea that it would take all day."

"I'm very glad that I went! What interesting folks and quilts. The lunch was delicious. Thanks so much for letting me come with you."

"I'm glad you were there with me. It was so interesting to see a man that passionate about quilts!"

"Unusual, that's what it was! What in the world will he decide to do from here?"

I shrugged my shoulders. We chatted about the unique experience all the way back to Augusta. I dropped Carrie Mae off. When I got to my house, I took the quilts from the car and put them on the back porch so I could air them out later. Some of them would have to be washed. I checked the shop to make sure everything looked normal. Once again, I stared at the cabinet, hoping for a miracle. As I settled in for the evening, I once again thought of Ellen and what she may be going through. It was only eight, so I decided to call her. "Ellen, it's Lily," I said.

"Oh, Lily, it's nice to hear from you," she responded.

"I keep thinking of you. How was your day?"

"Pretty bad, actually. I met with Mom's lawyer today concerning her will."

"Oh! Well, it's none of my business, but I hope she didn't leave everything to some unknown entity."

"I almost wish she had," she said with anger in her voice.

"I was the only beneficiary, but there was a pretty scathing letter about what I should do with everything. She always had to have the last word."

"I guess I just never understood her. I feel bad for you."

"She'd always been disappointed in me, especially when I took up quilting. I didn't get my degree, so that always came up, of course. I knew I could never make her happy."

"I'm so sorry, Ellen."

"Time will help, but I only have a few weeks to get her things moved or I'll have to pay fees. I don't know how I can get rid of everything."

"Is there someone who can help you?"

"I think so. I'm going to ask a neighbor of hers to take some of the things off my hands. I want very little of what she has."

"Just don't be too hasty, Ellen. You may regret it later."

"I doubt it, but I appreciate your concern. If there's anything you sisters would like, I'd be happy to save it for you. I'm so glad we got to visit before all this happened."

"I am too. We all really enjoyed it. I can't wait until you can come back to Missouri again."

"I will, of course, but not anytime soon."

I felt awful after hanging up with Ellen. What had her life been like having this love-hate relationship with her mother? Ellen was an only child. Was she feeling angry or guilty that Aunt Mary had engaged in an affair with my father? It was complicated, but I was glad that we had accepted her into the family.

Chapter 53

The next day was going smoothly until my phone rang and I saw that it was Butler. I reluctantly answered.

"How's it going?" he asked.

"Butler, how nice to hear from you."

"It's always nice to hear your voice. I'm calling to pin down our luncheon date. Since you're such a busy traveler these days, I think you should set it."

I paused and could feel my stomach begin to churn. "Oh, perhaps sometime later in the week. Have you checked with Carrie Mae?"

"Carrie Mae always wants to have lunch with me, remember? You're the one who hesitates. Besides seeing you, of course, I can visit those handsome quilts that now live with you."

"Sure. Where would you like to meet up?" I tried to sound enthusiastic, but the thought of Butler dropping by to see the quilts began to produce a landslide of anxiety in me.

"You once told me how fond you were of Wine Country Gardens when you first started coming out to wine country. Would that suit you?"

"It would. I haven't been there in a while."

"So, twelve on Friday?"

"Sure. I'll pick up Carrie Mae and we'll meet you there."

"How's everything else going?"

"Well, my sisters and I enjoyed going to Paducah for the quilt show last week, but then we got word that my Aunt Mary had passed. She's the mother of Ellen, the person we went to visit."

"Oh, I'm so sorry. Where did your aunt live?"

"In Florida, so it's a bit awkward."

"I see. Again, my condolences."

"Thanks. See you Friday." When I hung up, I knew that judgment day was coming. Should I tell Butler about the missing quilt before, during, or after lunch? I had to prepare myself in case he decided to take his quilts back. He had every right to do so. Hopefully Carrie Mae would let me keep the cabinet so the loss wouldn't be so obvious. I was in a daze when my cell phone rang again.

"Hello, Lily. It's Kitty."

"Oh, are you back?"

"No. We're in Cleveland, Ohio seeing my aunt, who is pretty ill. We had to take a little trip out of the way. I hope things are going well and that you're keeping my Baltimore Album quilt safe. I still can't believe that Ray bought it for me!"

"It is safe, and I hope it brought you a happy birthday. I think Ray is a keeper."

"Indeed! Is everything good at the cottage?"

"Yes, I check nearly every day. I recently went out of town for a few days, but I had Judy check on the place while I was gone."

"Thanks so much. I'm starting to get a little homesick, but I want to stay here until my aunt is out of the woods, so to speak. We still need to get to some of the auction houses."

"Have you found any bargains to bring back?"

"Not like we used to. Nothing is like it used to be."

"Well, have a safe trip back. I hope your aunt recovers."

"Thanks!"

I hung up thinking how happy Kitty would be to receive her quilt and how unhappy Butler would be when I told him I'd lost one.

Bored from a lack of customers, I pulled out my redwork quilt blocks in hopes of making some progress. With quilt class meeting the next day, I wanted to get as much done as possible. When this quilt was done, I wanted to display it on the wall in the quilt room.

A young woman came in the door and barely acknowledged me at the counter until I said something. She headed straight to the quilt room.

"Can I help you?"

"Not really. I just wanted to see the quilts that you have for sale."

"Are you looking for any particular kind or price range?"

"Not really. I hear your price range is huge."

I didn't know how to respond. I started by saying, "Well, as you might guess, some are nicer than others." As I observed her, I saw she was only checking the price tags rather than looking at the quilts. She was obviously scouting for something.

"What's the price range of the quilts in the cabinet?"

"Most of them are over a thousand dollars."

"And you have luck selling those?"

Chapter 54

This customer was quickly making me feel uncomfortable in my own shop! How should I respond? I said, "I try. May I ask why you're interested in the prices of my quilts? Are you pricing for yourself or for someone else?" The look on her face told me that there was more to the story.

"I just want to know if you can survive just selling quilts and antiques," she blurted out.

"How does anyone survive in any business? Are you thinking of starting a business like this?"

"Not from what I know so far. I can't believe you can get enough traffic through here to sell these quilts. No one has even come in the shop since I've arrived," she said accusingly.

I smiled. "I have some things to attend to, but if there's anything else I can help you with, just let me know." I really had to bite my tongue. I felt insulted. I'd barely made it back to the counter before the customer walked past me towards the door. "Have a good day!" I said as she left. I had to wonder if I had encouraged her or not. What I did know was that it had been an odd interaction. My cell phone rang, and I could see that it was Carrie Mae. "I guess by now you've heard from Butler," I said right away.

"Are you upset?"

"Let's just say I'm concerned. He actually said he wants to see his quilts again."

"It pays to be honest, Lily Girl. It will work out. Butler has a heart of gold. I'm calling for another reason. I want you to come over for dinner. I've been upstairs most of the day, making chicken and dumplings. It takes me so much longer to do things these days. Betty can join us. If you want to include Karen and Bonita, we can do that. I think Bonita is still here."

"No, let's just let it be the three of us."

"Just come on over at five when you close."

"Great. What can I bring?"

"Not one thing. Betty said she's made a Texas sheet cake, so she's going to bring some."

"Wine? Do we need wine?"

"Now, you know how well supplied I am. Let me have this chance to use some of it."

"Okay. See you after work."

I thought the business day was a total loss until a man purchased an antique walnut folding table that I'd brought with me from Rosie's shop. He was excited when he found a certain marking that I was totally unaware of. It had a small design of inlaid rosewood. The man didn't ask for a discount, so the price must have felt like a bargain to him. I was tickled to get the table out of the shop and free up some space.

Feeling good about my day, I freshened up to go to Carrie Mae's house. My cell phone rang, and it was Holly.

"Guess what?" she asked with excitement. "I'm going to

drive out to your place tomorrow!"

"You are?"

"I'm so anxious to see those special quilts that you have, and we have a lot to catch up on."

"Oh, Holly, tomorrow is my quilt class. Would you like to come with me? The class members would love it. I've told them all about you."

"I don't know about that. What time is the class?"

"It's at ten. If you leave by nine, it can work. We can go to lunch afterwards, which would be so much fun. We haven't done that in a while. The class will likely have many quilt questions for you."

"Well, it does sound like fun, if I can get myself going in the morning."

"They're all down-to-earth folks, and I know Susan, the teacher, will be delighted to meet you."

"Okay, if you're sure."

"Be at my place before ten. The library is close by."

I hung up and rushed to Carrie Mae's. It would be fun to see Holly again and introduce her to other quilters. Butler's inventory must have really gotten her curiosity up. Holly was famous for accepting a chance to lecture on quilts and then coming over to borrow selections from my collection. She'd better not ask to borrow any of these quilts, because I'd have to turn her down!

Chapter 55

Korine was leaving Carrie Mae's house when I arrived, so I went right on in.

"Oh, it smells divine in here!" I said as I inhaled.

"I know!" Korine nodded. "She's sending a nice bowl home with me."

"Great! Enjoy!" I went upstairs to Carrie Mae's apartment for only the second time since I'd known her. When she heard me coming, she immediately started apologizing.

"Please excuse my mess," she began. "You know I'm not a housekeeper."

"No worries!" I assured her.

"I have a pathway through the rooms. That's all I need. Have a seat and help yourself to the wine. I just need to finish up this salad."

"Where's Betty?"

"She'll be here any minute. We'll have to listen for her knock, because the shop door is locked."

"Carrie Mae," I said slowly as I took in my surroundings, "you keep so much stock up here. I thought that was what your basement was for."

She gave me a look of disdain. "Not for my precious things that are near and dear to me!"

"Yes, Butler hinted that you store all of your bears up in the attic."

"No, I have some on this floor as well. Butler was a big help to me when I needed to identify them. He also had connections with other dealers when I wanted to purchase one here and there."

"He's got connections, alright."

Carrie Mae smiled and nodded. "I can tell that he enjoys the hunt, you might say. I think I hear Betty at the door. Will you let her in?"

Betty was as chipper as always when she handed me her sheet cake to carry upstairs.

As soon as I poured Betty some wine, Carrie Mae announced that we should sit and enjoy the meal. Her red checked tablecloth was crowded with all the fixings, including a large soup tureen of chicken and dumplings in the center. She was using Nippon china that had chips here and there.

"I love this pattern," I remarked.

"I do, too, and I'm using it, as you can tell," Carrie Mae replied. "My Aunt Hilda used this set for years, and I always admired it."

"I'm using some of my china for everyday too," Betty added. "My kids sure don't want stuff like that, and I don't entertain anymore. Lily, I guess you don't have any news to share about that missing quilt, do you?"

I shook my head.

"Well, the Dinner Detectives need to get on that pretty

soon, because Butler's coming on Friday," Carrie Mae informed her.

"Speaking of our Dinner Detectives, I hear we'll be one short soon with Bonita leaving," Betty said.

"Already?" I asked.

"I saw Karen at Johann's yesterday, and she said Bonita would be leaving any day now," Betty claimed.

"I was hoping to spend more time with her," I said wistfully. "I was going to suggest that she visit our quilt class. I think that many of the class members would support her cause."

"Karen thought her visit had been very successful, so that's good," Betty explained.

"Is anyone hungry or not?" Carrie Mae said teasingly.

"Bring it on," I said, reaching for the ladle and smiling. "There's nothing like sitting at the kitchen table surrounded by some good home cooking."

As we enjoyed our dinner, Carrie Mae was delighted. She loved to cook and hadn't been doing it as frequently as she would have liked. As I looked at the countertops full of flour where she'd rolled her dumplings, I knew it would be a big chore to clean up. I decided to stay and help her.

Between the cleanup and our chatter, Betty and I didn't leave until ten. We both took home an adequate supply of chicken and dumplings that we could enjoy later. When I got closer to the house, Doc's office lights were flashing. That hadn't happened in quite a while. I ignored it and went inside. I was totally ready for a good night's sleep. The next day would be a full morning with Holly coming to visit. Before I crawled into bed, I checked my phone for messages.

In our group email was a message from Ellen. She said she

was still in Florida, going through her mother's things, and she'd come across a lot of pictures of our dad and wondered if we wanted them. She said that her mother's neighbor was a big help and that she had given the neighbor quite a few things. I was pleased to hear that.

It made me sick to think that Aunt Mary had so many pictures of Dad. They were likely pictures that she'd taken of him when they were together. That was a part of his life that I was not interested in. As far as I was concerned, Ellen could pitch them. It would be interesting to see how my sisters would respond.

Chapter 56

I couldn't believe that Holly was on time the next morning. We hugged and sat down for a quick cup of coffee before we went to quilt class.

"Lily, I don't know how you drive on those winding roads all the time. Even though today's weather was perfect and there was little traffic, I found myself hugging that steering wheel."

I nodded in agreement. "Since the day of the accident, I drive really carefully on the roads."

"Okay, before it gets too late, show me those quilts!"

I grabbed the key from the cash drawer.

"Mercy, girl!" Holly shouted when she saw them stacked in the cabinet. "I can tell that these are all dandy quilts. You know I'm a sucker for appliquéd quilts, so can we pull out a few of those?"

"This Baltimore Album quilt is sold. Kitty's husband put a deposit on it. She's always wanted one, and this one's really special," I explained as I pulled it out.

"There's more here than I thought there would be. Let

me see this one that has a lot of red and green."

I opened it up, and Holly's eyes widened.

"Get out!" she responded in disbelief. "This is awesome, and I'll bet it has many different names. The green is a bit fugitive, but not much. I think this is turn of the century, from what I see in these fabrics."

"If I recall, this is named Rose Wreath, but doesn't it remind of you of the pattern President's Wreath?" I asked.

"Yes, it does. This twelve-inch border is totally cool, but just look at the alternating white blocks. They each have a different trapunto design, mostly birds and leaves. How time-consuming that must have been! There's a slight fold line, but I don't see anything else wrong, do you? What else do you know about it?" Holly asked.

"Let me go get Butler's list and see," I said, leaving the room.

When I returned, Holly was examining the close quilting stitches. "I've never seen anything like this, Lily."

"There's not a lot here," I said, looking at the list. "It's pretty large. The size is 101" x 100". It was found in Mt. Carmel, Illinois, and the maker is unknown. It has a pretty good description, however."

"I would have guessed that it was from the East Coast from that style. Okay, I'm afraid to look at the tag. How much is it?"

"Keep in mind that I didn't set these prices, Butler did. He knows the market all over the world."

"I'm waiting!"

I chuckled. "Sit down," I advised.

"There's no place to sit down. This quilt is covering everything."

"It's twelve thousand dollars. Should I wrap it up, or would you like to put it in layaway?"

Holly looked shocked. "Would you take ten dollars a month?" she joked.

"For you, girlfriend, I would."

"Do you really think you can? I'm not arguing about the value."

"Probably not. I can do a ten percent discount, so that's twelve hundred dollars off, if that helps."

We looked at one another and burst into laughter.

"Yikes, Holly, we've got to get to class! Help me fold this back up."

Holly and I carefully folded the quilt so it would stack nicely back in the cabinet with the others. I locked the cabinet, and we made our way out the door. Holly couldn't stop talking about the quilt as we drove to the library. She asked if she could take a photo of it when class was over, but I told her no. Butler had told me not to allow any photographs.

Everyone was seated when Holly and I arrived.

"Oh, good!" Susan said, surprised. "I was worried that you'd forgotten. Who's your friend?"

"This is my friend Holly, who I have mentioned many times before. She's quite the quilt authority. She lectures on various quilt topics and does quilt restoration for people. A special plus for some is that she washes them as well."

"That's impressive, Holly!" Susan responded. "Welcome to the Wine Country Quilters!" I'd never heard anyone refer to us using that name before.

"I'm thrilled to be here!" Holly said. "Lily has talked so much about you. I'm looking forward to seeing your blocks for the wine country quilt."

"We're having a lot of fun with it," Susan assured her. "I wish you could lead a class sometime. I'm interested in quilt restoration."

Holly smiled. We got a cup of coffee and then sat down at the table. Holly was totally absorbed in what each quilter had to say about their block. Occasionally she would comment or give a piece of advice if it was asked for. When I showed my block, I received positive feedback from the group.

"You really are enjoying the redwork process on these blocks, aren't you?" Susan observed.

"I am!" I said happily. "It's like painting a picture. I particularly like that I don't have to change the colors of the embroidery floss!"

Chapter 57

"Holly, would you consider being a judge for us at some point?" Susan asked, catching everyone off guard.

"Sure!" Holly responded. "Are these blocks or the finished quilts going to be judged?"

"No, but I've always wanted to do a quilt show in Augusta," Susan explained.

"Well, Edna would win every time!" Heidi quipped.

All of us laughed at Heidi's remark because it was very likely true.

"I've been doing handwork much longer than any of you," Edna laughed. "Everyone has improved so much since you first started."

"I agree, Edna!" Susan chimed in.

"I think we could have a ready-made quilt show if Lily would just show everyone the beautiful quilts she's recently acquired," Judy said. "You don't see those kinds of quilts every day."

"Aren't they amazing?" Holly asked. "I had the pleasure of seeing them this morning."

"Well, those quilts don't belong to me, so I would never take them out of the shop," I explained.

"Lily, we're a small group, and we would be willing to meet at your shop sometime," Susan offered.

"That would be so cool," Candace said.

"You should think about that," Marilyn advised, giving me a friendly smile.

"I will think about it," I said, still feeling hesitant.

"Susan, they each cost thousands of dollars!" Judy explained.

Everyone looked shocked.

"Really?" Heidi asked in disbelief.

"They're more expensive than the quilts I typically carry in the shop," I replied. "We would have to sell our cars or houses to afford some of them."

They giggled.

Susan took charge of the group conversation by saying, "Before you corner Holly with your questions, I wanted to tell you that I met Bonita, Karen's friend, who is originally from Honduras. She has been visiting this area and has an interest in helping to promote sewing and quilting in her country so the women can have extra income, especially in the rural areas. She was sorry she missed our class, because she is new to the craft herself. She was asking for donations, and I understand that Gracie was very helpful and shared some sources that may donate free fabric and even sewing machines."

"Oh, that's wonderful!" said Edna right away.

"I have her information if you have any ideas for her," Susan added.

At that, the class was officially dismissed. Holly was

approached right away by Candace, who was trying to restore her grandmother's quilt.

"I hope you didn't mind me bringing up your quilts," Judy said to me. "I was just trying to help you sell them."

"I know," I replied. Thank goodness she hadn't known about the missing quilt, or she would have revealed that as well!

Holly and I were the last to leave, and Holly wanted to know where we were going to have lunch.

"How about we go to one of our favorites like we used to?" I suggested.

"Wine Country Gardens?" she guessed.

I nodded.

"That would be awesome. Why don't I drive separately so I can leave from there?"

"That's fine. We'll get your car and head on over there."

It was a pleasant day to go to Wine Country Gardens. I was hoping I could keep my secret about the missing quilt from Holly. I arrived a little early and tracked down Chris, the owner, asking her to come to our table on the large porch. By then, Holly had arrived and had found where we would be sitting.

"You remember Chris, don't you, Holly?" I asked.

"I sure do!" Holly said, shaking her hand. "I love your chicken salad. I hope it's still on the menu."

"It sure is," Chris assured her. "Welcome back!"

"Do you have time to join us?" I asked Chris.

"I wish I could, but its payroll day," she explained. "I've been out here way too long as it is. How's your niece Sarah?"

"She's getting her life together," I reported. "Thank you for asking. I'll tell her you that you asked about her. She really loved her visit here and thought it would be so cool to work here."

Chris chuckled. "We work pretty hard here, and the weather isn't always kind to us," she laughed. "It's a great place to work, but it's not easy most days."

"I'm sure," I said. "We don't want to keep you. Thanks for stopping to chat."

"Nice to see you again, Holly," Chris said. "Come back soon."

"I wish I lived closer," Holly said wistfully as we watched Chris go back inside.

"You could do that, you know. You can afford to build any kind of house you want. There's always land available somewhere."

She paused. "I guess it's just too soon for a big change. Now that I can finally do some things to the house, I'm learning to like living there all over again."

Chapter 58

Once again, Holly enjoyed our conversation, chicken salad, and iced tea. I remembered the first time I'd brought her here. I'd then taken her to Carrie Mae's, where we'd each bought a quilt.

"You know, I can't get that appliquéd quilt off my mind," Holly said out of the blue. "How much would it be again with the ten percent off?"

I looked at Holly quizzically and took a sip of my tea. "It would be ten thousand eight hundred dollars plus tax."

Holly paused. "None of my quilts are of that caliber, nor have I ever seen one that has gotten my attention like that one."

"Your quilts are beautiful! These quilts will end up going to collectors who are looking for certain quilts. They're in a different price range entirely."

"Excuse me, but are you trying to talk me out of buying it?"

"Sorry, Holly, I didn't mean it that way, but you can't be seriously thinking about buying that quilt, can you?"

"I think if you work with me, I can swing it. If I gave you five thousand dollars as a down payment, I could pay you the balance in six weeks or so."

"You have to be kidding! You're not poor, Holly, but you don't have money to burn either. I'm thrilled to sell it to you, but don't buy it to impress me. That's a lot of money, even for you."

"I brought my checkbook with me, because I really intended to buy something from your shop. After seeing the Rose Wreath quilt, nothing else compares."

"This is crazy! Are you sure?"

"That's no way to close a sale, girlfriend. Don't look a gift horse in the mouth! I can do this. Just watch me." Holly got out her checkbook and set it on the table, and I watched her write a check payable to Lily Girl's Quilts and Antiques for five thousand dollars. I stared in disbelief until she signed her name.

"Unbelievable!"

"Here you go. Now, I'd like a receipt, please."

I was caught off guard. "Okay, here you go. I'll use this clean napkin. Let me borrow your pen." I gently wrote the name of the quilt, the price less the discount, the tax, the balance due, the date, and Holly's check number. All I had to do was sign my name.

"Thank you very much," Holly said, slipping the makeshift receipt into her purse. We both broke into laughter.

"Thank you! I promise to put a sold sign on it as soon as I get back to the shop. Speaking of the shop, I have got to get back."

"Seeing that I just spent five thousand dollars in your shop today, I hope you're going to pick up this lunch tab."

"Absolutely! Congrats on owning half of a fantastic quilt."
We giggled again.

I laid the money for lunch on the table, and we walked happily to our cars. We gave each other a big hug before we parted company. I felt elated on the drive back. When I passed the Yellow Farmhouse Winery, I was sorry to see a sign out front indicating that it was for sale. It was one of the cutest wineries in the region. When I got back to Augusta, Ted was just leaving my place. The yard looked great, and I found myself feeling grateful for his sense of responsibility and work ethic at his young age.

As soon as I walked into my shop, I put Holly's check in the cash drawer. It wasn't a bad sale for not being open! I stepped into the quilt room. The light was on. I remembered that I had left it off. Why, oh why did spirits try to communicate with lights? I got the key to the cabinet and removed Holly's quilt. I refolded it a bit and admired it once again. I wished I knew about the maker. Because of all the quilting, I couldn't help but wonder if initials or a simple name might be quilted in the quilt. I examined each corner where I thought that could be found. Had the quilt been made for a special occasion? I guessed most folks were too modest to label their quilts. I decided to keep Kitty and Holly's quilts together. It would be better to take them upstairs where people couldn't see them. I was starting to realize that a layaway plan could be the answer to selling these high-dollar quilts.

Chapter 59

Friday morning, I felt sick at the thought of seeing Butler. I could start out by telling him I sold the Rose Wreath quilt to Holly, which would make him happy. My real concern would come when he'd want to check on the quilts. I couldn't eat breakfast, so when I thought Carrie Mae might be up, I would give her a call and ask for any advice she might have. I knew she could soften the news when it came time to tell Butler about the missing quilt. Rain suddenly started to pour down outside. This was not what we needed for our outdoor lunch at Wine Country Gardens. Eating inside there would not be the same. Because of the hard rain, I didn't even open the shop, but started on bookwork instead. At ten, I decided to call Carrie Mae.

"Can you believe this weather?" Carrie Mae exclaimed. "I think we should stay here and eat somewhere in town. What do you think?"

"Sure. I don't think the weather will make my day any more unpleasant after I tell Butler about the quilt."

"You've got to tell him, sweetheart. He may not be happy

that you waited this long to tell him, I'll grant you that."

"What will I say? Please stand up for me."

"Of course I will. You need to tell him at lunch. He may or may not want to come back to the shop after that."

"That's true. I hope he doesn't."

"I think I'm going to call and tell him to meet us at Ashley Rose instead," Carrie Mae suggested.

"Ashley Rose?"

"Yes. Is that okay?"

"Sure," I said reluctantly. My thoughts immediately went to Anthony. We hung up, and I rushed upstairs to get dressed. I had to look extra nice. Alex called while I was putting on my makeup.

"Lunch date with Butler, huh?" he teased.

"Carrie Mae is also going, so don't start with me," I warned, laughing. "What's up with you?"

"I just got some heat from Richard."

"Why?"

"I turned down an article he wanted me to do on a political issue that I disagree with. I don't do that very often, but doing this article would be very uncomfortable. I hate that I can't choose my subject matter like someone else I know."

"I know. I'm fortunate. I totally get it."

"I sure didn't score any points with him. It will probably be a while before he assigns me anything again, if ever."

"He won't want to lose you. You have a good following. Why don't you use this time to start that book you keep talking about?"

"Funny you should say that. If I could just start it, I would feel better."

"Surprise me! I have to go now, or I'll be late." I hung up and finished dressing, then said a silent prayer asking for guidance. I had to be brave and honest, and then take the consequences. If Butler decided to remove the quilts, so be it. Just as I was about to leave, Carrie Mae called to confirm that she had told Butler to meet us at Ashley Rose. With the rain, I didn't want Carrie Mae to walk, so I told her I would pick her up. I gave myself a last-minute look in the mirror and accepted what I saw.

Very few people were in the restaurant when we arrived. I said a quick hello to Sally and then chose a booth for us away from the bar.

"No sign of Butler anywhere," Carrie Mae observed.

"I don't think I can eat a thing," I said, taking a sip of water.

"Hello, I'm Marvin," the waiter said. "I will be your server today. What can I get you to drink?"

"I think they're going to have a glass of the best wine you have," Butler interrupted.

We smiled.

"Bring us some Vintage Rose," Carrie Mae suggested, since she knew I loved it. "It's quite good."

"That's what I hear," Butler said.

"That's what our wine expert recommends when he comes here," Marvin replied. "I'll bring a bottle."

"Good to see you charming ladies," Butler said as he sat next to Carrie Mae. "I haven't been here before. How is the food?"

"The specials are always good," I stated.

Chapter 60

Our conversation initially covered the niceties of the day and the weather. Butler said he'd driven through thunderstorms on his way to Augusta and had seen a couple of accidents, which didn't surprise me. At the restaurant, the specialty of the day, according to Marvin, was liver and onions. Butler was delighted and commented about how rare that was to find in restaurants these days.

"I think I'm tempted," Carrie Mae said slowly, trying to make up her mind. "I love it, but I'm rather picky. I used to make my own years ago."

"It's fairly popular here," Marvin bragged.

"If it's good enough for Butler, I'll join him," Carrie Mae said flirtatiously.

"I'll have your French dip," I decided. "I've never been disappointed." Of course, I remembered that it was Anthony's choice.

"I know that it's one of your favorites," Marvin commented.

"You must come here often," Butler teased.

"Not as much as I used to when I'd just moved here," I

explained.

"This wine is delicious!" Butler exclaimed.

"I'm glad you like it." I said with a smile.

"Lily, tell me how your customers are reacting to the quilts," Butler inquired as he looked directly into my eyes.

"Well, I'm pleased to report that I now have two quilts in layaway," I answered. "The Rose Wreath tugged at my friend Holly's heart, so she paid me half as a down payment."

"Congratulations!" Butler responded.

"Did you tell him that you sold the wholecloth quilt?" Carrie Mae interjected.

"I did," I said.

"Lily, I am so proud of you." Butler said as he reached over and patted my hand from across the table.

Our food was delivered to the table. I tried to find an appetite. I let Carrie Mae and Butler do most of the talking. They both were very pleased with the liver and onions.

"This is just how I fix mine," Carrie Mae bragged.

"I forgot how much I enjoyed this," Butler said as he took another bite.

The two of them then talked about cooking, which left me out, but I had other things on my mind, like the missing quilt and how I would tell Butler.

"How is your sister doing since the death of her mother?" Butler asked as he sipped his wine.

"Thanks for asking, Butler," I said, and then paused. "It's a strange situation that I won't go into, but she's dealing with it the best she can. The estate was quite simple, so that helps."

When the subject of dessert came up, we decided to share a piece of the chocolate pie Marvin had recommended. Sally made sure it was extra large, and it arrived with three forks.

"How is your foundation doing, Butler?" asked Carrie Mae with interest.

"Very well, thank you," Butler responded. "It's a cause that affects more families than you realize. I still miss James terribly."

"I'm sure you do," I sympathized.

Lunch was coming to an end, and I still hadn't told Butler about the missing quilt.

"I take it that your shop is closed today, or did you get someone in to watch it?" Butler inquired.

"I'm closed," I replied. "With this rain, I wouldn't have had many customers anyway."

"Perhaps I'll find something to purchase," he teased. "Is Korine keeping your shop open, Carrie Mae?"

"Oh, yes. She loves showing up every day. I think she's convinced herself that it's her shop."

We chuckled.

"You're fortunate to have her," Butler replied. "Well, unless you ladies want more coffee, I suggest that we head over to Lily Girl's Quilts and Antiques!"

When we got up from our seats, Carrie Mae gave me a look of warning. She had probably been hoping that I would have told Butler by now. Butler headed out and said he would meet us at the shop.

"I know, I know," I assured Carrie Mae. "I'll tell him when we all get there."

"You'd better! You don't want him to discover that it's missing and then try to explain it to him!"

I mumbled another prayer as we went out into the rain to get in my car.

"I hope this rain lets up before Butler has to drive home," Carrie Mae added.

Chapter 61

"Butler, I didn't want to spoil our lunch, but I need to share something with you," I said when we arrived back at the shop. Butler raised his eyebrows, interested. Carrie Mae busied herself looking at other merchandise while Butler and I talked in the quilt room.

"Okay." Butler nodded. "Continue."

"Do you remember the crazy quilt in your collection?" I asked.

"Sure, the one with the appliquéd woman's glove on it? That's a favorite of mine."

"Yes, that's the one. It's missing." I blurted out.

"Missing?" he repeated.

"I noticed it some time ago, but didn't say anything, because I thought there had to be a logical reason for it," I confessed.

"So, Lily, what's your logical explanation, or should I say theory?" he inquired.

"Believe me, Butler, there are no clues. Not one," I admitted. "I never forget to turn on the alarm. I've gone over and over your list, and it's just not there. I haven't found any signs of a break-in, either."

"Did you know about this, Carrie Mae?" Butler asked, fixing his gaze on her as she entered the quilt room.

"Yes, she told me right away," Carrie Mae acknowledged. "She's been just sick about it."

"Did you call the police?"

I shook my head.

"Why not?" he asked.

"Because of the publicity it would bring to both of us," I explained. "You would be pulled into any inquiry as the real owner of the quilts."

"I see," he said as he started to pace. "I assume that you keep this cabinet locked at all times?"

"Yes, definitely," I confirmed. "There's only one key to the cabinet, and it stays in my cash drawer. Honestly, Butler, there have only been a few people that I've opened the cabinet for, and I've stood right here beside them while they looked at a particular quilt. Most customers aren't interested when I tell them that they are all over a thousand dollars."

"Any suspects there?" he asked.

"Not really," I said.

"Butler, I may not have shared with you that Lily has a spirit or two in this house," Carrie Mae revealed. "The doctor who once lived here has literally moved things around. He even moved some of his things back to the basement after we'd brought them upstairs. I know it's hard to believe, but I can testify to those happenings."

"That is interesting," Butler admitted as he put his finger on his chin.

"I know it's crazy, but I had to factor in that it could be

the doctor playing with me again," I shared.

"Why would he do that?" Butler asked.

"I don't know," I said in frustration. "Frankly, my gut says it wasn't Doc. He's only moved things that belonged to him."

"And there's another ghost?" Butler questioned.

"Rosie. Remember Rosie from the antique shop?" I asked. "She's been totally harmless, and I sense that she is my protector."

"I do remember Rosie," he acknowledged. "You think she's here?"

I nodded.

"I don't think she would be creating this kind of stress for you, Lily," Carrie Mae said.

"Let me see this cabinet," Butler requested. He took the key out of my hand and opened it up.

"I check the quilts every day and refold them every now and then," I explained. "I do think they look good there. I can't have folks handling them unless they're seriously interested. I stay right with them when they look," I repeated for emphasis.

"Well, Lily, it sounds like you've done all you could to keep them secure," Butler stated as he lifted each folded quilt. "I can't condone or condemn your doctor friend. I have a spirit at my place as well; however, he or she only likes to misplace small things, like salt and pepper shakers and items of clothing. It drives me nuts."

"Oh my!" I exclaimed. "I'm glad you don't think I'm crazy!"

"So, you're certain that there are no suspects in the backs of your minds?" Butler questioned once more.

I shook my head. "I am so, so sorry, Butler. If you think

you need to remove the quilts from here, I totally understand. I'll pay you back in some way for the missing quilt."

"We're fortunate in that these quilts are insured, so don't worry about that," Butler informed me.

I began to feel relieved for the first time in a long time.

"I am very grateful to hear that," I said in a shaky voice.

"My biggest concern is that you might be hit again," Butler warned me. "The individual who did this has been successful, and it's only natural that they will try again."

"I've thought of that as well," I said in agreement. "This is my fault, but I don't know what I can do about it."

"Lily, Lily, things like this happen in business," he said kindly, moving closer. "We always want to blame ourselves. I think you and I had this talk when James took his life. Things happen. Besides, your sales on these quilts are going very nicely."

I looked at Carrie Mae, who gave me a comforting wink.

Chapter 62

Butler stayed another half hour as we discussed security. He was sympathetic in that he'd never had a brick-and-mortar store. He'd always sold online or during a direct visit to his clientele. Before he left, I thanked him for being sensitive about the matter and assured him that I would keep him posted on any news. We agreed at this point to keep the police out of the situation. When he closed the door, I sat on the chair near the door and began to cry. I was so relieved, and yet intensely disappointed at my inability to fix the situation.

"Oh, sweetie, that wasn't so bad, was it? I told you that Butler had a good heart. It would never be about the money with him."

While Carrie Mae was consoling me, my mind was giving thanks to God for His helping me tell Butler. "Thanks for supporting me, Carrie Mae," I said as I touched her hand on my shoulder. "I feel so foolish about all of this."

"I have a feeling this will be resolved in its own time. Try to get some rest. You have more quilts to sell tomorrow."

I smiled and gave her a hug. "Let's get you back home where

you'll be safe and sound," I joked.

"From the looks of this rain, you'd better, or I'll be spending the night."

I took Carrie Mae home in the pouring rain. When I returned to my place, Doc's lights were flashing in his office.

"Yeah, yeah, I know you're still there. If you had anything to do with the missing quilt, I'll never forgive you," I said aloud.

At the end of the day, I was ready to crawl into bed. The relief of Butler's forgiveness allowed me to fall fast asleep.

As I awoke the next morning, I had to remind myself of Butler's kind actions and made the decision to move on. I went downstairs, looking forward to that first cup of coffee, but first walked into the quilt room, once again hoping for a miracle. My landline rang, bringing me to the counter.

"Lily?" a somewhat familiar voice asked. "This is Meg, Marc's sister."

"Meg! How nice to hear from you."

"I probably don't have to remind you, but Marc has a big birthday coming up. You do know that he's turning sixty, don't you?"

"Yes, but thanks for the reminder. He says you're coming here to visit."

"I am. I want to throw a little surprise party for him, and I wondered if you could help."

"Sure!"

"I talked to his law partner, Joe, whom I've met once or twice, and he's been somewhat helpful. He suggested that I have a little something at the Missouri Athletic Club, where the law partners go every now and then for drinks. I did as he suggested, because Marc will be less suspicious if someone takes him there."

"Good idea. How can I help?"

"Well, you know another side of him, so I want you to tell me who else I should invite."

"I see. He's very close to my brother-in-law, Carl, and some of my friends as well, so I can send you some of those suggestions."

"That would be great. You have my email address, correct?"

"Yes, I do."

"If the weather is nice, I hear the club has a lovely patio where we could gather. The second thing is, what can I give him?"

"I could ask you the same thing. He has everything he could ever want. By the way, I hope you can get out to Augusta again while you're here."

"It depends on how much time I have."

"I really appreciate your asking for my input. Let me know if you think of anything else that I can do."

"I will. See you soon!"

Marc's birthday was close at hand. I had been too busy thinking about my own problems. It was a good thing Meg had called and reminded me that he was turning sixty. I wondered if I should be the one throwing him a party, but when we had spoken about it earlier, he hadn't seemed to like the idea. Thinking of a gift for him would be challenging. The first thing I'd ever given Marc was an antique toolbox that Rosie had had in her inventory. He'd hinted that he was a handyman in a secret life and had always wanted a toolbox when he first saw it at Rosie's shop. I had put it aside and given it to him later as a thank you gift for helping me move.

Chapter 63

The next day, I was in the mood to rearrange some things in the shop since I'd sold some pieces of furniture. I had learned a few tricks about how to move bigger pieces by placing a rug under the feet of the piece to be moved. Then I could more easily push the piece into place on the hardwood floors. I was slowly selling off much of Rosie's furniture and was not replacing it with more. I was turning more and more into a quilt shop with a few antiques. I heard the door open, and I couldn't believe who walked in.

"Jenny! What a surprise!" I exclaimed. I hadn't heard from her since I'd visited her in her apartment on The Hill.

"Hi, Lily! I should have probably called first, but I agreed to meet with someone in Washington, so I thought I'd just stop by and say hello."

"Well, I'm glad you were able to find me!"

"I have to admit that the yellow house was a dead giveaway."

I laughed and nodded in agreement. "That's what I hear! Hey, how about a glass of iced tea? It's really getting hot out there."

"That would be so refreshing! I don't want to keep you from your work."

"Nonsense. I'll get some tea from the kitchen. Have a seat out here on the porch so we can talk."

"Sounds great, but I want to look around your shop before I go. So, you live upstairs?"

"I do! It's cozy and just the right size for one person. It's a bit messy, but if you'd like to see it, I'll show it to you."

"No, no. I'm just fascinated that you made this change from the apartment on The Hill."

"It was a big change, that's for sure. Take your time and have a look around."

Jenny went to the quilt room. "You have so many quilts in here!" she called. "Now I know why you dedicated a whole room to them."

"These are just the ones that I have for sale. I have my personal collection upstairs. Let's go sit."

"Listen, if someone comes in, just ignore me, okay?" Jenny said.

"Most customers don't come in until after lunch."

"This view is amazing. I love your plants out here. This place looks bigger once you're inside."

"I thought the same thing when I first saw it," I agreed.

"Oh, before I forget, I brought you a few more things from Bertie."

"Oh, I thought I smelled something delicious!"

She giggled. "Yes, of course! I brought you a few cannoli from Vitale's Bakery, too."

"Wonderful! How sweet of you. It's like a taste of home."

"I can imagine. I found the other things in an old dresser

in the attic. There are little unfinished pieces that didn't make it into a quilt block like the other ones did. Perhaps I should have pitched them, but since they were made by Bertie or belonged to her, I thought you might like them."

"Yes, these are sweet, and I wonder what the story is behind them. Some of the fabrics in the finished blocks are very old. Perhaps Bertie's mother left them to her. These other hexagon pieces are from later, perhaps the 1930s. They were to be sewn into a Grandmother's Flower Garden block like the two here that are finished. All of these were pieced by hand, of course."

"That's interesting. I wonder why she never finished any of these."

I chuckled. "There will always be things left behind, I'm afraid. All antique quilts have been left behind, when you think about it. Sometimes they end up in good hands and sometimes they don't. Quilters refer to leftover blocks as 'orphan blocks' because they didn't end up with a home or a purpose. Sometimes they were a practice block for the quilter."

"Please don't feel like you need to accept them. I just felt I should show them to you first."

"I would love to have these, especially since they were from Bertie. She knew I loved quilts, and she'd tease me all the time when I'd bring another one home."

"It sounds like she didn't miss much," Jenny said, smiling.

"I could hardly ever go up those stairs without her saying something," I said.

"I'll bet she cared a lot for you."

"She really did. When I told her I was moving, she was very hurt and was even angry. Our relationship was never the same after I told her."

"Hello! Is anyone here?" The voice sounded like it could be Judy.

"Hi, Judy," I responded. "I'm back here visiting with a friend."

"How nice!" she said, joining us. "I'm just stopping by on my way to work. I don't want to keep you from your friend."

"Not to worry. What's going on with you?"

"Well, Randal cut my work schedule back a day," she began as she looked at the floor. "I wondered if you need any help or if you have another trip planned."

"I'm so sorry to hear that," I said. "Right now, no trip is planned, and I certainly can't take anyone on my payroll at this time. You know how slow the days get around here."

"I know. I just wanted to put a bug in your ear," she replied.

"Have you tried Gracie's Quilt Shop?" I suggested.

"No, there isn't really anything available in town. I guess I should try a few places in Washington. Oh, I'd better get going or I'll be late."

"Okay. Tell Randal and Marge hello. If I hear of any openings around town, I'll let you know."

Judy nodded and left. While I had been talking with her, Jenny had kept herself busy trying to make sense out of the little quilt pieces. She was trying to create the Grandmother's Flower Garden block.

"Jenny," I said, catching her off guard. "You'd better watch it, or the quilt bug will get you!"

Chapter 64

"I don't think I would make a very good quilter. I was going to ask if you could give me any leads on freelance jobs. I would like to slowly exit from what I'm doing. I can't imagine doing this for the rest of my life."

"I totally understand. I'm afraid I'm pretty removed from the networking world of freelance writers. My friend Alex is very well-connected with other opportunities. He freelances and is also a great writer. I could give you his contact information."

"I would really appreciate that! Is he in the city?"

"Yes, the Central West End." I jotted down Alex's contact information on the back of one of my business cards and handed it to her.

"Wonderful. Thanks so much. It's almost time for lunch, and I'm not familiar with Washington, so I'd better get going."

"Thanks so much for the cannoli and for Bertie's quilt pieces. I'll have fun with these pieces that she left behind."

"You are so welcome! I hope you come back to The Hill

soon so we can do lunch."

"I would love that."

I gave Jenny a big hug. I was so lucky to have met her. I put the cannoli in the refrigerator and took the bag of goodies from Bertie to my counter. I examined the unfinished quilt blocks, which were all neatly hand pieced. Some of the patterns I could identify, like Missouri Star, Broken Dishes, Log Cabin, and the simple Nine-Patch. These orphan blocks had not been put into a quilt for a reason. Maybe the quilter tried the pattern with some scrap fabric, but it was too difficult or didn't fit in with her plan in some way. I supposed you could compare it to a human orphan who was left behind in the same way. One could always hope there would be a situation where they would fit in, be accepted, and be wanted.

As I separated the blocks, it appeared that most were around ten inches square. Would it be possible to put them all in one quilt as a remembrance of Bertie? There might be enough for a full-sized quilt. Maybe I'd show the quilt class and get their feedback. When I looked at the older fabric, I had to think beyond Bertie and where she may have gotten it. I was not a fan of hexies like most people, but I would find a place to use them if I could.

I then got a text from Marc.

. . .Heads up! Need to fly to Memphis for a couple of days. Any Elvis questions I should ask?

. . .No, just Love Me Tender! Haha! Work, I presume?

. . .Two meetings. Let's meet up when I return.
I love you!

. . .Love you, too!

I realized that I had a smile on my face. I really appreciated Marc keeping me informed of his whereabouts.

Surprisingly, Karen and Bonita arrived at the shop. "Ladies! Nice to see you!" I greeted them.

"Lily, I came by to say goodbye," Bonita said.

"I had heard that your stay was coming to an end," I replied.

"I'm really going to miss her," Karen added.

"It was a very productive and pleasant stay," Bonita said with a smile. "Karen has been a wonderful hostess. She has introduced me to so many generous and friendly people."

"Your efforts to help the poor in your country are commendable," I said. "I hope you're able to take back good information and supplies."

"Oh, yes!" she said with excitement.

Chapter 65

"I can't believe all the help I received!" Bonita exclaimed. "Gracie provided me with contacts for free sewing machines and quilting supplies from some of the vendors she buys from. That is huge. I'm also in debt to you for your sharing about your quilts and how the quilt market works. You are truly an inspiration to me."

"I was pleased to do it, Bonita," I said.

"I also wish I could have been more help with the spirits you have inside your house," Bonita joked. "I have a feeling that things will work themselves out, and I will keep you in my prayers."

"Thanks so much," I responded. "God bless you on your mission."

"I'm sending some wine with her, of course," Karen chuckled. "She has to remember the wine country!"

"Indeed!" I agreed. "Thanks for coming in to say goodbye. Keep us posted on your mission."

Bonita nodded. We hugged at the doorstep.

"I sure hope I can continue to be one of your Dinner

Detectives even after Bonita is gone," Karen teased.

"Of course!" I chuckled. "I feel like there might always be a mystery concerning Doc—and who knows what else?"

As I stood at the door and watched them leave, I thought about how quilting had such a wide purpose in the world. I certainly was lucky to have it in my own little world.

As the day went on, I could count on my hand the number of customers I had. I sensed that I should be doing much better in the middle of the tourist season. After locking up the shop, I decided to get a little exercise and check on Kitty's guest house. The temperature was very warm, but a lovely breeze made my walk much more comfortable. As I walked toward the busier part of town, I noticed how the dinner hour was bringing in more cars, even as the tourist customers were leaving. Ashley Rose and Silly Goose were definitely benefitting from the influx of those wanting to have dinner in Augusta. Kate's Coffee was also open. I was tempted to stop, but stayed on my course to get to the guesthouse.

Once there, before I opened the tiny white picket fence's gate, I stood there to admire the cuteness of the place. The front porch and sidewalk were lined with pretty flowers that Johann had offered to water while Kitty was gone. The front porch swing brought back fond memories of the one night I had stayed there. For five seconds, I wanted to think of a way to buy the place from Kitty. It was too small for anyone to want to live there, but it served its purpose of being a good place to stay for one night. Holly was the only person I knew who had pockets deep enough to write a check for the place. The timing for doing such a thing would not be good right now for me. Perhaps when Kitty returned, I would have a conversation with her about the possibilities for the little cottage.

I looked around outside and checked the back door. Everything seemed fine. I knew the locals would keep an eye out for any odd activity as well. I opened the front door, and other than a musty smell, everything seemed fine. Without the air conditioning on, I knew the place could heat up pretty quickly. As I exited, I noticed Johann.

"Is everything okay over there?" he asked.

"It seems to be!"

"Why don't you buy the place?" Johann teased. "It's such a shame to see it sitting empty."

"I agree," I said as I waved goodbye. As I continued to walk home, I wondered if it would be a safe financial investment. I knew through the grapevine that some of the B&Bs were struggling, especially in the winter. I was tempted to have a glass of wine at Augusta Winery, but I decided that a glass of cold iced tea was what I needed.

When I arrived home, I fixed my tea, turned on the alarm, and went upstairs. That alarm had sure done nothing to catch my quilt thief! As much as I didn't want to, I had to start suspecting Doc and Rosie. Maybe Doc wanted revenge, and maybe Rosie was trying to teach me a retail lesson. Would I ever know?

I checked my laptop as I sat down to enjoy my drink. The only email that I had was from Lynn. She wanted to know if I had plans for Marc's birthday. I responded by telling her about Meg's visit and the party she was planning. I told Lynn that I had asked for both of them to be invited. Then I asked if she knew Marc was turning sixty. Lynn was quite surprised, which I found amusing. I closed the laptop and went to bed. Once I was settled in, I still felt bothered by the missing quilt. I decided it was time to have another heart-to-heart talk with Rosie and Doc. I said aloud, "Listen up, you two! If you're playing games with me, please stop. Instead, use your resources to help me find the thief that took the crazy quilt!"

Chapter 66

The next morning, I felt ambitious and attempted to do some cleaning before opening the shop. Alex interrupted my plans with a phone call. "What's up with this early call?" I asked jokingly.

"You're up, aren't you?"

"Absolutely! I even have my dust cap on."

He chuckled. "Hey, first of all, thank you for referring Jenny Jordon my way. We met up last night to do a little networking. She is so interesting—and not bad to look at either!"

"Oh dear! What did I just do?" I asked, laughing.

"Well, we both want to write that book one day, so we mostly talked about that. I can also help her to get some freelance gigs, although they may not pay a lot. I have to admit, she's got a cozy job right now that pays well, but like so many of us, she wants more freedom."

"So how do you think she feels about you?"

"Well, I must have scored big, because she asked me to dinner. We seem to have a lot to talk about, and who doesn't want a free meal?"

"Well, that sounds pretty aggressive, since you just met."

"I didn't take it that way. She's so soft-spoken and sincere."

"If that means she's not loud or full of herself, I agree."

"We both love to cook, so she's making some kind of pasta dish. I'm bringing the wine."

"How romantic! You'd better not fall in love too quickly, my friend," I warned.

"Quit being so jealous. Besides, I'm dying to see your old apartment again."

"Okay. I'll take the blame if she breaks your heart."

Alex laughed.

I continued, "By the way, you're on the invitation list for Marc's sixtieth birthday party. His sister is throwing a little happy hour at the Missouri Athletic Club."

"Man! Just think, Lily! You'll be dating a sixty-year-old guy!"

"Yes, and I'm not far behind, so be quiet."

"So, are you certain about not going to Fish Creek for your joint birthday with Laurie?"

"We both can't afford the luxury. Besides, we're grown women who can't expect that to happen every year like when we were kids."

"Yeah, I guess that's really true. Well, thanks again for sending Jenny my way."

"You're welcome!" When I hung up, I couldn't quite decide how I felt about Alex's new friendship with Jenny. I didn't want him to affect my friendship with her. Jenny didn't seem like the flirtatious type. I just hoped that Alex would behave himself.

I looked at the clock and saw it was already time to open

the shop. I rushed to put out Rosie's rocker, then went to the quilt room and chose a pink-and-green Dresden Plate quilt to place on the back of it. As I arranged it, it reminded me of sherbet.

"That's a very pretty quilt," a woman said as she watched me arrange it. She would be my first customer of the day.

"I think so, too! It's for sale along with many others inside the shop. They all need a good home."

She smiled. "I'm afraid that I have plenty of my own to get rid of. I'm really here to check out your antiques."

"Please come in!"

"Oh, I see you have some handsome costume jewelry in this case. I'm afraid that it's a weakness of mine."

"Yes, I have quite a bit that I purchased from a previous shop owner. She had great taste."

"I love this turquoise-and-purple necklace and that matching bracelet. They're quite striking. May I see them?"

"They are quite unique," I said, handing them to her.

"Some things are so gaudy that they become beautiful. Do you agree?"

I laughed and nodded.

Chapter 67

The customer was delightful and had a ball trying on various pieces of jewelry and admiring them in my small mirror. At the end of her visit, she had spent seventy dollars. It had been fun to revisit Rosie's jewelry collection. It was rare that anyone even took time the time to glance at it.

While the customer was still there, several others wandered into the quilt room. No one asked to see any of the quilts in the cabinet. I thought about my missing quilt again and wondered if I had been distracted by another customer while someone stole it. No, that wouldn't have been possible, since the key was kept at the cash register.

I looked up to see Gracie. "Well, hello!" I said, surprised to see her. "Who's running your shop today?"

"Mom is there this afternoon, so I took some time off to run a few errands," she explained. "How's your day going?"

"Good," I responded. "What's on your mind?"

"You! You're the point of my visit," she said with a wide grin. "I wondered if you would teach a redwork class at my shop. Just something simple for beginners, of course."

"Oh, Gracie, I'm a beginner myself," I explained. "I don't think I'm good enough."

"Yes, you are!" Gracie stated. "I even ran this idea past Susan, and she thought there would be interest in such a class. I would supply everything, and I think it should be a night class so it will attract those who work during the day."

"You're serious, aren't you?" I asked in disbelief.

"I am!" She nodded. "I can pay you per student or by the hour."

"I don't need to be paid," I protested.

"Of course you do! So, when can I start advertising it?"

"I guess I could try one class and see how it goes. Make sure it's for beginners."

"Deal!"

"How are things with you and Anthony?" I asked bravely.

"Pretty good, actually, except for one thing," she said.

"What's that?"

"He likes talking about you too much."

"What? That's crazy!"

"I couldn't agree more! He compares everything I say and do to you."

"I sure don't know why. Just ignore him."

"Anthony is pretty hard to ignore, if you know what I mean. Like you said, he's quite the charmer. He's entertaining and warm. Since I'm not looking for a husband, I don't mind him hanging around."

We burst into laughter.

"I understand completely."

"I need to go, but thanks again for agreeing to teach the class."

"I hope I won't disappoint you!" I said as she left.

What had I just gotten myself into? I'd never taught anything in my entire life! I would first have to think of a very simple design, and then the stitches it would require. I knew Gracie sold an embroidery pamphlet with instructions for basic stitches, so students could purchase that, and Gracie would have some income from the class. I supposed that teaching a class could be fun—or not!

When the shop was empty, I got out my embroidery block for my wine country quilt. I needed to think about my third block before the next quilting class. Since the cottage had been on my mind lately, perhaps I could do a simple sketch of the front porch, which I loved. It had certainly been a significant place for me in wine country. The straight lines of the picket fence would be easy.

"Howdy, Lily Girl!" a boisterous voice said. It was Chuck, the traveling quilt buyer. "I just thought I'd stop by since I picked up some quilts at an estate sale in Marthasville. They aren't worth a hoot, so I thought maybe I could pick up one of those highfalutin quilts that you're selling these days."

"Oh, Chuck, you know those aren't the kind of quilts you'll pay for, and I can only give you ten percent off on them."

"Now, little lady, I have contacts who may take it off my hands, so don't judge me," he replied. "I was here when you sold a white wholecloth to a lady for a pretty penny. You were on cloud nine! Wouldn't you like to sell another one?" He began walking towards the quilt room. "Go get your key."

I looked at him oddly, wondering if he was serious. I took a deep breath and got the key from the drawer.

Chapter 68

When I got to the quilt room, Chuck was already messing with the displayed quilts.

"How about you get that red-and-blue one out of the cabinet?"

"The one on the bottom?"

He nodded.

I gave in with a sigh and unlocked the door. I carefully took the quilts out one by one and placed them on a table nearby. When I got to the red-and-blue hexagon-patterned quilt, Chuck abruptly grabbed it from me.

"Be very careful with this, Chuck," I warned. "It's pretty fragile."

"This isn't my first rodeo," he responded. "This one is too old for me to get rid of. You can put it back. What about that one with the little stars?"

"It has a medallion star in the center with smaller ones around it," I described as I tried to be gentle with it. "It's circa 1900."

"Now that's a beauty. I could move that one." He nodded

like he already owned it. He then looked at the price tag. "It's not twelve thousand dollars, is it? Did you mean to put twelve hundred dollars?"

"No, Chuck. I told you that these are out of your range. I didn't price these, by the way, so I have no power to change the amount on the tag."

"Okay, I'll bet you'll settle for half of that amount. Six thousand dollars is nothing to sneeze at."

"No way. Let me fold this back up. I warned you about this." I took the quilt out of his hands, and his face took on a hard expression.

"Okay. Have it your way. When you still have these sitting here a year from now, you'll change your mind."

"I'm doing just fine with them," I retorted.

My landline was ringing, but I was not about to leave Chuck alone in the quilt room without locking the cabinet.

"Your phone is ringing," he said.

"Let it ring," I said, continuing to put the quilts back into the case.

"Suit yourself! Just so you know, these quilts are a ripoff. You should be ashamed of yourself! Whoever you got these from is making a fool out of you."

"Chuck, just leave. Don't come back again if you just want to insult me," I said firmly. "I should never have done business with you."

"Likewise!" he said as he tipped his ball cap in mock politeness.

He stormed out of the room and slammed the door as he left the shop. I took another deep breath and finished putting everything back into the cabinet. I shouldn't have let things go that far. Chuck had been hoping I'd have a weak moment and take his filthy money. When I locked the cabinet, I had a scary thought about him. What if he tried to get revenge on me and came back to steal a quilt? What if he was the one who had the crazy quilt? No, that would be impossible. I decided to call Carrie Mae and warn her about him. She finally answered after a few rings.

"No, he didn't stop here," she reported. "He knows I carry very little in quilts since you opened the store."

"He was so, so angry today. I wonder if I should report him."

Carrie Mae chuckled. "And say what? It's not a crime to be unhappy about a business encounter. Did he threaten you?"

"No, but his tone of voice did."

"He'll just cross you off his list and won't return. I wouldn't worry about him. He's a rough kind of individual."

"I think I insulted him when I indicated that these quilts were too expensive for him. I should have refused to show him anything in the cabinet."

"A domestic issue like the Hatfields and McCoys, that's what you've got here. Cops don't want to hear about those types of things. If you report him, you may make him even angrier."

"I even wondered if he'd had anything to do with my missing crazy quilt."

"Unless you have good reason to think so, you'd better forget it."

"He knew about my nine-thousand-dollar sale to the woman who bought the wholecloth from me. What if I was so excited about the sale that I forgot to lock the cabinet after it sold?"

"I doubt that you would forget that. Quit second-guessing yourself. It will all come out one day. I still think it's the spirits' nonsense that's going on in your house. I have a couple of folks here at the counter, so I need to go," Carrie Mae said. "I think they have something lovely in their hands that they intend to purchase." She chuckled.

"Sounds good. Sorry I kept you. Thanks for listening. Happy sales!"

"Bye, sweetie," she said as we hung up.

Chapter 69

"Oh, look, honey, she's here!" a woman said to the man accompanying her.

"Welcome," I said. "If you need some help, just let me know."

"Lily?" the woman asked with a big smile.

I nodded.

"I'm Karen O'Hare," she said. "I freelance for a few neighborhood papers and I'm doing an article on writers. We were on our way to a wedding at Chandler Hill Winery, and I told Harvey, my husband, that we should stop by to see you. Do you have a few minutes?"

"Honey, you should have given her some notice," her husband interjected. "She has a business to run here."

"I don't see any customers," Karen noted as she looked around.

"I'm not sure I can be helpful, but I suppose I could answer a couple of questions," I said with hesitation.

"Can we sit down somewhere?" she asked.

"Sure, come out here to the back porch," I suggested.

"Oh, it's lovely out here," Mrs. O'Hare said as she looked out over the backyard. "May I take a few photos?"

"I suppose," I agreed. "Look, I have all my information on my website with *Spirit* magazine, as well as photos."

"I know." She nodded. "I looked at those things on our way out here."

My cell phone rang, but I let it go to voicemail.

"Honey, get on with this, please," Harvey insisted.

"Okay, okay," Mrs. O'Hare said, positioning herself on the couch. "I've asked everyone some of the same questions," she explained. "Why do you write?"

I paused. "I need to write," I shared. "I always have. That's just the best way to describe it. When I was a child, if I had a pen and some paper, I was happy."

"Oh, that's precious," she said, busying herself by taking notes. "Why haven't you written a book, or do you have one started?" she asked, reading the question from her paper.

I smiled. "I keep very busy making a living, so a long-term project like a book may never happen," I explained.

"So it isn't on your bucket list, as they say today?" she asked with a chuckle.

"Not right now," I answered.

"Honey, may I remind you that you said just a couple of questions," her husband warned.

"Okay, just one more question," she stated, "Who is your favorite author?"

"Jane Austen always comes to mind," I replied. "She's not always easy to read, but I like her stories. Her persistence to write at a difficult time when women weren't recognized as writers was huge. She wrote under a different name at first. Her style and observations were quite unique and have become more and more appreciated over time. That's a real legacy!"

"So well said, Ms. Rosenthal," she replied. "I must look into her history. Thanks so much for your time today."

Surprisingly, Mr. O'Hare said, "Now, if I may ask Lily a question, it would be, 'How come the bright yellow house?'"

I smiled. "The previous owner had it in this color," I explained. "Some even call it the John Deere house because of the dark green shutters. My friend owned it and had it available for storage until I decided to open a shop here. People can certainly find the place. It's really grown on me."

"Interesting!" the man said as he stroked his beard.

"I think I heard someone come in," I said to move them along.

"Well, we'll be on our way, then," Mrs. O'Hare said, moving towards the door. "I'll email you when I finish this."

"I would like that," I said, seeing them out. I then turned to the man who had just entered the shop. He was looking at my assortment of walking canes.

"This inlaid pearl handle is quite unique," he pointed out as he walked a few steps with one of them.

"Yes. If I recall, the tag said it was made in 1920. I bought it with a collection. The really nice ones that were more ornate already sold. Canes are a fun thing to collect."

"Well, I'm pretty picky about the ones I buy, but I haven't seen one like this before, and the price is certainly reasonable."

"I can make that happen!" I said as I started to wrap his purchase.

"I should have looked at your quilts," he said as a second thought. "My wife loves antique quilts."

"Well, why don't you take a look in the next room?" I encouraged him.

Chapter 70

"I can probably give you a good deal on certain ones," I teased.

"Sure, that never hurts. She loves blue and white," said the man.

"So does my friend. I happen to love red and white. I think I have a couple of patterns here that are blue and white. Here's a Drunkard's Path quilt, for example. It's in really good condition."

"She actually has one like that. I can remember because I teased her about the name."

"Okay, here's an Ocean's Wave pattern," I said, holding it up. "It's more worn but is still very graphic, which is important. I can give you twenty percent off that one."

"I like it!" he said right away. "I don't remember seeing one like that. If the back is nice and clean, I'll take it. I know it's one of the first things my wife checks on a quilt."

We turned it over, and there was only a very slight fold line that was hard to notice. Of course, the customer saw it right away. "That's where your twenty percent discount comes in," I laughed. "It's really pretty nice for the price."

"Okay, you sold me," he agreed. "My wife will love that I was thinking of her."

"Absolutely! Blue-and-white quilts are getting harder to find these days."

After the man left feeling happy, I was happy to have made two sales. My landline was ringing. It was Jenny.

"Oh, Lily! Thanks so much for sending Alex my way," Jenny said with excitement. "He is so knowledgeable and so much fun. We've gotten together twice already! He's given me some very good leads."

"Happy to hear it! It's nice to share the same interests with someone." I said, suddenly feeling a bit hesitant about having connected the two of them.

"Maybe the three of us can get together sometime. He thinks the world of you. It seems like you two have been friends for a very long time."

"Yes, we have. I also admire his work."

"Since I've met him, I've taken the time to look up some of his work. His topics are really diverse."

"Yes, they are, and he likes the travel that goes with the job as well."

"I just had to call and tell you. We're going to meet up at Rigazzi's tomorrow night after work."

"Well, give him my best."

"I will!"

When I hung up, I felt like I had just given my best friend away. Going to Rigazzi's for pizza and beer was something Alex and I always did together. I had to admit that the two of them could be a perfect couple. Jenny spoke his language and was as cute as a button. I was never worried about Mindy, but this Jenny was a different animal! I sighed. The day was about to end when a UPS driver pulled up in front and came to the door.

"Ms. Rosenthal?" he asked as he handed me a large box.

"Yes, that's me. Thanks." As soon as I accepted the package, the driver was quickly on his way back to his truck. I looked to see who the package was from and was surprised to see that it was from Ellen.

I brought Rosie's rocker inside and locked the door, then began to work at getting the package open. When the cardboard broke loose, I saw a note attached. The contents of the package appeared to be a quilt wrapped in tissue. The note read, "Lily, I found this quilt among Mom's things. It's obviously quite old, so I have no clue who made it. I can see why she would like it, with all the fancy stitches and trims, but I have no clue as to where she got it, so I thought you would like it. P.S. Do you know anything about old dress gloves? Mom loved to collect them, and I have shoeboxes full. Still in Florida. Love, Ellen."

In seconds, I knew that the quilt was a crazy quilt. I gently took it out of the tissue and placed it on the counter. It was in very good condition compared to most crazy quilts. Perhaps there would be initials, dates, or names on the quilt to identify it.

The embroidery was exquisite. Susan and the quilt class participants would love to see something like this! There were Kate Greenaway-like illustrations, spiders for good luck, and hand-painted designs that were as beautiful as the elaborate feather stitching around each piece. So far, I hadn't found any personal information about the quilt. Why Ellen hadn't seen this quilt before was the real mystery.

Chapter 71

I folded the quilt back up and decided to go upstairs. If this quilt was a gift, then I certainly did not want to sell it. For all I knew, it may have been made by someone in my own family! As I went upstairs, I felt sad at the thought of someone doing all that work and not getting any recognition for it. No assumptions could be made under these circumstances. When people buy quilts, most of the time the quilts have no provenance. Just because a quilter leaves a quilt behind doesn't mean that she or her family made it. Many folks assume there is a strong connection.

This quilt that Aunt Mary left behind could be researched or could just be accepted without question. I supposed that could apply to people and their opinions as well. Should I just accept the quilt or do justice to the maker and research its history? This thought process was making me think of my next magazine article that was due next week. I could call it "To Question or to Accept?"

I personally gave my quilts and antiques unconditional love. If the spots and wear were insignificant, it did not affect my willingness to accept them. The same applied to my social life and customers. I didn't want to second-guess or question who they were. It came down to trust, I supposed. If someone or something made me suspicious, then I asked questions. If there were signs they were misrepresenting something or misleading someone, I asked questions then as well. Was it our nature to be one or the other—trusting or cautious? How could we strike a healthy balance in our business and personal lives?

I placed the crazy quilt on the sofa upstairs. While it was on my mind, I opened my laptop and started writing the article. A quick fifteen minutes later, I sent it to *Spirit*. It was shorter than most, but it was to the point.

I went over and looked at the quilt. Should I share the news of this newly acquired quilt with my siblings? I wasn't the only one who liked quilts. Loretta would have been thrilled to have received it, and Lynn could certainly appreciate the fancywork on it. In the end, I decided to call Ellen to tell her I had received the quilt.

"What a delightful surprise!" I announced when she answered.

"Do you like it? If you don't, just sell it."

"Oh, Ellen, I wouldn't do that. Yes, it's lovely! Are you sure you don't know where it came from?"

"Nope, not a clue. It was tucked away in Mom's closet along with some other blankets. She had never mentioned it to me. I have no use for it, so I thought of my sisters who love quilts."

"Well, I feel a little guilty receiving this. Loretta and Lynn like quilts as well."

"I owe you so much, Lily. Your initial acceptance of me as

part of the family made it easier for the others. You decide, but I thought it had your name on it."

"Okay, I guess. I may offer it to them if it's okay with you. If they decline, I'll keep it."

"That's fine. I'll also ask my mother's neighbor if she'd seen it before."

"When are you going back to Paducah?"

"In a couple of days. I've also decided that I'm going to offer to volunteer at the quilt museum. I have a friend who is also going to, so it might be fun."

"That's good to hear. Let me know how you like it. Have a safe trip home."

"Thanks, Lily. I love you!"

"I love you too, Ellen."

Even though the hour was late, I decided to go ahead and email my siblings about the quilt that Aunt Mary had left behind.

Loretta and Lynn had emailed earlier that they had received an invitation to Marc's party. Lynn and Carl had accepted, of course, but Loretta seemed especially pleased to be included.

Knowing I would not get a response back from them this late at night, I closed the computer feeling sleepy and ready to get some rest.

Chapter 72

Why wasn't I very excited about receiving the quilt? Was it because my feelings about Aunt Mary had changed? Was it because it had a busy design and I preferred two-colored quilts? Crazy quilts were complicated. They were made to thrill the eye, not warm the body. Holly once told me they'd referred to them as "parlor quilts" in the Victorian era. She liked them very much and even lectured about them. They were "crazy" because the pieces were not organized. They were randomly pieced on the background fabric in any way, shape, and fashion. I did admire the beautiful skill applied to the embellishments and appreciated the intricate embroidery. The hand painting was also to be admired. Not everyone referred to crazy quilts as quilts since most were not really quilted. They were usually tied, and typically, there wasn't a filling between the layers because the layers were already very heavy. Therefore, many crazy quilt tops were never quilted. Many gave up on making them, thinking they would add more to them as time went along. The tops alone did have a place in the market, but a collector would want the entire quilt completed. It was hard to find a crazy quilt in good condition. They contained delicate fabrics like silk, and silk just did not hold up. Velvet and wool fabrics held up much better.

Butler's crazy quilt was close to perfect despite its age. Its condition, design, and rarity gave it its hefty price. Investing in crazy quilts could be risky because of how they deteriorate. Butler's quilt had extreme detailing. One could easily personalize a crazy quilt. As a shop owner, I saw many folks who thought their crazy quilt was unique. They soon found out otherwise. They are more common in households than people think. The arrival of Aunt Mary's crazy quilt caused me to think about Butler's quilt. I would probably dream about crazy quilts that night!

The next morning, I was pleased to have gotten a good night's sleep. The next day was Marc's birthday party, so I needed to plan accordingly. Marc was getting back from his trip that day and then was picking Meg up at the airport. I still wasn't sure what I planned to give him. I was sure Meg would be closely watching my choice of gift for him, but I also knew that Marc wouldn't mind if I showed up without a gift. I decided to call Lynn to see if she had any advice or suggestions for me.

"Oh, you just caught me going out the door for my Rotary meeting," Lynn said, sounding breathless.

"I didn't know you were a Rotarian. So is Marc!"

"Someone talked me into it, but it's a pretty good marketing tool. Two weeks ago, I hosted a business-after-hours gathering here at the studio and sold a pretty pricey painting."

"That's great. Do you have just a second?"

"Sure. What's going on?"

"I have no gift for Marc, and his party is tomorrow," I shared.

"And what am I supposed to do about that?"

"Suggest something!"

She giggled. "Carl finally suggested a special scotch that Marc likes, so that's what we got him."

"He'll love that. I've never been to this club, have you?"

"Yes, it's pretty upscale. Why don't you come to our house and go with us?"

"I would like that. Now think of a gift for him!"

"I'll try. Be here around five, okay?"

"Okay, but I may show up empty-handed."

"You could always buy a sexy little piece of nightwear that he may enjoy," Lynn teased, giggling.

"Now, Lynn, you know I'm not that kind of girl," I retorted.

"Yeah, right, Lily Girl. You are all heart!"

"Goodbye, sister."

When I hung up, I started looking over my own shop merchandise. It had rescued me more than once. Marc's place was contemporary. I'd lucked out by giving him an unusual wine rack from Gallery Augusta at Christmas. I knew a quilt was not the answer. Now, if I had a Cardinals quilt, he would love it! Perhaps I could do that for him one day.

When I came back to the main room of the shop, I stared at something I had practically hidden in a dark corner. Rosie'd had a very old globe on an antique stand and had marked the year 1875 on the price tag. The price she'd had on it was twelve hundred dollars. I had been baffled by it because I knew nothing about globes, but trusted that Rosie knew what she had. I walked over to it and gave it a twirl.

Chapter 73

It was obvious from the layers of dust that I had ignored this piece of merchandise. I did have to admit that for its age, it was in very good condition. I pulled it out of the corner and wondered how Marc would react to such a piece, trying to picture it in his den. I got a dust cloth and some lemon oil from under the counter and began wiping it down. The wood brightened up enormously. Because of the globe's price, I was uncomfortable trying to sell it. A knock at the door interrupted my activity.

"Snowshoes, good morning! Time has gotten away from me today!"

"I have a small package for you and didn't want to leave it on your porch. What have you got there?"

"Oh, it's an old globe I've had for sale since I moved here. I thought it was time that I cleaned it up a bit."

Snowshoes walked over to take a closer look. "Boy, they don't make them like that anymore. I guess now, you can get on your phone and pull up a map of anywhere in the world."

"You're right. No one has ever asked to see it. It has a date of 1875 on the tag."

"You don't say! Well, it will take the right person to take it off your hands, I suppose. You have a good day now. Maybe you'll have some luck with it today."

I chuckled as Snowshoes left the shop. I stood back to admire the cleaned-up globe. As uninformed as I was, I could tell that the countries on the map had looked a lot different back then. I still wasn't sure it was right for Marc. I moved some things around, putting the globe front and center in the shop for a change, and placed an antique chair in the corner where the globe had been.

Betty entered the shop, and the globe immediately captured her attention. She stood there admiring it for a bit before she said, "Lily, I didn't see your rocker outside. Are you open?"

"I am. I just haven't had a chance to set it out. I've been cleaning up this globe."

"It's a dandy. I think the only place I've seen something like that is in libraries. Did you just get it?"

"No, I moved here with it, but I had it tucked back in the corner. It has a hefty price, so I kind of kept it back."

"It's right nice here where you have it. I think it will sell."

"Well, now that I've given it some love, I'm thinking about giving it as a gift."

"Giving it away?" she questioned. "I can see it in some really nice office or library."

"Marc is celebrating his sixtieth birthday, and I keep wondering if he would like it."

"It's a manly kind of gift. Would he have room for it?"

"Yes. I can actually picture it in his office."

"It sounds perfect, then." Betty paused. "Are you sure he's

worth it?" She winked.

"He really is, and I've run out of ideas for anything else to give him."

"Price?" she asked, picking up the ticket. "Oh my! Well, Rosie knew something we don't know, I guess." She continued, "The reason I'm here is to pass on a few garden veggies. I don't eat like I used to, and I need to give stuff away."

"Thanks so much! I always appreciate what you bring."

"So, when are the Dinner Detectives going to meet again, Lily? I can bring my beef stroganoff."

"Oh, that sounds so good. Let me get through this week, and we'll set something up."

"Karen wants to make sure we will still include her."

"Why, sure, but I think we'll all miss Bonita. I'm so glad she was able to get some help from various people for her mission."

"I know. I hope we helped her. Well, I'm off. Wish Marc a happy birthday for me. I think he'll love the globe!"

As she left, a nicely dressed couple walked in. "Welcome!" I greeted them as I put my dust cloth away.

"You look like you have a nice project there," the man said, peering at the globe.

"Yes, it needed a bit of cleaning," I explained.

"It's beautiful!" the woman chimed in.

Chapter 74

"I sure haven't seen one like this before," the man commented. He reached over and gave the globe a spin. "How much is this?"

"Twelve hundred dollars, sir," I stated.

"Not a bad price!" he said as he stood back to admire it.

"Are you two looking for anything special?" I asked.

"Yes, I would like to see your quilts," the woman answered.

"When my wife saw quilts on your sign, she got so excited," her husband explained.

"Come in the quilt room and look around," I offered. "If I can answer any questions, just let me know."

"Thanks, I will," the woman said. Once in the quilt room, she immediately started touching some of them. The man stayed in the front room, so after a few minutes, I went to check on him. He was stooped down and was giving the globe a closer look. Should I tell him that it was officially sold? Was I sure? I told him to holler if he had any questions. With that, I went back to the quilt room. The woman was holding up a scrappy Jacob's Ladder pattern on a white background.

"I've always liked this pattern for some reason," she said. "Maybe it's the name."

"It's in excellent condition," I replied. "I don't think it's ever been washed."

"The price is so reasonable," she said as she looked at the tag. "My, these quilts in the cabinet look very old."

"Yes, they are," I confirmed without offering any further information.

"That's not my taste," she stated. "I want to really use my quilts, and I don't want to be afraid to wash them."

"I totally understand," I replied. "Quilts mean different things to different people. It's nice to hear that you enjoy using them."

"My children grew up with quilts on their beds and always preferred them over blankets," she said.

"I always had quilts on my bed, too," I replied. "When I was a young child, I loved running my hands across the stitches."

"I'll take this one if you can ship it," she decided. "We're in a rental car and are flying home."

"I'd be happy to," I said, taking the quilt from her. We walked into the front room, and I observed the man still examining the globe. He had his finger on his chin as if he were assessing something.

"Honey, I think I'm going to buy this quilt and have it shipped home," the woman said.

"Great idea!" he agreed. "I'd buy this globe if it wouldn't cost a fortune to send."

I nearly fainted. "Frankly, I'm glad to hear that, because

I should have told you that it is likely sold," I said with a smile.

"Well, I hope that works out for you," he laughed. "I saw underneath here that it's marked with the name of the company that made it. It's also printed on laid paper, which gives it a ribbed texture. This wooden stand alone is worth a pretty penny, and the globe still shows the Russian territory where Alaska is found today. I know a little bit about maps. The condition is everything. I hope the buyer has an appreciation for it, and most likely he does."

After I got the mailing instructions for where to send the quilt, I thanked the couple for the sale and for the information on the globe. I now realized that this globe was special. I felt that Marc would most likely appreciate it. A big bow and a sweet card would do nicely. If I kept this on the floor for sale, it would most likely sit there for a long time. I put the globe aside and answered a call from Holly coming in on my cell phone.

"Hey, girlfriend! I just wanted to tell you that I'm sending you another payment on my quilt. I need a little more time on the balance, but I'm anxious to bring it home with me."

"There's no hurry, Holly. I told you that. How are things going with Clete?"

She snickered. "It's fine. I haven't seen him lately, but that's okay. I've been really busy. Frankly, Lily, he isn't my type."

I laughed. "Really? Aren't you getting independent?" I joked.

"Like you said, I'm finally free, so let's see what the world has to offer."

"Congrats! You finally get it!"

"Hey, Marc's party is coming up. Be sure to tell him happy birthday for me."

"I will. Thank you, and thanks for another check. You know the shop can always use it."

We hung up promising to get together soon, as we always did. I was so pleased that Holly seemed to be moving on and didn't feel like she needed a man by her side at this point in her life.

Chapter 75

The next day, I found it hard to concentrate knowing that Marc's party was taking place so soon. Carrie Mae called at eleven. I had not opened the shop yet.

"Are you with a customer?" she asked.

"No, I haven't opened. I've been so busy doing other things."

"Has anyone from the sheriff's department been around to talk to you?"

"No, why?"

"They wanted to know how well I knew Chuck Waller."

"Did they say why?"

"Not exactly. They asked if I ever did any business with him and if I'd had any problems with him. I told them I hadn't, but I thought of you."

"Did you tell them about me?"

"No, I didn't. I don't know how they got my name. I wasn't sure you'd want to get involved. They may not know anything about you since yours is a newer shop."

"He's in trouble, I suspect. That doesn't surprise me, as

arrogant as he is."

"If it's pretty serious, I'm sure we'll hear about it."

"He won't be back to see me, I can guarantee you that. Thanks for alerting me. I'm ready to go into the city for Marc's birthday party tonight."

"Wish him a happy birthday for me. Be careful driving, especially if you come back tonight."

"I'll be staying at Lynn's, unless I get a better offer," I said with a chuckle. "Guess what I decided to give Marc?"

"I couldn't say."

"I'm giving him the old globe and stand that I had in the corner. I cleaned it up, and it looks really nice."

"My goodness! That had a hefty price on it, as I recall."

"Yes, and I've never had anyone even look at it until I wiped it off yesterday. I think it's worth even more than Rosie was asking. I'll tell Marc to sell it if he doesn't want it."

"Can you handle getting it in the car by yourself?"

"I think so. I'd better get moving."

"Have fun, sweetie!"

"I will."

With that reminder, I began the task of getting the globe into my car. It was awkward, but I eventually succeeded. As I began getting dressed, I was once again disappointed in my clothing selection. I got out every piece of jewelry Marc had given me and held it up to some my black pieces of clothing. I decided on a simple black dress and worked to put my hair up. My hair was getting quite long, and I hoped to look more sophisticated by wearing it up for a change. When I added dangling earrings, I was pleased.

Off I went. I was anxious to see Meg and her sweet brother Marc. I had been really beginning to miss him. The weather cooperated, and in no time, I arrived at Lynn's house. I loved being back on The Hill. I supposed it would always be my real home.

Lynn and Carl were ready to go when I arrived. They insisted that I leave my car with the giant birthday present inside in their driveway. I agreed since it would give me a chance to visit with them privately before joining the birthday crowd.

"What is his sister like?" Carl asked. "Do you like her?"

"Yes, she's great," I replied. "Marc thinks she walks on water." I drew in a deep breath. "I hope Marc is surprised."

"The club is fabulous!" Lynn bragged. "I love your hair up like that."

"By the way, Lynn, you look pretty good yourself," I replied. "We rarely see each other all dressed up."

"She's a looker, alright," Carl said with a wink.

We parked the car in the club's garage and took the elevator to the party floor. Meg was there greeting everyone. She had on a gorgeous yellow sundress and looked like she'd come off the cover of a high fashion magazine. Her bouncing hairstyle and pleasant smile made her very approachable.

"Lily, it's good to see you!" she said, giving me a slight hug. "Marc should be here in about twenty minutes."

I introduced Meg to Carl and Lynn before we walked toward the open bar. I had been hoping to recognize more people, but there were lots of unfamiliar faces instead. As Carl played host to Lynn and me, I saw Alex walk in with Jenny on his arm. They looked attractive in their party attire. Jenny looked so different than when I'd seen her in jeans. Her perfect figure was accentuated by her choice of a simple, elegant white dress. Alex glanced our way. I knew he would be joining us soon.

"Hey, what's up?" Lynn asked me as Alex made his way towards us. "A new girlfriend?"

I could feel myself flinch a bit at Lynn's question. It wasn't like her, particularly, so I felt the need to rescue the situation before Alex and Jenny came within earshot. "Alex's date is Jenny. She lives in my old apartment," I explained as they greeted us. "Remember when I told you about her? She's also an editor, which is so ironic."

"Nice to meet you, Jenny," Lynn said.

"I'm happy to be here," Jenny responded.

Chapter 76

We chatted with Alex and Jenny for a brief time, but all the while, Alex kept sneaking looks at my hair. After a few minutes, he looked at me and winked, as if to signal his approval.

"You guys sure know the right people," Jenny was saying. "This place is lovely. I can't wait to meet Marc."

I was about to respond when the lights dimmed. Meg announced that Marc was on his way up in the elevator. My stomach churned. I hoped that all would go well.

"Surprise!" everyone yelled as Marc entered the room. Judging from the look on his face, he truly was surprised. Meg immediately gave him a hug, and the two engaged in conversation.

"You should have been there with Meg," Lynn commented.

"No, she's the hostess of the party, and they haven't seen each other for a while," I explained. "He'll find me eventually." By the time I finished speaking, the chatter had gotten louder, and it seemed that the party was off to a good start. In the back of my mind, I hoped that Marc would know that I was there. He seemed to personally greet everyone before he noticed me. I was in a group of about four people and I stayed there, hoping he would make a point to quickly approach me. When he got to our group, he spoke to everyone else before even looking at me. Finally, I got to say the same words as everyone else. "Happy birthday," I said with a big smile.

"Thank you!" he said, giving me a peck on the cheek. It would turn out that I was one of many such pecks as I followed him for the next few minutes. "I'm glad you could make it in," he said.

I felt like I lived in that faraway state again. I fought back those feelings, knowing they would not help me enjoy the evening. "Meg did an amazing job organizing this gathering," I said.

"Didn't she? I don't think I've ever had a surprise party before!"

"Neither have I," I replied. "Enjoy!" I wasn't sure he'd heard me due to the noise, but as more people approached him, I lost him. Hugs, kisses, and greetings were coming from every direction, and Meg wasn't far behind him. As I watched Meg lead Marc away to more well-wishers, Lynn and I made our way to the food table.

"Does Carl know most of these people through the law firm?" I asked Lynn.

"It seems so." She nodded. "Many of them look familiar to me as well. Meg is charming. She's certainly playing the hostess with the mostest. She and Marc must be close."

I nodded in agreement. My nervous stomach was not in the mood to enjoy much food, although it seemed as if Meg had ordered every delicacy under the sun. An artistic form of a six and a zero was sculpted in ice in the center of the food table.

"Is that all you're going to put on your plate?" Lynn asked, frowning at me. "Two pieces of shrimp won't do it for me. This is dinner!"

I chuckled. "I'm just not hungry right now," I said quietly.

"Honey, I want you to meet some folks over here," Carl said as he took Lynn's arm and led her away from me.

I left the buffet table wondering where to go next.

"Wanna get away?" Alex said from behind me.

I jumped.

"Where's Jenny?" I asked.

"In the ladies' room," he responded. "Are you okay?"

"I don't belong here, Alex," I said, trying not to make eye contact with him.

"What are you talking about?" he asked as he nudged my elbow.

"I feel uncomfortable, and I really don't think Marc even knows I'm here," I said, taking a sip of wine.

"Stop it," Alex said firmly. "He has a lot of distractions, and his sister's presence here makes him a bit obligated to her."

"Oh, I understand," I lied. "However, I still would like to get away."

Alex looked at me with concern.

"Excuse me, Alex. I'm going to the ladies' room."

I made my way through the crowd and finally found a fancy sign on a door that I presumed meant it was the women's restroom. There was only one other woman in there, so Jenny must have left. I freshened my lipstick, washed my hands, and spoke to myself in the mirror, consoling myself that the evening would soon be over. I would spend the night with Lynn and Carl, and everything would be fine. I readied myself to join the crowd once again. Suddenly, Meg entered.

"Oh, Lily, I hope you're having a good time," she said pleasantly. "I'm so pleased that Marc was surprised and that so many people showed up."

"It's wonderful, Meg," I replied. "You did a marvelous job putting the party together. The food is delicious."

"They'll be bringing in a large birthday cake in a few minutes," she said excitedly. "That's when we'll sing to him."

"Oh, how nice," I said, taking a deep breath as I readied myself to rejoin the party.

Chapter 77

I entered the main room and looked frantically for Lynn. Several people greeted me with a quick nod or a hello, making me feel as if I should know them, but I was certain I had never met them.

"Lily!"

I heard Alex's voice, which was a relief. I looked at him like I was lost. I felt lost. "Oh, the cake is here," I said as the lights dimmed.

A waiter rolled a large cake with what had to be sixty lit candles into the center of the room. Meg quickly ushered Marc over to it so he could check it out. Suddenly the crowd broke into boisterous singing. I moved my lips but wasn't sure anything was coming out. I looked at Marc, feeling a rush of love and admiration as his beautiful smile showed his delight at the whole effort. Meg hung onto his arm as they finished singing.

"Thank you, thank you," Marc started. "I really appreciate everyone coming to my party, and I want to thank my sister, Meg, for all of her hard work." With that, he gave her a hug and a kiss.

Marc didn't even catch my eye. It was a memorable moment in his life, and he didn't try for the two of us to share it together. I blinked back tears as I looked to find Lynn or a glass of wine, whichever came first.

"Here," Alex said as he handed me a glass of champagne. "I think this is what you might be looking for."

"Yes, thank you," I responded without looking at him.

Jenny approached the two of us.

"I think your guy is having a pretty good time," Jenny commented.

"Yes, it does look like he is," I agreed. "He has a lot of friends. Have you seen Lynn?"

"She's getting a piece of that gorgeous cake," Jenny said, pointing in the direction of the crowd who had now surrounded the dessert.

I spotted Lynn and interrupted her as she was about to take her first bite.

"Don't you want some cake?" Lynn asked, dishing a forkful of cake into her mouth.

"Can I stay at your place tonight?" I asked.

Lynn looked puzzled. "Why, sure, but..." she stopped as Marc approached us.

"How's that cake, Lynn?" he asked, smiling broadly.

"It's delicious!" she responded. "I was just trying to convince Lily to have some."

"Can I get you a piece?" Marc asked kindly.

"No, thanks. I'm stuffed," I answered. "It's beautiful."

"What a great surprise this has been," Marc exclaimed. He was beaming with excitement.

"I'm glad you're having a great time," I said.

"I can't believe Meg went to all this trouble," he said as he watched the crowd. "Lynn, did you get to meet Meg?"

"Yes." Lynn nodded. "She knows how to throw a party! This has been a lovely evening."

Carl joined us and asked Marc about one his law partners. Soon, the two of them were off to discuss something, so my time with my sweetie was up. I then gave Lynn a look to get her attention. She followed me to the buffet table.

"Lynn, I want to leave as soon as possible," I whispered. "Do you think we'll be going soon?"

"What's wrong?" Lynn asked.

"I don't feel well, but please don't tell Carl," I pleaded. "Just tell him you're ready to leave."

"I'll see what I can do," she agreed. "Go and talk to Alex in the meantime."

I looked for Alex and Jenny, but it appeared that they had already left. It wasn't hard for me to see that the two of them were becoming romantically involved and wanted to have some time to themselves. I went ahead and put some food on my plate as I watched Lynn talk to Carl. In seconds, they walked towards me.

"So, are you ready to go, Lily?" Carl asked. "Lynn isn't feeling very well, so I think we need to leave. Do you mind?"

"Oh, sure!" I said. "I told Lynn not to eat that spicy avocado dip. She doesn't do well with that."

"I'll be fine," Lynn said fanning herself. "I just need some fresh air."

"You girls go on out while I say goodbye to Marc," Carl instructed. "I'll meet you in the hallway."

When we got to the hallway, Lynn grabbed my arm. "Aren't you going to say goodbye to Marc?"

"No, I don't want to bother him," I said flatly. "It's a night for him and Meg. He won't even miss me."

Carl joined us at the elevator. When we got outside, I took in a deep breath of fresh air. I had escaped.

Chapter 78

Carl was worried about how Lynn was feeling, which took the focus off of me. That was a great relief. I got my bag out of the car when we pulled into their garage and went straight to the guest room, where I'd stayed a few times before. Lynn followed me. Rather than chastising me, she surprised me with a warm hug.

"Thanks, Lynn. I owe you one," I said, hugging her tightly.

"It's okay. I love you."

"I love you, too. Thanks for taking care of your little sister tonight."

She released me from the hug and gave me a big smile. Knowing I was upset, she gave me a soft pat on the arm before leaving the room. I got ready for bed and settled in. I tried to justify what I had just done. Was I jealous of Meg? I couldn't decide. Forgetting the Meg factor, I had been just plain ignored by Marc, and as his girlfriend, I just wasn't ready for that. I'd been surprised and disappointed by his lack of attention to me. I didn't consider myself a needy person, but that had hurt. Perhaps I had inflated our relationship.

No one there would have ever noticed that Marc even had a girlfriend! It had been all about Meg. My cell phone rang, and I jumped. Could it be Marc realizing that I was gone? I grabbed my phone off the bedside table to see who it was. It was Alex. "Alex, where are you?" I asked.

"I'm at Jenny's apartment, and we were worried about you. What happened tonight with you and Marc?"

"Nothing, absolutely nothing. That happens to be why I'm here in Lynn's guest bedroom. Marc didn't care one bit that I was there. It was a Marc-and-Meg night, it seems. I don't know. I guess it just hurt my feelings a bit."

"Well, that was a big mistake on Marc's part. I watched you all night, and you looked like you were about to jump right out of your skin. He definitely screwed up, but don't be too hard on him. He had a lot of folks competing for his attention tonight."

"I realize that. It also made me realize how unimportant I am in his life. You're so sweet to call. I'll be fine. He doesn't even know that I've left the party yet."

"Okay, then. Get some sleep and call me in the morning. Do you hear me?"

"Yes, I will. Thank Jenny for sharing you with me." I hung up, realizing once again how Alex always had my best interests at heart. He knew me like a book. We were pretty good soulmates. I puffed up my pillow while asking God to guide me regarding my very rocky relationship. I did manage to doze off, but woke up when I heard a firm knock at the bedroom door.

"Lily, it's Lynn," my sister said as she opened the door.

"What's wrong?" I asked in a daze. "Is it morning?"

"Marc is at the door asking for you. Here, use this robe.

He looks pretty upset."

"Outside the door? What time is it?"

"A little past midnight."

"Hmmm. It took that long for him to realize that I was gone," I muttered, feeling sad and aggravated at the same time.

"Lily, just go talk to him," Lynn insisted.

"Okay. Let me comb my hair."

I took a deep breath, not knowing what to expect. Once again, I asked God to come with me. As I approached the front door, Marc's eyes were penetrating. Was he angry, sad, or what? I honestly couldn't tell.

"Why did you leave the party without saying goodbye?" he asked, sounding frustrated.

"It was time, and there didn't seem to be a purpose in me staying," I said firmly. "There was a lot going on, and it was obvious that you would never miss me, so we came home."

"What was I supposed to do?" Marc asked sharply.

"You've just made my point. It was a party for you and Meg, and I'm so glad you enjoyed it. I really am."

From there, we began to argue. We exchanged lots of words, but the ones I wanted to hear were "I'm sorry." "Sorry" wasn't mentioned.

"Why are you staying here at Lynn's instead of at my place?"

"Did you hear anything that I just said to you? For starters, you didn't ask me to stay, and hardly noticed me at all, so it made sense that I would come here. Why don't you go home and get some sleep? We can talk about this tomorrow. I think we're waking up the neighborhood."

Marc gave me a look. He was so aggravated with me.

"What the heck do you have in your car?" he asked, glancing at my vehicle.

"Your birthday present, which can easily be returned, by the way," I said sarcastically.

He took long strides to reach my car. He peered in the window and turned around in wonder. "You got me a globe? An antique globe?"

"I know, crazy idea. I was afraid I was off base, but you have everything you could possibly want."

"I'm fascinated by old maps and globes," he announced to me. "I want to see it."

"Well, I'm not so sure now that I want to give it to you," I said defiantly.

He took a deep breath, and I could see that he was fighting to control his anger.

Chapter 79

"Quit trying to play hard to get and let me see the globe," he demanded. "The car is locked, so get your key fob."

"No, it's late. Just go home."

"I'm not leaving until I get my birthday present," he said.

It was then that I realized that he'd likely had more to drink than I'd supposed.

"I'm serious. I don't think Lynn and Carl will appreciate me staying out here all night." His gaze darted toward a window.

I turned around and saw Carl and Lynn watching us from inside. "Okay," I hissed. "I'll get the fob. Then take it and go home, and don't bother sending me a thank you note!" I returned inside, seething with every step I took. Lynn and Carl remained silent. I returned to Marc where he stood by my car. His hands were on his hips. I didn't say a word. He awkwardly helped me to maneuver the globe onto the sidewalk.

"This is awesome, Lily! Where did you find it?"

"Just never mind. Put it in your car and leave." I blinked. I was so angry with him that I was beginning to shake. At that moment, his face broke into a wide smile, and he enthusiastically pulled me into his arms. After a second, he pushed me away and gave me the most passionate kiss I'd ever received from him. It completely took my breath away. Gasping for air, I didn't know how to respond.

"Thank you so much, sweetheart!" he said, looking into my eyes. "I love you so much!"

After another one of his kisses, my mind was recalculating. "I'll talk to you tomorrow," I said, turning to go into the house.

"Yes, you will, and every day after that," Marc shouted enthusiastically.

This was not the Marc I knew. He picked up the globe with both hands and took it to his car. I turned around in disbelief as he drove away. When I went inside and closed the door, Lynn was standing there.

"That was quite a display of affection for someone who doesn't know you're around," she teased.

"He was still in party mode, I suppose. At least he liked my gift. I'd had second thoughts about giving it to him."

"Oh, Lily, he's a man! Don't you know by now that they aren't the sharpest knives in the drawer when it comes to behaving properly? Look at what I had to put up with from Carl! The bottom line, sister, is that Marc loves you."

"How did you get so wise all of a sudden?"

She burst into laughter. "Get some rest, and we'll talk in the morning at the coffee bar. This has been fun, but I'm going to bed."

I swallowed hard and went back into the bedroom. I could still feel the impact of Marc's kiss on my mouth. Why hadn't I seen this side of him before? Had I totally misread him at the party? I still wasn't convinced that I was mistaken about his behavior. I did give myself credit for picking out a pretty darned good birthday gift.

A soft knock at the door startled me out of sleep. Daylight was coming in through the window. "Get up, sleepyhead. It's ten," Lynn announced.

I immediately sat up in bed and tried to get my bearings. I got dressed and joined Lynn and Carl at the coffee bar. Carl was looking at his phone, and Lynn presented me with hot cinnamon buns. I was hungry, especially since I hadn't eaten the night before.

"I guess I missed some of the party in my front yard last night," Carl teased.

I snickered.

"It's nice to know that there are still lover's quarrels at any age," Lynn added, smiling.

"Okay, you two," I said, taking my first sip of coffee. "I have no comment."

"You aren't going to see Marc before going on back to Augusta?" Lynn asked.

"No. I'm done," I said, feeling tired. "I need to get back to work and get the shop open."

"She's going to play hard to get, Lynn," Carl joked. "What did I tell you?"

"That's a great idea that you have there, Carl," I said with a grin.

Lynn gave me a wink and then helped me get my things together so I could leave.

"Thanks for everything," I said, giving her a hug before I climbed in my car.

"I'm glad you got rid of that big thing in the back of your car before driving home."

"I am too! I think he loved it. I hope he remembers how he ended up with a globe in his car."

"Just keep listening to your heart, sister," Lynn advised.

"Thanks. I'll try. I love you!"

"I love you, too!"

Chapter 80

I had a lot to think about on the drive home. So far, there had not been a peep from Marc. What could that mean? Thank goodness that the globe was out of my hands. How could he give that a twirl and not think of me? I'd almost gotten to Augusta when my phone rang. It was Alex, so I pulled into an American Legion parking lot.

"Where are you now?" Alex asked.

"I'm not with Marc, if that's what you're asking. I'm nearly to my front door."

"Good heavens, Lily! What happened?"

"When Marc finally realized that I wasn't at the party, he came over to Lynn's house after midnight and got me out of bed."

"Oh, I love it. Please continue."

"There was yelling and even a touch of passionate romance, but no conclusion about anything. He loved my gift and took it home, so that was the best part of the evening."

"What did you give him?'

"An antique globe with a beautiful stand."

"Impressive! So, he liked it?"

"He loved it. He was overwhelmed, actually."

"Jenny and I felt so bad for you. He was so engaged with the attention from his sister and everyone else that he forgot about you. Not good."

"I appreciate those thoughts, but I'm not proud of myself. I didn't realize that I had a jealous bone in my body until last night. One part of me said, 'You go, girl,' and the other part said, 'Grow up, you big baby.'"

Alex chuckled. "You are a Gemini, and you do have a birthday coming yourself, remember."

"Don't remind me. I've had enough birthdays for a while. I'm glad you and Jenny are getting cozy. That early part of the relationship is at its best right now, you know."

"I think you're right. I'll admit that it's been fun getting to know her."

"Thanks for calling, Alex. You're the best."

"Best what?"

"Goodbye, Alex!" I hung up and drove the few blocks to my house. I passed a sheriff's vehicle on my way. Had he been to see me? Sure enough, a note was attached to my front door from a Deputy Ernest Becker. I stopped to read it before removing it. It said that the sheriff had stopped by to see me regarding Chuck Waller and that if Chuck should contact me, then I was to notify the sheriff's office. What on earth had Chuck done to require this search? I placed the note in my cash drawer when I got in the shop. I left the front door open to get a little fresh air, took my things upstairs, and then came down to place

Rosie's rocker on the porch. My cell phone was ringing. It was Marc. I decided to let it go to voicemail. There wasn't much to say right now. To my surprise, Judy and a friend entered the shop.

"Lily, I want you to meet my friend Cora," Judy said. "Cora, this is my friend and sometimes boss, Lily."

"Nice to meet you, Cora," I responded.

"Likewise," she said. "I live in Washington, and we take turns taking each other to lunch. Judy has talked so much about your shop."

"How nice," I replied. "Feel free to show her around, Judy."

"She loves quilts, Lily," Judy assured me. "I told her about the exquisite ones in the cabinet."

"Do you collect or make quilts?" I asked Cora.

"I just buy them when I can afford them."

"It's a buyer's market right now," I responded.

The two went into the quilt room, and I could hear them chattering with one another. I went about my business by taking care of some paperwork.

"Lily, Cora would like to see the quilt with all the bright cheddar in the cabinet," Judy requested. "May I have the key?"

"Judy, you know I don't show those quilts unless someone is seriously interested."

Judy looked disappointed. "Well, you never know," she said as she shrugged her shoulders.

I reluctantly got the key and went into the quilt room. The quilt Cora wanted was the third from the top of the stack, so it didn't disturb too much. When I pulled it out, I relocked the cabinet. I carefully unfolded the requested quilt.

"Oh my goodness!" Cora gasped.

"Isn't it dynamite?" Judy exclaimed. "Lily, tell her about the color cheddar."

I sighed. "Well, first of all, it's not dye-fast," I began. "If it gets wet in a quilt, it's likely to bleed through to the backing. The date on this quilt is 1850, which is the right era, except you don't typically see this much cheddar in one quilt. Usually, you will see small pieces of it used with green and red. This quilt is unique. I like the contrast with the indigo blue."

Chapter 81

"What's the price?" Cora asked.

I picked up the tag. "It's ten thousand five hundred dollars."

She nodded, looking unimpressed.

"Now, should I wrap it up for you to take home or put it back in the cabinet?" I asked with a smile.

"Thanks for showing it to me, Lily," Cora said politely.

Before she could ask to see any others, I folded the quilt, placed it on the top of the stack, and locked the cabinet.

"Can I show you any others in this room?" I said as I looked around.

"They're all unique in their own way, aren't they?" Cora commented.

"Yes, they are." I nodded. "With any piece of art, no two are alike."

"Cora, we must be going," Judy urged. "Cora is interested in a barn quilt, so we want to go by Karen's shop."

"Well, have a nice day," I said. Admittedly, I was ready for them to leave. "It was nice to meet you, Cora." I felt sure that Judy had picked up on my unwillingness to open the cabinet.

Even though it felt mean, I really wasn't here to entertain people and their friends.

Then, in a total turn of events, I couldn't believe who had just parked in front of the shop. It was Meg! Now what?

"Good morning, Meg," I said as she came in. "What a pleasant surprise."

"I didn't want to head home without paying you a visit as I had promised," she began.

"How nice! You must be very pleased at how the party went."

"I really was. The best part was pulling off the surprise," she said.

"I loved seeing Marc's face. I suppose he's back at work today."

"Yes, he is, but we plan to meet up for dinner. We want you to join us," Meg said kindly.

"How sweet, but I really can't. I have plans."

"Lily, I want to apologize for occupying so much of Marc's time at the party."

"You don't have to do that. There were so many people that he wanted you to meet," I said, still feeling conflicted.

"Marc felt horrible when he realized that you had left."

"Perhaps he should have," I said coldly.

Meg's eyes widened.

"He had a lot of people to meet and greet, so I get it. I'm just a friend who cares for him more than most of the people who were there, that's all!" I felt winded and hot as I choked the words out.

"Lily! Marc cares for you a great deal! I tease him all the time about asking you to marry him, but he says you have an agreement to the contrary."

I nodded. "That's right. We do have an agreement."

"Do you know how close he came to giving you an engagement ring at Christmas? He didn't because he was worried that it would scare you, and if that happened, he knew you would turn him down."

"It surprises me to hear that, and he was probably right. As I watched him last night, I realized how unimportant I am in his daily life."

"Nonsense!" Meg protested, positioning her hands on her hips.

"I'm the sweet woman that he met who loves sweet little quilts and lives in a sweet little town. That's it."

"You are so wrong, Lily—although I do think you are very sweet."

I smiled. "Look, Meg, I really appreciate what you're trying to do. You're a good sister to drive all this way and try to fix things, but last night was a wake-up call for me."

"I hope you won't stop seeing him over what happened on just one evening. He feels terrible about neglecting you."

"Just so you know, I'm not a jealous or needy person, but there are times when I expect certain behaviors from those I care about."

"Can I tell him that you're not angry with him anymore?"

"You can tell him that I'm a big girl and that I was very pleased to see that he had a good birthday party."

"So you accept his apology?"

"Yes, you can tell him that."

"Don't hesitate to change your mind about coming to dinner tonight."

"Thanks."

"Lily, you're the best. I'll be in touch," Meg exclaimed.

Chapter 82

I closed the shop door and gave Marc credit for using Meg to smooth things over. I sat behind the counter and wondered what the rest of the evening would have been like had I stayed until the end of the party. Marc lived in a world so much more sophisticated than mine. I'd never have enough black outfits to wear for his social activities. Would I even enjoy such a life? I opened my laptop and decided to check on my siblings. They were my go-to people when I felt a bit down.

The first email was from Laurie. She was enjoying a robust retail season with so many tourists coming to her town. Lynn embellished Marc's birthday bash, but thankfully didn't tell everyone about her baby sister getting jealous. Loretta said she had been babysitting Lucy a lot recently. She seemed happy to do it because she approved of Sarah's relationship with Lance. She mentioned that she had sent Marc a birthday card, and then asked what I wore to the party.

Ellen mostly responded to Laurie, which was good. It sounded as if visiting Door County was on her bucket list. Ellen also told Loretta that she had boxes of fabric from her mother and that she wished one of us would take them off her hands. Aunt Mary had not been a quilter, so her fabrics were likely satins, silks, and wool, which quilters generally didn't use. Ellen noted at the end of her message that it was her first day to volunteer at the quilt museum.

It was my turn to respond. I told Laurie that I was jealous of her tourist business, as I was somewhat disappointed this year in Augusta. I encouraged Ellen to get to Door County. I said artists were in abundance and told her that the cherries grown in Door County were to die for, and reminded her that there were charity groups that could take that fabric off her hands. At the end, I returned to Loretta's question about what I wore to the party. I said that I'd decided to wear something different—so I chose a simple black dress. I knew she would get a chuckle out of that. I closed the computer and noticed that it was four in the afternoon. It had been another disappointing retail day, so I brought the rocker and quilt inside, signaling the official end of my business day.

I grabbed my purse and decided to check on the guest cottage. I had nothing to eat for dinner, so in the back of my mind, I planned to stop at Ashley Rose for something to eat or perhaps to take home. I walked up the hill to Carrie Mae's shop, certain that she would still be open, but she wasn't. I knew she would be curious as to whether Marc liked his globe. I continued on my way, wondering if I should also stop at Johann's, but decided against it. I opened the gate to the tiny yard of the cottage and noticed that all the flowers looked dry. Did I need to remind Johann of his duties? It seemed odd that he had forgotten after all this time.

I walked inside, and it seemed extremely warm. I went ahead and turned on the air conditioning, looked out the back window, and then checked the lock. All was well, so once again I admired the cottage's charm and went on my way.

"Hey!" Ted shouted as he got out of his truck. "I just remembered that Johann asked me to do the watering today at the cottage."

"Oh, good! I was about to scold him! Things are so dry."

"He's been using me to do some deliveries now that I have this nice truck," Ted reported with pride.

"Wonderful! Have you applied or registered for school yet?"

"Don't you start on me too! I've got plenty of time."

"You do?"

He didn't answer but busied himself with his watering job instead. I waved goodbye and proceeded down the street to Ashley Rose. It wasn't Thursday, so I had no worries about running into Anthony. When I entered the restaurant, I had to eat my assumptions. There was Anthony, sitting at the counter with several other people.

"Hey, Lily!" Sally called from behind the counter.

Before I could respond, Anthony turned around. "Hey, Lily! Not to worry. I just stopped to get a drink before I pick up Gracie."

I nodded and smiled. "What's your special today?" I asked Sally.

"Oh, it's all about Italian today," Sally replied. "You can have lasagna, spaghetti, or fettuccini. You could have a smorgasbord!"

Several people at the bar chuckled.

"I'll just start with a glass of wine, please," I said, selecting one of the stools at the counter.

"Put that on my tab," Anthony requested.

"Thanks, but that's not necessary."

Chapter 83

"Put her dinner on there too, unless she orders the whole Italian menu," he joked.

Everyone with hearing distance laughed.

"I hope all is well, Lily. Sorry I can't partake with you tonight, but perhaps another time. See you later, Sally."

I didn't respond or turn around as he exited.

"That fella misses you so much," Sally said with a wink.

"I'd like to purchase a bottle of Vintage Rose to take home with me, so don't let me forget," I instructed her.

"Consider it done," she said as she went to help another customer.

I enjoyed lasagna as my choice for dinner. My cell phone rang. It was Marc. I wondered if I should answer. Feeling relaxed from my wine, I responded. "Hi, Marc."

"Well, I'm glad you're still speaking to me," he said quietly. "How are you?"

"Pretty good. I'm enjoying an Italian meal at Ashley Rose."

"That's nice. I wish we could be enjoying dinner

together. I want you to know how much I love the globe you gave me. At first, I thought I might take it to the office, but I think I'll enjoy having it right here in my office at home. Thank you again. It was very generous."

"I'm glad you like it. I wish I had more information about it."

"Can I come out to see you this weekend?"

I hesitated. "I suppose."

"You're not sure?"

"I do think we have to talk. I can come in if you're too busy."

"Stop. I am never too busy for you. How about if I come around on Friday when you close? We'll go to dinner at one of the wineries."

"Fine. That will be fine."

"Lily, are we okay?"

"We'll talk. I'll see you on Friday."

We hung up, and I felt good about not expressing my feelings. I needed more time. I had to think seriously about whether Marc and I should continue our relationship. He lived in a different world. I might as well have been living in another state. I wasn't certain that Marc loved me the way Meg had described. I thought she had just been trying to smooth things over for us. Had he really thought about purchasing an engagement ring, or was it just a crazy thought he'd shared with her?

"How about dessert, Lily?" Sally asked as she wiped the counter.

"I'd better not. I've had too much garlic bread, I'm afraid."

"When is Kitty coming back?" Sally asked. "Has she

let you know? I guess you're still keeping an eye on the cottage."

"I am still watching it. Kitty said she'd let me know when they arrive. I think it will be soon. I can't believe that no one has bought that cute little place."

"I would love to buy it, but I could never afford the price they're asking," Sally said, shaking her head. "I hate the drive from Washington every day. I've always wanted to live in Augusta."

"Why don't you talk to them about renting it? I think they might be open to that."

"I doubt if I could swing it. It's perfect for one person. I got to see it one time when one of the guests showed it to me."

"Sally, Kitty knows you. When she gets back, you need to talk to her about it. I think they're worried about who will be the next owner, so they may work with you."

"I guess it doesn't hurt to ask them. I'm supposed to get a raise next month, so every bit helps."

"Good. Well, I'd better get going. I need to take my wine."

"You just owe me for the wine. Anthony took care of everything else. He's a good man, Lily. I don't know what he's thinking dating Gracie. Nothing against her, but they are not a match."

I chuckled and smiled at her as I gathered my things and prepared to leave. I left Sally a generous tip and went on my way. Her comment about Anthony and Gracie was interesting, and I had to admit that I agreed with her.

When I arrived home, I got a text from Alex.

. . .How wounded is Marc?

> . . .*He's limping, but that's okay.*

. . .You are cruel, Lily Girl.

> . . .*How is Jenny?*

. . .Cool.

> . . .*When will she wise up?*

. . .Jealous?

> . . .*Maybe!*

. . .Hmmm...

Alex was a gem. I loved to tease him.

Chapter 84

The first thing I did the next morning was stitch some more on my block for quilt class. The Cottage Guest House was looking better and better. If I did another block like it someday, I could give it to Kitty. Thinking about Kitty, I would have to be sure to give Sally a good recommendation. I didn't have much hope for getting her in there as a renter, but it wouldn't hurt to try to help her. It was starting to rain, so I grabbed my umbrella by the door and took it with me to the library. I made a dash inside and saw only Susan standing there.

"Where is everyone today?" she asked. "You and Judy are the only ones here."

"Hi, Judy!" I said.

"I brought some coffee cake that Marge just baked this morning," Judy announced. "Help yourself."

"Thanks, I will!" I responded, eager to taste Marge's baking.

"Edna and Marilyn are at an out-of-town wedding, I think," Judy offered. "I don't know about the others."

"Well, all the more coffee cake for us!" Susan joked. "Did you bring your blocks?"

"Mine is almost finished, so I'm happy to just sit here and stitch," I hinted.

"I'd love to work more on mine, too," Judy agreed.

"Can I see your block, Judy?" I asked, interested.

"It's Johann's sign." She blushed. "It's old and tattered, but I love it. Everyone knows Johann's sign here in wine country."

"What a great idea!" I exclaimed. "I like it very much! Susan, are you keeping up with us?"

"No, I'm afraid not," she admitted. "I may have enough to do a small wall quilt when I'm done."

"Mine may not be very big either," Judy shared as she helped herself to another piece of coffee cake.

"Hey, I heard that Gracie has a pretty serious boyfriend," Susan mentioned. "I met him at her shop last week. I've seen him around."

"Oh, yes!" Judy nodded. "He's known as the 'wine guy' around here."

"Well, I wish her the best," Susan said. "Do you know him, Lily?"

"Yes," I said, nodding.

"What about your guy?" Susan questioned. "Is it serious?"

"No, but I am very fond of him," I answered.

"You've been seeing him for some time now," Judy teased. "I'll bet you end up marrying him."

"I wouldn't bet too much on that, Judy," I countered.

"Lily! Lily!" Korine shouted as she ran into the library. "They just took Carrie Mae to the hospital in Washington!"

"What happened?" I asked.

"When I arrived this morning, I called and called to her and then I heard a groaning sound, so I went up to check on her. She was slumped over in her chair," Korine explained. "Her voice was slurred. I think she's had a stroke! I called 911 right away."

"Thanks, Susan," I said, hurriedly gathering up my things. "I'll go there right away, Korine."

"Be careful not to hurry, Lily," Susan warned. "These roads can be slick when they're wet. Maybe you can just call and check on her."

"No way! She'll need me to be there," I responded. "Goodness knows where her daughter is right now." I opened the umbrella and rushed to my car. "Please, God," I said aloud. "Don't let her die. Please keep her alert and comfortable."

Traffic was slow, but that was probably a good thing under the circumstances. Carrie Mae was in her eighties, so anything could happen. When I finally arrived, I parked and found my way to the emergency entrance. Once inside, trying to find someone to help me was frustrating. Finally, someone showed up at the desk.

"Are you a relative?" the nurse asked curtly.

"No, but I am about the only family she has," I explained. "I need to see her."

"Let me check for you," she said. "If they just brought her in, you may not be able to see her for a while."

"Please check. She'll want to see me," I insisted.

Betty rushed in. She looked as rattled as I felt.

"What do you know, Lily?" she asked.

"Nothing, other than what Korine shared with me," I

said, about to cry. "I think she's had a stroke."

"Good Lord, Mary, and Joseph," Betty said as she crossed her heart. "Please, God, have mercy on her."

We hugged, sat down in the nearest chairs, and attempted to gather our thoughts.

Chapter 85

"Betty, I don't know much about Carrie Mae's family. Is there anyone who should be called?"

"I assume that her daughter was called," Betty said with tears streaming down her face.

"Was Carrie Mae upset about something that could have brought this on?"

"Not really. The last time we talked, she told me about the sheriff's department coming by to ask her questions about Chuck Waller."

"Yes, they came to my shop while I was gone. I wonder what that crazy guy did?"

"The rumor is that he was selling stolen goods, but I don't know that for sure. Carrie Mae always said he was a shady character. She also mentioned a long time ago that there must be a black market for quilts that he was likely a part of."

"Yeah, I often wondered what he did with the quilts he bought for next to nothing."

"Ladies, the doctor said you can go in now to see Mrs.

Wilson, but you need to go one at a time, and don't stay very long," the nurse instructed.

"You go first," I insisted as I nudged Betty.

She didn't hesitate and obediently followed the nurse. I didn't want to let myself think about losing Carrie Mae. Certainly, the doctors would give her something to help her. In no time, Betty returned. Tears were rolling down her cheeks.

"Sit down, Betty," I said softly. "Tell me what to expect."

She blew her nose and shook her head. "I hate seeing her like that."

"Like what?"

"One side is paralyzed, and it shows on her face when she tries to smile or talk. You can tell that it's scaring her to death."

"Oh. Did you get to talk to a doctor?"

She shook her head.

"Stay here and calm down. I'll go in now. Is she coherent?"

"Yes, she knows what's going on."

"Well, it's good that she's still with us," I said to encourage Betty.

Randal and Marge arrived. Word of Carrie Mae's situation was spreading around town. I asked them to sit with Betty while I paid my visit to Carrie Mae.

I entered the area slowly. Carrie Mae was hooked up to an immense variety of tubes. The bun on her head had disappeared into long, flowing gray-and-black hair streaming down her shoulders. She was still her in cotton housedress. When she looked up at me, she shook her head, and I could see that she was upset. "Don't try to talk, sweetie, just listen to me," I said, touching her hand. "I know this is scary right now, but you're getting help, and there's already been some improvement. This place will help you get back to normal again. Don't worry!"

She pointed to the numb side of her face with her unaffected hand. I nodded, understanding what she was telling me. "Now, I happen to know that half of one of your smiles is bigger than most others' full smiles."

Her eyes glistened.

"Are you comfortable now?"

She nodded as a nurse came in to check her vital signs. Without thinking twice, I asked the nurse if Carrie Mae was going to be okay. Carrie Mae stared intently at her.

"As we said, there's already been some slight improvement, but we'll have to see," the nurse said gently. "The doctor will be able to tell you more. Can you please step outside while I work with her? It won't take long."

"Of course. She has many friends outside who would like to have a report," I explained.

The nurse nodded and smiled.

"Don't worry Carrie Mae, I'll be right here." I left the room and, once in the hallway, I leaned my body against the wall. I couldn't hold back my tears. I knew her strong will; Carrie Mae would fight this tooth and nail. However, if she remained handicapped in any way, I felt that it would devastate her. I pulled my emotions together and joined the others in the waiting room. Korine and Karen had joined them.

"I think that she was glad to see me, but I don't think she's ready to see everyone at this point," I advised. "I think she's embarrassed and needs to take some time to come to grips with this. She knows there's been some improvement, so that's good. I'm sure she'll be getting some therapy right away."

"I just can't believe it," Korine cried. "When I left her yesterday, everything was normal."

"I'm glad she has you, Korine," Karen said, giving her a hug. "She'll need you more than ever now."

Chapter 86

It was at least another forty-five minutes before a doctor came to see us. He asked who was family. We all nodded our heads, and he smiled.

"We are her family," I responded. "How is she doing?"

"I'm hopeful," he began. "It will be slow, but that's to be expected. I'd like for her to stay another day or so to make sure nothing reoccurs. I suggest that you all go home and get some rest. We'll see about a release date tomorrow."

"Thank you, doctor," Betty said with a sigh. "I'd like to stay with her a little while longer. We've been through a lot of tough times together, and I need to be there for her right now."

"She's right, doctor," I agreed. "They're seldom apart, and Carrie Mae is frightened right now."

"Very well, then, but try not to get her to talk right now so she can rest," he advised.

Betty agreed.

We all said goodbye to Betty and asked her to keep us informed. Korine said she would keep the shop closed until Carrie Mae instructed otherwise. I left, feeling very sad. It was Monday, so my shop was closed. If something happened to Carrie Mae, I wasn't sure I could ever open again.

I put my quilt project away. I had no interest in it right then. I put some laundry in the machine and slowly walked into the quilt room. I thought of the Dinner Detectives and how we couldn't solve the mystery of the missing crazy quilt. I owed it to Butler to try harder to solve this crime.

I took my laptop to the back porch. The rain had stopped, and the sun was shining brightly now. I checked for any word from my siblings, and there wasn't a peep. Was everyone as sad as I was? I knew I had to tell them about Carrie Mae. They knew how important she was to me. I then thought about Butler. He was like a son to her. She'd voiced that on more than one occasion. I looked for his number in my phone and decided to call him.

"Butler here," he answered, as if he were in the middle of something.

"Butler, it's me, Lily," I said slowly, hoping that my racing heart wouldn't cause me to ramble incoherently to him as I gave him the sad news.

"Lily! How nice to hear from you! Do you have good news to tell me?"

I knew he was either referring to his missing quilt or hoping I'd sold another one of his quilts. "No, I really don't. In fact, the reason I'm calling is to tell you that Carrie Mae is in the hospital. She's had a stroke."

"Oh, Lily! How bad is it?"

"I really can't answer that, but she's still with us and is paralyzed on one side of her body. The good news is that there's already been some slight improvement, so perhaps she'll progress back to normal."

"Well, that's good news. Is she in Washington?"

"Yes, but I don't know for how long."

"I'll get there as fast as I can."

"Butler, I know you think the world of her, but I don't know how comfortable she'd be with you popping in. She's very self-conscious and frightened right now. Her speech is slurred, which breaks my heart. Betty has insisted on staying with her, so I think that will be comforting."

"I'm coming out, even if she doesn't want to see me. I want her to know that I'm there for her. I recently found a rare teddy bear and purchased it for her, so I can bring that to cheer her up."

"That just may do it, Butler. You've been so kind to her. You're a gem!"

"I'll settle for being told I'm a gem by someone who already is one. You don't know how pleased I am that you thought to call me. Thanks so much."

"Let's pray that she'll have a full recovery."

"With her drive and spirit, she likely will," Butler said with confidence.

I hung up feeling like I had done something good for Carrie Mae. Hopefully her daughter was also on the way to see her. I heard a knock at the shop door, so I went to answer it. Two ladies were standing there with disappointed looks on their faces. I unlocked the door.

"Are you really closed?" one asked. "We've come all the way from Alton, Illinois to see your shop. We both read your column and wanted to see where you live."

"I am closed, but I'll be happy to let you in," I said

reluctantly. "I'm doing some work, but feel free to look around."

They practically cheered as they stepped inside.

"Do you write from this yellow house or at another location?" one asked.

"Usually from this house," I answered. "I do appreciate your reading my articles and subscribing to the magazine."

"We share. My favorite is the your article called 'Fall Back in Love Again.'"

Chapter 87

"That was such an inspiration to me," the woman continued, patting her chest to indicate that it had affected her heart. "I applied your message to my job as well as to my husband! You really know how to touch people's hearts."

"Thanks so much," I said, feeling flattered.

The other woman chimed in, "Well, my favorite is the one called 'Living Without the Written Word.' Ever since I read that, I've been better about writing thank you notes. I even started a journal; however, I'm not very faithful about keeping it current."

"So you improved some things about your practices. That's wonderful!" I commented.

"Now, another thing," the first woman said. "Laura and I had never been that fond of quilts until now. We never disliked them, but now we look at them differently. Oh! We should have introduced ourselves. This is Laura, and I'm Elizabeth. We've been friends since grade school."

"Oh my goodness," I said with admiration. "I'll bet you

have stories to share."

"We sure do!" Laura said as they giggled.

"Well, feel free to look around, and let me know if you have any questions."

Elizabeth asked, "Will you sign the magazine that we brought with us?"

"Sure!" I said, getting my pen off the counter.

"Make it out to The Twilight Girls," she requested. "There's a story there, of course."

They giggled some more.

"It's a secret and a story that we will take to our graves," Elizabeth confided.

I went about my business as they started looking around the shop. They wandered into the quilt room, but weren't there very long.

"Why is it freezing cold in that room?" Laura asked as she came out rubbing her arms.

"Freezing cold?" I asked, mystified. "It's always the same temperature as in here."

"No way!" Elizabeth said, still shivering. "Go see for yourself. I've got to get warm!"

To please them, I walked into the quilt room, and the temperature was the same as in the front of the shop. I came out and looked at them.

"Sorry, ladies. I didn't feel any difference," I said, shrugging my shoulders.

"Let's go, Laura," Elizabeth insisted. "I have got to get warm. There's something odd here."

"Yeah, nice to meet you, Lily," Laura said as they rushed to depart.

After they left, I had to check again for myself. Again,

there was no temperature change. I knew Rosie or someone else was up to no good. "This isn't nice. Please stop it," I said aloud. I shook my head and locked the door before I went upstairs. Things had been reasonably calm around the place lately, so what had that stunt been all about?

I munched on some snacks I had upstairs. As I stared out of the back porch windows, I thought of Marc. I would have to wait until Friday to see him, but I missed him. The day after this, there was an estate sale that I was determined to get to in Dutzow. It was time that I replenished the merchandise in the shop, or no one would return. The sale flyer I'd seen had mentioned quilts and antiques. I could go by there after I paid a visit to Carrie Mae.

As I undressed, I made a mental list of things I could use for the shop. I wasn't interested in big pieces of furniture. I could use linens, quilts, glassware, and kitchen items, if they were the right style. With the farm equipment being sold in the morning, the auction should work with my schedule. The directions sounded easy, and it would be something fun to do. I was about to turn the lights out when my cell phone rang. I hadn't been expecting a call from Lisa, of all people. Carrie Mae and I had traveled to her home prior to her divorce and purchased some quilts from her. Since the divorce, she'd settled into a lovely home in a housing development, and we occasionally caught up with one another.

"How are you?" I asked.

"I'm doing well, thanks. I'm having a cocktail patio party this weekend and wondered if you'd like to come. You're welcome to bring Carrie Mae or another guest, if you'd like."

I thanked her and then gave her an update on Carrie Mae. She was terribly sad to hear the news and said she would send flowers. I then explained that I had plans with Marc on the weekend and likely wouldn't make the party. It was a nice thought, but honestly, I didn't know how things would evolve between Marc and me.

Chapter 88

When I hung up, I pictured Lisa in her fancy house in Augusta Shores. She lived alone but had had a pretty active social life since she'd moved into town. I wondered if she was dating anyone. She was nice, attractive, and very rich.

The rain had picked up again. The weather seemed to be crying for Carrie Mae. I had to talk to someone, so I decided to call Betty, who was likely feeling sad as well. There was no answer, so I assumed that she was still with Carrie Mae. My cell phone rang again, and I was pleased to see that it was Lynn.

"I'm so sorry to hear about Carrie Mae. I know how much she means to you," Lynn stated.

"Thanks. I think she's out of danger, but at her age, you never know."

"I know how much guidance she has given you, and I think she's been close to being a mother to you."

"Well said, Lynn. I wouldn't be here right now without her."

"By the way, Carl had a drink with Marc yesterday, and Marc is concerned about you."

"Really? In what way?"

"He thinks you may foolishly give up your relationship for the wrong reasons. Are you really thinking of breaking it off with him?"

"No, not really. I'm glad he's concerned, but it's my own insecurities that have given me pause."

"I can see where you had reason to be concerned at the party, but Marc's world is not going to change, and neither will yours."

"I know, and that's what I'm trying to envision for us. It's difficult to speculate on what the future holds."

"Well, keep the faith. I'm here for you."

"Thanks, Lynn. I appreciate your call and your concern." Lynn was right. Nothing would change. Would I be okay with Marc and me if nothing changed? I had to sleep on it, which I did.

The next morning, I opened the shop on time and looked forward to the estate sale. I called Betty to find out where Carrie Mae might be. The phone rang and rang before someone finally picked up.

"Hello!" a voice sounding like Ted's answered.

"Ted, it's Lily. Is Betty home?"

"No. She stayed at the hospital all night again to be with Carrie Mae. She doesn't like driving at night either."

"I see. Do you know if Carrie Mae is improving?"

"No, I can't tell you."

"Okay. It looks like I'd better check on them. Thanks, Ted." I changed my mind about opening and closed the shop instead. Off I went to Washington. Thankfully, the rain had stopped. Traffic was slow and heavy all the way. When I finally parked and got inside the waiting room, there sat Butler.

"Oh, Lily, I'm glad you're here," Butler said, putting his magazine down. "Carrie Mae's daughter just left to check on the shop, and Betty is with her now."

I nodded and sat down next to him. "How is she today?"

"She's a fighter, I'll say that," he said with a grin. "Betty thinks there's been some slight improvement. She put Carrie Mae's hair in a bun and put some makeup on her. I think Carrie Mae felt better after that, so I take that as a good sign."

I nodded and smiled weakly. "I never knew how long her hair actually was! I love her so much!" I started to cry.

"I know. I do too," Butler said as he circled his arms around me.

His hug lasted a bit too long, and it felt more intense than it should have. We were interrupted when Betty came into the room.

"You can go see her now, Butler," Betty announced. "I have her all prettied up, and when she sees that teddy bear, it will make her day."

"Thanks, Betty," he said as he left us.

"Betty, you look exhausted. Please go home and get some rest."

She nodded in agreement. "I think they're going to release her tomorrow. I'll be back to get her in the morning, if that's the case."

"That's good. I hope she's doing okay with Butler. I know how embarrassed she was."

"I know."

"I'll spend a little time with her, and then I'm going to an estate sale in Dutzow."

"Oh, I saw that flyer. It should be a good one. Carrie Mae most likely would have gone to that. I think she knows those folks." Off Betty went, and I waited until Butler came out.

"I'm afraid she went to sleep," Butler informed me. "The nurse said the medication wipes her out. She may not know you're there, Lily."

"Did she love the teddy bear?"

"Her look was priceless! It didn't matter that she couldn't say a word."

Chapter 89

"I'll wait for you if you'd like to get some lunch."

"I really can't, Butler. I'm leaving here to go to an estate sale in Dutzow, but thanks."

"That sounds intriguing! Would you like some company?"

"No, not really. I feel guilty being away from the shop, but I need to beef up my inventory."

"Very well, then. I'll leave you with Carrie Mae. I'd appreciate it if you kept me informed."

"Thanks. I'll let you know if anything changes."

"Take care, now," he said as he gave me a quick kiss on the cheek.

I waited until he left the waiting room before I went in to see Carrie Mae. I took a deep breath as I entered her room. A nurse had just left after taking her vitals. Carrie Mae was indeed sound asleep. Betty had done an excellent job applying blush to her cheeks, putting lipstick on her lips, and fixing her hair, which included a flower in her bun. Carrie Mae liked to do that, and it reflected her cheery personality. I stood and stared at her. Finally, I said, "Carrie Mae, I know you're asleep right now, but I want you to know that I'm praying for your speedy recovery. I love you!" I patted her hand, but she didn't flex a muscle. I felt I was intruding on her privacy, so I decided to leave.

As I got close to my car in the parking lot, I saw Randal and Marge arrive. I decided not to call out to them. I was eager to get to the sale, and since I had only seen Carrie Mae sleeping, I really didn't have any new information to share.

The drive to Dutzow was about twenty miles or so. It turned out to be a beautiful day, and I was eager to think about the sale instead of about Marc and Carrie Mae. Cars were parked everywhere when I arrived. There was no question that I had arrived at the right place.

I walked up to the charming farmhouse to which the signs directed me. Items inside the house had predetermined prices, and the outside items would be sold at the live auction. I started in the house, where I knew I was most likely to find the things I was interested in. People were walking around with armfuls of merchandise to purchase. It was obvious that the first to arrive were getting the cream of the crop!

I was amazed at the volume of items that this family had accumulated. Stacks of doilies and linens were being uprooted by careless lookers. Quilts and blankets were getting unfolded and not refolded. The dining room was filled with tables of glassware that was mostly Depression glass. Cake plates were stacked everywhere. Who would collect cake plates?

A man in front of me had a box full of teapots. I watched him put it down. Had he changed his mind? "Are you taking these?" I asked.

"No," he said, shaking his head. "Help yourself. Some of

those don't have lids, just so you know."

I nodded and happily lifted the heavy box. Teapots always sold well, even if they didn't have lids. They could be used for flowerpots and even as pencil holders. A young man from the auction service offered to carry the box to the checkout lane until I was ready. I gave him my name so I could continue shopping. I decided to give the quilts another look. I saw a friendship quilt with yellow-and-blue prints that caught my eye. The names were embroidered in red, which I thought was odd. Even though I knew friendship quilts were hard to sell, I noticed that it had never been washed, which was a good thing. The sizing was still evident, and the embroidery was well done. If any of the names ended up being familiar, it could help the quilt sell. I figured I could at least make a hundred dollars off of it from the asking sale price. I put it on my pile.

In the dining room, I chose glass creamers that did not have sugar bowls to match. I found four of them. There was a precious pink glass child's plate that had the imprint of teddy bears around the rim. I thought of Carrie Mae and knew she would buy it in a second. At the other end of the table, I found a child's cup that matched. I wondered how they had gotten separated. I was getting concerned about my total, so I headed to the checkout line. At the last minute, I added a cute birdhouse that was yellow with a red roof. I saw it fitting perfectly in the little tree in the front yard. I was pleased with my purchases and reached for my checkbook.

Chapter 90

I asked the same young helper at the auction to help me load my things into the car. He was surprised to receive a tip and acted as if that had never happened before. A mile down the road, I stopped at a small roadside stand located on someone's farm. I loaded up on beautiful red tomatoes, sweet corn, and freestone peaches. I was starting to get hungry. In tomato season, I was perfectly happy with an onion and tomato sandwich with mayo, salt, and pepper. I might add an ear of corn to top it off!

It took me a while to unload the car, but it was exciting at the same time. I may have missed some good sales at the shop while I was closed, but this trip had been worth my time. Just as I took in my last load, Karen pulled up in her car.

"Hey, it looks like you've been shopping!" she teased.

"Yes, I have. There was a great sale in Dutzow today."

"How is Carrie Mae? Have you heard anything?"

"I saw her this morning, but she was sound asleep. She may be coming home soon."

"That's good news. Is she still paralyzed on one side?"

I nodded. "All of us have hope, since there's been some improvement."

"I was going to call you, but since I see you here, I wanted to ask you about two ladies from Alton, Illinois who came into your shop."

I paused, remembering them. "Yes, Laura and Elizabeth were their names. Why?"

"I'm pretty sure that they stole some things from my shop."

"Seriously? What makes you think so?"

"I had several small items missing right after they left that I knew were there before. I don't get that much traffic. One of the items was a small painting. One of them asked the price and said it was too expensive. Well, now it's gone."

"Oh, that's awful, Karen. Their visit was strange. We first talked about them reading my articles, and then they went into to the quilt room to look at quilts. They were in there for a few seconds when they came out shivering. They said it was ice cold in there. I was shocked, so I checked it myself. It seemed normal to me, so I don't know what was going on."

"Cold?"

"Yeah, they truly were shivering."

"Was anything missing after they left?"

"No, I don't think anything was missing. They said a quick thank you for the autograph, and off they went. I think they were spooked."

Karen chuckled. "I'll bet Rosie caught onto them and scared them."

"I have to admit that the thought crossed my mind. It was too weird," I said.

"Has she done that before?"

"No, never! She's done other weird things, but never the cold chill! Did you ask Vic or any other shop owners if they're missing things?"

"No, but I will," Karen said. "When Carrie Mae gets home, we need to make things as normal as we can for her. How about a dinner for the Detectives?" She grinned as she waited for me to answer.

"Sounds good."

Karen seemed better after she left. I felt for her. I guessed I was lucky that the two women had gotten chilly and left!

I eagerly fixed my tomato sandwich and cooked one of the ears of corn. It was delicious! I cleaned up the kitchen and was about to head upstairs when I heard a loud siren. In a small town like this, it had to be for someone I knew. I tried not to think about it. I turned to my phone and saw that I had received a text from Alex.

. . .I can't sleep. Are you in bed?

. . .I was about to try. What's on your mind?

. . .Work, mostly.

. . .And Jenny?

. . .No comment. It's almost birthday week. Any suggestions?

. . .Beer and pizza at Ragazzi's.

. . .You are simpleminded. Be more creative.

. . .I'll think about it. Go to sleep.

. . .Don't let the bed bugs bite.

. . .☺

I pulled down the covers and began to get ready for bed. I was pleased that Alex thought of me when he was troubled. I was sure that Jenny must be getting to him. He sure liked his independence, though. I thought of me and Marc. A relationship developed in stages, as it was with Marc's and mine. Taking it to the next level brought risks. Was I ready, or would I risk the status quo?

Chapter 91

I got up early the next morning. Despite the beautiful day, Augusta was relatively quiet until around nine, when the everyday noises of a community waking up could be heard. As I was enjoying coffee on the front porch, I was surprised to see Barney coming my way instead of Snowshoes. "Well, good morning, stranger!" I greeted. "Where's Snowshoes today?"

"Haven't you heard?"

I shook my head.

"He had a heart attack yesterday. I thought you would have heard the ambulance."

"Oh! I did hear it. I'm so sorry to know that Snowshoes had a heart attack. It's easy to forget that he's the age that he is."

"I suppose we're all getting older than we actually feel inside," Barney said as he wiped his forehead in the heat.

"Is he at the hospital in Washington? I'll send a card."

"Yes, he is. I hear Carrie Mae will be with us again soon."

"I hope so."

"I'd best be on my way, Lily," he said, giving me a wave.

Knowing that Snowshoes had encountered a health setback caused me to begin to think about the older citizens and their impact on the entire area. The older generation in Augusta continued to contribute to the town in positive ways. As I thought about Carrie Mae and Snowshoes, I wondered who would tell of their contributions once they were gone. It was probably true that many older folks never got recognized or thanked for their contributions. What if I wrote about the pillars of the community in my next column? Perhaps that would make people more aware of those who had made a difference, and then others would remember to thank them. I could call the column "Who Are the Pillars of the Community?" They likely all had similar styles of leadership and a passion for the town and neighborhoods. Some worked in the background and some became more visible by investing financially in the community like Carrie Mae and her husband had. She'd brought life to places that would have been torn down and forgotten. She'd invested in newcomers like me, probably hoping that we would carry on the traditions. Not everyone thought that way. Some people just wanted to know what someone else could do for them. I thought I had the gist of the column in my mind, so I went to my laptop to write. I was interrupted by Korine, who came running in the door.

"Lily, Lily, did you know that Carrie Mae may be arriving home as soon as this morning?" she said with excitement.

"You'll be there with her, right?"

"Oh, sure. I thought I would spend the night, if she'll let me."

"Good idea. She'll depend on you more than ever now, Korine."

"I know, but she'll never want to admit it."

"I sent flowers, so keep an eye out for them."

"How nice. She'll like that. Are they lavender?" Korine smiled.

"I told the florist that it was Carrie Mae's favorite color."

"I guess you know about Snowshoes."

"Yes, Barney told me. Listen, if you need anything, please call me, okay?"

"I will. Thanks, Lily."

I went back to my writing until an elderly couple arrived. The woman used a cane. When she got to the porch and saw Rosie's rocker, she sat down.

"I won't be long, honey," the man said to her.

"Good morning, folks," I greeted.

"Thanks so much for having this chair handy," the woman said. "Do you mind if I rest my head on this lovely quilt for a minute?"

"Not at all. Enjoy!" I couldn't believe my own words! The weary woman created a sweet picture. I hoped that Rosie wouldn't mind. I checked on the man. He was strolling through the shop. I couldn't help noticing that he looked very sophisticated.

"Are you looking for anything in particular?" I inquired.

"Smoking memorabilia, perhaps," he said. He spoke with an English accent.

I responded, "There are some things in this case over here. They're mostly advertising pieces. I also have this 1920s smoke stand."

"Thank you," he responded.

Chapter 92

"Are you visiting from England?"

"Yes. We're having a lovely trip," the man said as he examined the smoke stand.

I sensed that he did not want to engage in much conversation, so I went about my business. I decided to check on the woman. I could see the chair rocking at a pretty good pace, which seemed to please her. The smile on her face seemed to show a hint of surprise. Her smile widened when I came out to see her.

"A bit of a nice rock, I say," she said.

I nodded, knowing that Rosie must be up to something. I went back inside to check on the Englishman and was pleased to see that he had put about five things on the counter. Three of them were unique ashtrays. "Good choice!" I commented as I began to wrap them up.

"Tally in the quilt on the rocker if you would, please," he requested.

"Are you sure?"

He nodded and got out his credit card.

"The quilt is an Irish Chain, and it's three hundred and twenty-five dollars," I informed him.

He didn't bat an eye or respond, so I rung up all the items. After I finished the sale, we walked to the porch, where we found his wife dozing off. Her head was comfortably turned to one side. Rosie had rocked her to sleep.

"Sweetheart," the man murmured to her as he nudged her arm.

She opened her eyes and began to get up as she held on to his arm. I put the cane in her hand and carried the quilt to the car. Her husband carefully helped her inside and put the quilt on her lap, as if it had belonged to her all along. It was the sweetest sight. "Thank you so much," I said, shaking the gentleman's hand. "Safe travels home!"

"Thank you," he said as he tipped his straw hat.

I stood there in awe as I watched them drive away. What had just happened had a lot to do with Rosie. I walked back to the porch and was reminded that the rocker needed another quilt. Perhaps I shouldn't discourage customers from using the rocker! I went inside and brought out a lavender-and-white Drunkard's Path quilt. I hoped it would bring another sale.

My landline rang. It was Korine, telling me that Carrie Mae had arrived home. She reported that Carrie Mae was resting and that the lavender flowers had been delivered and were beautiful.

"She wanted me to thank you," Korine said. "I think I'm starting to understand her speech."

"When would be the best time for me to stop by?"

"I honestly don't know. Why don't you call first? Either

Betty or I will be here."

"Very well. Tell her I'll be coming by soon."

The day was so beautiful that I got out my embroidery block and sat on the front porch to work on it. I was nearly finished, so I had to start thinking about what my next block would be. So far, I had grapevines on the hills, The Ebenezer Church, and now the Cottage Guest House.

I thought about how much I was enjoying the quilt class and how important it had become to me since I'd moved here. If I could embroider something to do with the library, I could then add all the names of my quilting friends who attended class with me. Surely there would be a sketch or photo of the library that I could copy. I finally made the last stitch in my block and held it up to admire it. I wondered if I had given it enough stitches. My mother had always said, "If in doubt, do without." Considering that sage advice, I decided that it looked fine.

"Hello, Lily!" Vic said as he approached the shop. "It's a pretty day, isn't it?"

"Yes. It's too nice to stay inside. What's on your mind?"

"Karen said that you had two female customers stop by your shop, and she thinks they stole from her. She asked me if I had anything missing, but I didn't notice anything gone until this morning. When I think back about their visit, I think they may have been the ones who took it. Did you know them?"

"No. They wanted to talk about my column. They were very chatty until they went into the quilt room. They quickly exited, telling me that it was freezing cold in there. When I checked, it seemed to be the same temperature as the rest of my shop."

"Seriously?"

"I'm afraid so. You know that I occasionally have things happen here that I honestly can't explain."

He snickered. "I understand. I just thought there might be a way to check those women out. I'm glad you didn't have anything taken."

We chatted a little longer about Carrie Mae and Snowshoes before he went on his way. I felt bad for him and Karen. How could people get away with stealing like that?

Chapter 93

The next afternoon, I called Korine to see if it was okay to visit Carrie Mae.

"Come on ahead, but she's refusing to see some people, just so you know. When I tell her who's here, she either nods or shakes her head. Betty just left after fixing her hair. They had a cup of tea together."

"Okay. I'll take my chances and come by. It's not been busy, so I'll just close the shop." I brought in the rocker and officially closed. I needed some exercise, so I decided to walk to Carrie Mae's and then check on the guest house after that. When I arrived at Carrie Mae's shop, Korine was assisting a customer. She nodded and pointed to the stairs, indicating that it was okay for me to go up. I proceeded upstairs and called out Carrie Mae's name. When I entered her bedroom, which I had never seen before, I was flabbergasted. It was so full of clutter that I almost didn't see Carrie Mae sitting up in bed! Her face was trying to smile as tears rolled down her cheeks.

"Oh, Carrie Mae, don't worry so. You'll be back to

normal before you know it."

She shook her head in dismay. There was paper and a pencil nearby, and she reached for it. She then pointed to the flowers I'd sent and blew me a kiss with her left hand.

I nodded and smiled. "Are you in pain?" I asked as I touched her hand.

She shook her head.

"That's good! Let's be thankful for that. I understand that somebody will be coming by to give you therapy, which will be a tremendous help."

She nodded.

"You must do everything they advise you to do!"

She gave me a stern look. I then decided to get her mind off things and began to tell her about the English couple that had come into my shop. She listened intently, and those glistening eyes of hers expressed delight when I told her that the couple had bought the quilt on the rocker.

"It's time for your medicine," Korine announced as she joined us. She said to me, "It makes her a bit drowsy, so you may want to cut your visit short."

"Well, I need to go anyway and check on Kitty's guest house before I go home," I responded. I then turned to Carrie Mae and said with an impish smile, "The Dinner Detectives need to get together, so get ready for us to invade you, Mrs. Wilson."

Carrie Mae half-grinned. She reached for her pen with her left hand and managed to draw a heart.

I smiled and nodded.

She then blew me another kiss.

"I love you, Carrie Mae," I said, blinking back tears. "I'll see you tomorrow."

I went down the stairs, and with each step, more tears began to flow. Korine followed me and gave me a hug.

"It's so hard to see her this way," I whispered.

"I know, but we have to have hope for her complete recovery," Korine insisted. "The Lord will help her through this. I just know."

"Thanks, Korine. God has sent you here for a purpose."

Then off I went, sniffling still, hoping not to run into anyone on my way to the guest house. When I arrived at the house, a couple was on the porch looking in a window. They looked shocked when I opened the gate and joined them.

"Are you the owner?" the man asked.

"No, I'm the housekeeper while the owner is gone," I explained.

"We were told that the building is for sale," the woman said. "Will you show us inside?"

"No, I'm afraid I can't do that without the owner's permission," I responded. "But as you can see from looking in the window, there is only one room besides the bathroom."

"One room?" the woman repeated.

"Yes."

"Honey, that will never do," she complained to her husband. "Thanks anyway."

"Are you looking for something for sale in the area?" I asked, curious.

"My wife would like to open a bed and breakfast out here, but in my opinion, there are too many to begin with."

I sensed that it was going to be a losing battle to continue the discussion, so I said goodbye and excused myself. I went inside and adjusted the temperature on the thermostat. There was something different in the room, but I couldn't put my finger on it. I unlocked the back door and checked everything. All was well and secure there. I finally went out the front door and was pleased to see that the flowers had been watered.

Chapter 94

The next morning before I opened the shop, I called Gracie to see if I could come in early to buy some floss and fabric. Since she lived in the same building as her shop, I hoped she wouldn't mind.

"Sure, come on ahead," she responded. "Just please make time for a cup of coffee."

"Great. I will. I just need to make myself presentable."

I was excited to tell Gracie about my new library block for the wine country quilt. I was hoping she would give me some helpful ideas. When I arrived and walked in, I was shocked to see that Gracie had a new haircut. It was very short. "Hey! I see that you've gotten a new hairstyle since I saw you last."

"Do you like it? I'm not sure that I do. When I look in the mirror, I wonder who she is!" she chuckled.

"What brought on the change? You always did so many unique styles with your long hair."

"Actually, Anthony suggested that this style would be better for me. Maybe he's right. Maybe I was in a rut."

"So he likes it now?"

"Seems to."

I couldn't help but wonder about someone making such a bold suggestion about someone else's choice of hairstyles.

"Coffee?" Gracie offered.

"Sure!"

"Mom made some banana bread yesterday. Would you like a slice?"

"Absolutely. I remember her banana bread. She's quite the baker."

I then told Gracie about my next block for the wine country quilt. She loved the idea and thought there was a sketch of the library on one of their brochures. She made some suggestions as to how I should position the names and told me to stitch the writing with one strand of floss and use two strands for the rest of the block. It was great having her undivided attention. As she refilled my coffee cup, she brought up Marc.

I shared, "He just turned sixty, so there was a grand party in his honor that his sister Meg planned for him."

"How nice! I take it that all is well?"

"To my knowledge, Gracie, but as in any relationship, I don't think anyone should take anything for granted. I think one has to recalculate every now and then."

She laughed quietly. "Recalculate is the perfect word for it. I couldn't agree more."

"Are you recalculating?" I asked.

She blushed and then said, "I am. Anthony is wonderful, charming, and sexy, but he's not a person I would think of settling down with. After my affair, it was nice to know that I could be attractive to someone like Anthony, but now that

I've spent time with him, I see some controlling habits that I saw in my previous relationship. I simply don't want that in my life."

"You mean like him influencing you to cut your hair?"

"Yes, like cutting my hair. What was I thinking?" She touched her hair and laughed shyly.

"That's a very personal suggestion for someone to make, I agree. I once dated someone in high school who said he'd want to marry someone just like me, except that he'd want me to lose a little weight, to work harder, and to go boating more often."

Gracie almost choked on her mouthful of coffee.

I continued, "I honestly don't think he realized how obvious it was that he didn't want me at all! Thank goodness I was smart enough to see it."

"Good for you!"

"So, have you told Anthony how you feel?" I asked.

"Not exactly, but I will. Recently, I've been giving him questioning looks when he's being controlling. I think he knows that I'm not pleased when that happens. He won't be surprised when we do talk about my feelings."

"I think there's something about Italians that make them feel they need to be macho and Mr. Romantic at the same time."

She giggled and nodded. "I think you're right. I think his father was that way, too. I'll admit that some of it is sexy and mysterious. You don't meet someone like that every day."

"I know. I felt the same way when I met him. He has a kind of power—something that just comes over you."

"I'm so glad to hear you say that, because I know you like him very much."

"Oh, Gracie, I'm not the one dating him. You are. He's knowledgeable about so many things that I'm interested in, like wine. However, we were never a couple. You're a smart woman, so you'll know how to handle it when the time comes."

Time had gotten away from me, but it was always good to visit with Gracie. I finished my purchase, and she made sure that I left with some extra banana bread. I then made my way back to the shop, put the rocker on the porch, and placed a scrappy Six-Point Star quilt on the back of it. I was hoping it would bring me luck like I'd had with the English couple. I took time to water the flowers in the front yard and reminded myself that I would be seeing Marc the next day. Had I made any decisions about what I would say or do?

Chapter 95

Marc was on my mind when I woke up the next morning. Was he missing me as much as I was missing him? I hadn't been awake for very long when my cell rang. It was Lynn, who was not an early riser.

"Good morning," she greeted me.

"The same to you! What's on your mind this early in the morning?"

"I've got a big day planned. I have a sale this weekend, so I'm getting an early start."

"Good luck! Is there anything I would want?"

She chuckled. "Well, perhaps, because you do have a birthday coming up, which is why I'm calling."

"Let's hear it!"

"Since you're not going to Fish Creek this year to celebrate with Laurie, why don't you come to our house for a nice dinner? Carl wants to boil lobster, which will be fun. I know you would like that, and if you want to invite Marc, that's fine too."

"How sweet! Lobster would be awesome!"

"Actually, we've wanted to do that all summer, so we're

using you as an excuse to do it."

I laughed. "Sure! It sounds delightful," I said, then added, "I'm seeing Marc tonight after work."

"I see. That will help you decide whether you want to include him in your birthday dinner. Lily, I hate to remind you, but he has become family."

I sighed. "No promises, Lynn. A relationship takes two people. I'll be interested in what he has to say since our little separation."

"Okay. We'll have your birthday celebration at our house on June seventeenth."

"I can't wait! Thanks so much!"

Lynn was a dear. For being the middle sister, she held her own as a strong, creative woman. It was sweet of Carl to think of me and suggest his lobster dinner plan to celebrate my birthday.

The temperature was supposed to get into the high nineties. It would surely impact the foot traffic for the day. I turned down the air conditioning and heard someone enter the front door.

"Good morning! Are you Lily?" a young girl asked.

"Yes. How can I help you?"

"My name is Kandi Ross, and I'm looking for a part-time job. A couple of shop owners suggested that I might talk to you."

"Kandi, I wish I could give you a positive response, but I really don't need anyone right now. As you may know, the business here is seasonal and is very affected by the weather."

She nodded. "Yes, Karen at The Cranberry Cottage said the same thing."

"Tell me a little about yourself," I said, just to be polite.

"I live in Defiance. I'll be leaving for college this fall, and I need to make some money."

"What are you going to major in?"

"Journalism. I love to write. I was the editor of our school newspaper last year and even journaled through my grade school years."

I smiled. "I also love to write. I was an editor for Dexter Publishing until I moved to Augusta."

"Really? That's cool! I dream of having my own publishing company one day. I want to be the one who decides what's being written. I had a taste of that with our school newspaper."

"My advice is to keep writing and focus on your goals. Write your contact information on this paper. If anything changes here, I'll give you a call. I'm curious; have you had any retail experience?"

"Just at the local Dairy Queen, where I worked one summer in high school."

"I see you that you drove here, so do you have your own car?"

"Yes. It's not much, but when my brother went off to school, I got his car."

"That's helpful. By the way, do you like quilts?" I was hoping she would know what I meant.

"I grew up with quilts and have a favorite that I'll take to college with me. It's pretty worn, but my Grandma Ross made it for me, and I love it. I was only nine years old when she passed, but she had put my name on this quilt. I'll cherish it forever."

"That's lovely. I'm so glad you stopped by." Just as Kandi was about to leave, Ted walked in. "Hey," I said. "Ted, this is Kandi Ross. I don't suppose the two of you know each other, do you?"

They looked at one another and both seemed embarrassed.

"No, we really don't," Ted said.

Chapter 96

"Ted does my yard work, some painting, and of course some snow shoveling," I explained.

"And whatever else," he teased.

I nodded and laughed in agreement.

"That's cool," Kandi responded. She turned to Ted and said, "I came in here looking for work. You're lucky to have something. You almost have to go into the city now to get work during the summer."

"Lily is a cool boss," Ted said, smiling shyly at Kandi. "Hey, Lily, since Korine is working for Carrie Mae, don't you need someone to clean for you and do odd jobs like she did?"

Kandi looked at me with hope. "I can clean!" she said. "I do windows, too! My grandma taught me that!"

"That's good to know, Kandi," I said, smiling. "I'll call you if there's something I need."

"That's all I ask," Kandi said. Then she smiled at Ted and said, "I need to be going now."

"Nice to meet you, Kandi."

I noticed that Ted suddenly sounded like a gentleman

and not a young man. When Kandi left, I grinned at Ted. "Look at you! She's pretty cute, isn't she?"

He smiled shyly. "I think you should hire her."

"I do have her phone number if you need it," I teased. "So, what's on your mind today?"

"I wanted to tell you that I can't mow your lawn this week. Grandma wants me to so some things for Carrie Mae. Is that okay?"

"Of course. Is there anything new with her progress that you know of?"

He shook his head. "Grandma is doing everything she can to help her. I think it's getting her down, if you ask me. I came into the kitchen this morning and saw her crying. She wouldn't say why, so I just gave her a hug."

"That was the best thing that you could do. She's worried to death about the possibility of her best friend leaving her."

"Okay, so I guess I will take Kandi's phone number, if you don't mind," he said with a twinkle in his eyes.

I laughed. "Not at all! She is a sweet and intelligent person." Ted left with Kandi's number. Perhaps she would be a good influence on him. He was still waffling about registering for college, while Kandi had already set her goals.

The remainder of the day was full of customers who just wanted to look. Many walked in and then walked out. One young couple did purchase an antique stepstool for their kitchen. I was grateful for the sale.

I closed at four to go upstairs and get ready for my big date with Marc. The weather might be chilly later, so I'd need to bring a wrap of some kind. I had many wraps—both prints and solid colors. I needed to look summery while I could. I decided to wear my hair up again. I'd worn a similar style to Marc's birthday party, but he hadn't noticed.

I called Carrie Mae's store, and Korine answered. She reported that the visiting nurse had been there but reported nothing different. I didn't want to think about it all right then.

I took one quick look in the mirror and then gave myself a splash of perfume. I never seemed to think about wearing it, but Laurie had thought that this scent suited me. I went downstairs and checked my phone in case Marc had sent me a text. Hopefully he hadn't forgotten. I checked my emails, and then five o'clock came and went. This was not good. At ten after five, I started to pace, thinking of all the reasons Marc could be late. At twenty minutes after five, he pulled up in front of my place. I took a deep breath, promising myself that I would not mention the time. I answered the door, and there was the smiling face that I had missed.

"Sorry I'm late, Lily," he said. "I'm afraid I got caught in the Friday night rush."

"It's okay. Do you want to come in, or shall we leave?"

"I made reservations at the Montelle Winery. I hope that suits you. They have music tonight, I believe."

"It sounds great. They have such a splendid view, and it's still light out."

"Let's get started! You look great, by the way."

I smiled. The compliment was nice, but this was the first time that Marc had not greeted me with a kiss. Had that been on purpose? The ride to Montelle consisted of small talk, and I felt a bit awkward. Hopefully, after we'd had a glass of wine, things would loosen up between us.

Chapter 97

"This is a fabulous place with a view in every direction," Marc mentioned as the waiter took us to our table. Once we were seated, he exclaimed, "Oh, this spot is great!" Then he asked, "Are you okay with the temperature out here?"

I nodded. Without hesitation, Marc ordered a bottle of merlot that I'd never heard him mention before.

"I think you'll like this, Lily," he said. "If you don't, we'll try something else."

"I'm sure it will be fine."

"So, have you been catching the Cardinals lately?" he asked out of the blue.

"You haven't mentioned the Cardinals lately. I haven't been watching much, but every day, I check the standings. I'm pleased that they're doing well lately."

"It's about time. They sure started the year poorly. We should go to a game soon. Would you like that?"

"Sure." Why did I feel like I was on a first date with him?

"I had a drink with Carl recently. Did Lynn tell you?"

"She did."

There was silence.

"She's having a sale at her gallery this weekend," I shared.

"Really? I've never known her to do that."

"She says that summer is a slow time for her," I explained.

The wine was served, and I really liked it. Marc knew me pretty well, actually. I asked the name of it. He said it was a California wine called Red Bliss. I smiled at the name and told him that he had chosen well.

The special for the evening was a filet and lobster combo with a fancy name. Marc jumped at the suggestion, so I ordered it as well. The lobster made me think of the lobster dinner Carl was planning. Should I ask Marc to go or not?

"Did Meg make it home okay?" I asked, hoping to generate a conversation about the party. "It was nice of her to come out and see me before she left. I take it that her visit to me was your idea."

He smiled slowly and looked down. "She wanted to do it. I thought it wouldn't hurt. We felt pretty lousy about you leaving."

"I felt lousy about leaving as well." He seemed shocked by my directness. I continued by saying, "I don't regret leaving. You had your hands full. There was a great turnout, and Meg did a wonderful job with it all."

Marc looked crestfallen. "I don't know what else to say other than that I screwed up."

"You were quite taken with it all, in other words."

"I suppose. I'd never been in a situation like that before. By the way, I can't believe you gave me such a generous gift. I don't deserve it."

"I'm glad you like it. Let's drop the topic of the party and move on. Your apology is accepted. I'm really not that needy,

Marc, but it did hurt my feelings."

He touched my hand and was about to say something when the waiter placed our dinner in front of us. Marc kept looking into my eyes.

I looked at the food. "This looks wonderful!"

"You are wonderful. I love you, Lily."

I'd wanted to hear those words so badly. I looked up from my plate and met his gaze. "I love you, too, Marc," I said softly.

Suddenly, nothing felt rushed or uncomfortable anymore. It was just the two of us in this warm and satisfying moment. When we did begin to eat, the food tasted better than I'd ever imagined. I suddenly felt very hungry and happy. Perhaps it was the wine, but God had answered my prayer for forgiveness and had provided a pleasant evening with Marc.

The music wasn't so loud that that it drowned out our conversation. Marc asked if I wanted to dance, but as we got up, the music stopped. Marc already had his arm around me and suggested that we dance anyway. I embraced him instead. The music didn't start up right away, so we sat down.

"So, dear Lily," he started, "You have a birthday coming up soon. What would please you?"

I chuckled at his formal approach. "Actually, there is something," I replied.

"Anything sweetheart, anything," he said, smiling.

"You can be my date for a lobster dinner that Carl and Lynn are giving me for my birthday."

He looked shocked but interested. "You aren't kidding, are you?"

"No. Since I'm not going to Fish Creek this year to celebrate with Laurie, they offered to prepare dinner for me."

"It's your first birthday without Laurie, right?"

"Right, and it won't be the last time this happens, I'm sure."

"I'd be honored to be your date," he finally answered.

"Was it the lobster that convinced you?"

He laughed. "Lobster and your birthday are both pretty irresistible," he said, giving me a wink.

Chapter 98

The rest of the evening was nearly perfect. There was no question that Marc and I needed to reacquaint ourselves with one another. Perhaps that was normal in a relationship after a while. We were lucky that neither of us were making any additional demands on the other. Marc ended up staying in Augusta for the night, and to my surprise, he was in no hurry to leave the next morning. He suggested that we go to Kate's Coffee to get some breakfast. I agreed. We decided to walk, and the heat of the day was already upon us. It was interesting watching others watch us. Were they wondering if Marc had spent the night, or would they think that he had just arrived? It was a small town, and people seemed to be interested in everyone else's business.

"Well, good morning!" Randal greeted us as we entered the coffee shop. "Marc, isn't it?"

Marc nodded.

"I met you at Karen and Buzz's New Year's Eve party," Randal said.

"Right!" Marc replied. "Why does that seem so long ago?"

"Because it was freezing cold then, remember?" I reminded him. "Randal, we're going to have breakfast. What would you recommend?"

"Today, we have bacon and spinach quiche and fresh blueberry muffins right out of the oven."

"I'll have both!" Marc said quickly.

"I'll just have the muffin," I answered. "I'm still full after that marvelous dinner we had last night."

We walked to the back room of the café, where Ruth Ann and Vic were just leaving. We said hello and chatted a bit about Carrie Mae and Snowshoes before they left. Marc and I sat down at their table, and Marge was quick to clear it off.

"Are you going to see Carrie Mae today?" she asked before she went back to the kitchen.

"Yes, but I'm not sure when," I replied.

"I'm so worried about her," Marge said, shaking her head. "Will you take her some blueberry muffins from us?"

"Sure! I know she'll love them," I answered.

"They're one of her favorites, and I thought of her as I made them," Marge said.

"Everyone knows and looks out for one another here, don't they?" Marc asked.

"They do. I learned that very quickly when I moved out here," I said. As we ate our breakfast, other familiar faces came and went. I acknowledged some and not others. There was that small town feel here that Marc was largely unaccustomed to.

"You'll let Lynn know that I'll be coming to dinner, won't you?" Marc asked when he was finished eating. "Do you want me to get you, or do you want to drive in?"

"I think I'll play it safe and meet you there."

He chuckled and shook his head. We needed to get back

to work, so we reluctantly said goodbye to Randal and Marge. We took our time walking back to my place. Had Carrie Mae been in her shop and in good health, we would have stopped to say hello to her. Our farewell was said on the porch before I went inside. We held each other as if we wanted to hold onto the moment as long as we could. I waved as Marc drove off. God had lined up the moon and the stars just right for us to be together again.

As I began my day, I knew I had the weekend to look forward to. Lynn's dinner would be the perfect way to spend my birthday. After I put Rosie's rocker on the porch, I checked for any emails on my laptop.

Loretta's email stated that she thought Sarah and Lance were getting serious. She added that Lucy had become quite fond of Lance, which made everyone happy. Ellen said she loved volunteering at the quilt museum. She was especially thrilled that she got to assist in putting up a new exhibit. She marveled at how much work and planning went into it. She ended by saying she hoped she would be seeing all of us soon. Laurie hadn't written anything. I hoped she wasn't pouting since I wasn't coming to see her for our birthdays. I made a short comment about Carrie Mae's condition and said that Marc and I had enjoyed a wonderful dinner at Montelle Winery. I ended by saying that I was happy for Sarah and looked forward to meeting Lance someday.

I was then interrupted by four girls entering the shop together. They got my attention immediately. They were very chatty, but I managed to get in a hello.

"We love quilts!" one of them said as she looked around the shop.

Chapter 99

"Most of the quilts are in this room," I said, indicating where the quilt room was located. "I'll be happy to help you."

The girls scattered about, grabbing and unfolding seemingly every quilt they touched. The comments ranged from good to bad.

"Oh, look here!" one of them called out when she saw the cabinet full of folded quilts. "I want to see those!"

"They're pretty pricey, but if you want, I'll get the key." I knew I shouldn't have made the offer. As soon as I unlocked the cabinet, the girls each want to grab a quilt.

"I'd prefer that you look at these one at a time," I stated firmly. "They have to be handled very carefully. Just tell me which ones you want to see opened, and I'll be happy to show them to you."

"That one!" one girl shouted as she pointed to a red-and-green President's Wreath.

"I want that third one down," another requested.

"I want to see the one underneath that one," another said.

"One at a time, ladies," I reminded them. "I'll read the

tag, which will give you the name, size, and price. Is that okay?" There wasn't a response, so I started with the first request. The others quickly became impatient.

"This is the President's Wreath. It is eighty-eight inches by ninety-two inches, and the price is eight thousand five hundred dollars."

Their mouths dropped open.

"This one is probably one of the least expensive, so should I keep going?"

"Nah, not on my account," one girl said quickly.

"That's ridiculous," another said. "How can that be? You actually sell quilts that cost that much?"

"Not often, but collectors know what they want and will pay the price," I explained.

"What a ripoff," one of the girls said, walking away.

"We'll pass, but thanks anyway," another girl was kind enough to say.

"This Snail's Trail here on this chair is a great pattern, but it's so worn!" one said. "I like the price."

"Forget it," another said, sounding frustrated. "I think we pass another place that has quilts on the way home."

As soon as I got the quilts back in place, I locked the cabinet. I then followed the girls to the door. None of them seemed very happy. "Come back again!" I said with my fingers crossed. I was so glad to see them go! I watched them make their way to their car. I was frustrated that I hadn't made a sale between four customers, but it hadn't happened. I sometimes wondered if having such a large price range of quilts hurt or helped my sales.

I poured myself some iced tea before I went back to the quilt room to refold the quilts the girls had unfolded. Why did some people think they had a right to mistreat items that were for sale? When I shopped and unfolded a shirt, I always tried to put it back the best I could.

I rearranged some of the quilts and was once again reminded of the missing crazy quilt. There had to be an explanation. Had it been a mistake to not report it to the authorities when it had happened? How long had it been missing before I'd discovered it? The more time that passed, the less I seemed to remember.

"Hello, Lily! Anyone here?" a voice called out.

"Hey, Lisa! How are you?"

"I'm doing well. I'm glad to see that your shop is open. I'm on my way to visit Carrie Mae."

"How nice. Did you call first?"

"No. Should I have?"

"Well, Korine says Carrie Mae doesn't always agree to see visitors. She's very self-conscious about her speech, for example."

"I can understand that. We just go back a long way. I found a new book on teddy bears, and I figured she didn't have it, so I bought it for her."

"How sweet and appropriate. She's likely pretty bored."

"Well, if she doesn't want to see me, I'll leave the book for her anyway."

"Good idea."

"You missed a good party, by the way. There was a handsome man there who asked if you were coming."

"How odd!"

"Karen and Buzz brought a man with them whose name is Anthony Giuliani. You must know him pretty well. He was interesting."

I chuckled. "Boy, this truly is a small town, isn't it?"

Lisa laughed and nodded. "It's interesting that you should say that, because it's a blessing and yet a curse at times. I always try to have a mix of friends in my life. When I was married, our friends were mostly from the city, so now I try to blend the two."

"Does it work?"

"It generally does. Each person I know has such a unique lifestyle. The grass is always greener to everyone. Have you noticed?"

"You're so right."

"I'm going to take a look at your quilts while I'm here. I'm really curious about the collector quilts you just got in."

"Sure! I'd be happy to show them to you. Let me get the key."

What a difference it was to show Lisa the quilts as opposed to the young girls who wanted to be entertained. Lisa knew quilts and loved them, and she had the money to buy these kinds of quilts.

Chapter 100

Lisa immediately spotted a green-and-red star medallion that had a bright cheddar background. The tag called it a Starburst, circ. 1830, made in Pennsylvania. The price was fourteen thousand five hundred dollars. The more of it I showed her, the more she fell in love with it. I reminded her of how risky the color cheddar could be.

"I'm finding that at forty-nine, I like brighter colors now more than ever. The dark quilts of the turn of the century don't do anything for me. I want to hang something 'wowsy' in my foyer that makes a statement."

"Is it on an inside wall?"

She nodded.

"Does it have any direct light coming in from anywhere?"

She thought about it and shook her head. "I know where you're going with this, but I really don't want to put a large painting there. It wouldn't create the warm effect I want."

"This is a knock-yourself-out kind of quilt, that's for sure. I didn't price it, but if you're seriously interested, I can give you a ten-percent discount."

"Sold!"

"Sold?"

"It's a burst of happiness and joy! Does it have a sleeve on it for hanging?"

"If it doesn't, I can sew one on for you while you visit Carrie Mae," I said agreeably.

"Great! I hope you'll take a check."

My heart was beating so rapidly that it scared me! I'd just sold a quilt for over fourteen thousand dollars! Butler would be thrilled, and it might soften the pain of the missing crazy quilt. As soon as Lisa left, I went to my drawer of white and muslin fabrics to find a piece long enough for the sleeve. My plan was to carefully whipstitch a sleeve to the top edge of the quilt. Thinking of stitching on a quilt this valuable made me nervous. I closed the shop so I could work uninterrupted. Having this quilt hang in Lisa's foyer would be great advertising for me. It would certainly be a conversation piece! When I was finished, I opened the shop again and brought out Rosie's rocker. Lisa drove up just a few minutes later.

"How was Carrie Mae?" I inquired.

"There's probably been no change since you last saw her, but she seemed to enjoy my visit. When I asked if she knew about the new teddy bear book, she shook her head. I think it will occupy her for a while."

"That was a great gift, Lisa. I think being normal around her right now is good medicine. She wouldn't want to be an invalid in any way."

"No question!" she agreed. "Is the sleeve on?"

I smiled and nodded. "Do you have someone to hang it?"

"Yes, Andy still comes around and does odd jobs for me like he did on the farm. Here's your check."

"Thanks so much, Lisa."

"You've been a good friend, and I hope the owner of the quilt will be pleased."

"He will indeed!"

Off Lisa went, taking the quilt like it had been an impulse purchase from a department store. God was being very generous to me by sending me some nice sales like that. I couldn't wait to call Butler right away.

"Butler here," he answered.

"It's Lily!" I said, excited.

"It's always a pleasure to hear from you. Are you calling regarding Carrie Mae?"

"No, but she's doing okay right now. I just wanted to tell you that I had the good fortune of selling another one of your quilts."

"Seriously?"

"Yes! I sold the medallion Starburst with the cheddar background."

"Oh, the one from Pennsylvania?"

"Yes. It was just the spectacular look my friend Lisa wanted for her foyer. She's a great gal. I met her through Carrie Mae. Lisa was a customer of hers, and then I bought some quilts from her when she was moving."

"Sounds like it went to the right person."

"Yes. I'd like you to meet her sometime. She's single, rich, and very attractive."

He chuckled. "Lily, Lily, you are something!"

"Will you be coming to see Carrie Mae soon, or shall I mail your check?"

"Hang on to it. I always look for an excuse to come and see you two!"

Chapter 101

A day had passed, and I wanted to check on Carrie Mae before the day's activities picked up speed. I needed to stop at Johann's for some things on my way. I called Korine to tell her I was coming, and she had a bit of good news.

"I'm pleased to say that the speech therapist said Carrie Mae was making good progress! When I brought her breakfast this morning, she even used her right arm just a bit. She'll be as good as new in no time."

"That's great news! You might tell her that I'll be coming by."

I hurried to get on my way. I did a quick lock check on the guest house and then stopped by Johann's. He was pleased to hear that there had been some improvement with Carrie Mae.

"Lily, please take her some of these fresh blackberries I got in. She loves them. I usually tell her when they arrive."

"Sure. That is so sweet. We're all going to spoil her! Now, if I happened to be an ambitious friend, I would bake her something using these."

"Now, Lily, I happen to know that you're a good pie baker."

I chuckled, thinking of Alex's help with making fruit pies one Thanksgiving. "Okay, add some berries to my groceries. I could give it a try. By the way, thanks for keeping Kitty's flowers watered. They look so pretty. Have you heard anything from our traveling friends?"

"No, but they should turn up any day now. You and Judy are doing an excellent job making regular checks."

It was nice that he'd remembered Judy from when she'd checked on the cottage while I was in Paducah. "Thanks for the berries, Johann. I'll tell Carrie Mae that you said hello and that you want her to enjoy them."

I pulled up in front of Carrie Mae's, where it looked as if Korine was busy with customers. Anyone who came to Augusta came to the Uptown Store. It was the cornerstone of the town in some ways.

Korine motioned for me to go on up. As I went up the steps, I called out Carrie Mae's name. She was sitting up in bed, and next to her was a pretty tea set. She then pointed to a small plate that had a cupcake on it with one candle. She smiled and awkwardly said, "Happy Birthday."

"Oh! How sweet! You remembered! My birthday shouldn't be on your mind." I took the plate and pretended to blow out the candle. I told Carrie Mae how much I thought she was improving, and she nodded. I then went on to tell her about Lisa buying the expensive quilt. She put her left hand on her chest and gave it a pat, indicating that she was grateful. She seemed happy for both Butler and me. I told her that Butler would be coming to see her soon. When I showed her the luscious blackberries from Johann, her face really lit up. I was tempted to tell her that I might make a pie, but chose not to in case it didn't turn out well. I stayed longer than I should have, so I didn't get my shop open until after noon.

While I waited for customers to arrive, I opened my laptop to check for emails from my siblings. I decided not to tell them about my big quilt sale. This was our family time, and I wanted to keep it that way on my end. Just like always, many birthday wishes were expressed. Everyone wished they could be at the lobster dinner that Lynn had told them about. Laurie finally acknowledged that we couldn't be together every year. I knew that she had been struggling to come to terms with that recent change.

Sarah sent a separate email with a happy birthday message. She hinted that there may be some exciting news coming from her soon. It sounded like it could be an engagement announcement.

With sparse customer activity and only a few sales, I decided to tackle the blackberry pie before the berries sat too long and got mushy. I would make one for Carrie Mae and one to take to Lynn's for my birthday dinner. Hopefully, I could accomplish successful pie-making without contacting Alex!

Chapter 102

From memory, I put everything out on the counter that I would need. I opened my cookbook to a page that pictured the perfect fruit pie. In no time, I had created the biggest mess from one end of the kitchen to the other! Finally, I got to the part where I filled the pie shells with berries. After that, I got fancy and cut strips of pie dough to arrange across the pie. I even took a photo before they went into the oven. So far, so good.

I stood by the oven window and watched them bake. I wanted to take them out at just the right time. The fruit was bubbling, and the crust was light brown. They looked pretty good. Out came my phone to take another photo. Now I could send something to Alex. It was after eight that evening before I got everything cleaned up. Satisfied, I texted Alex to see if he had received my photos.

. . .**Good job, Lily Crocker. What's the occasion?**

. . .*One is for Carrie Mae and the other is for Lynn.*

. . .None for me?

. . .None!

. . .Cruel!

I had to laugh. The pies looked nice, but goodness knows how they would taste!

I crawled into bed knowing that just in a few hours, I would be a year older. There had been times in my life when I'd felt like I was living in slow motion—like when I'd worked at Dexter Publishing. Living in Augusta, however, sometimes made me feel like I was on a treadmill and never catching up!

I was really looking forward to seeing Marc the next evening. I remembered to check on the Cardinals game so when he'd ask me about it, I would know. He was truly my baseball man.

It wasn't until I was taking a shower the next morning that I remembered it was my birthday. Perhaps I had been trying to forget it. I was sure Laurie was thinking of me. I certainly did find myself thinking about her.

I dressed casually for my shortened workday but knew that I would get dressed up for the lobster dinner later that evening. Of course, I also knew I would be wearing another little black dress with accents of jewelry from Marc.

When I saw Barney coming toward the house, I quickly opened the door.

"I'll bet you're anxious to get your hands on some of these birthday cards," Barney teased.

"I have cards?"

He smiled and handed me some envelopes, saying,

"Happy birthday! I know them when I see them!"

I smiled. "Thanks so much. How is Snowshoes doing?"

"Much better, from what I hear. How is Carrie Mae? Have you heard?"

"Doing better. It sure would be nice for them both to get well."

"It sure would. Well, you have a nice birthday!"

"You have a nice day, too."

I went into the house and opened the cards. I expected them to be from my siblings, but that was not the case. One was from Butler, one was from Karen, and one was from a woman I'd met at Dexter Publishing who shared the same birthday as me.

Later, as I was dusting the shop to kill time, a young woman came into the shop with shopping bags full of things. "Good morning!" I greeted her.

"This sure is a bright little place you have here," she complimented me.

I smiled. "Thanks! It looks like you've been doing some shopping."

"I have, a little, but I'm actually collecting things for the Lion's Club trivia party coming up. Are you familiar with it? It's at the American Legion Hall this year. Do you have anything to donate? It's pretty good advertising, and it's for a great cause."

"Sure. Do you have any suggestions?"

"You have so many pretty things here, but most people just give me a gift certificate. I see that you have a lot of pretty teapots over there!"

"Yes, I got quite a few at an auction recently."

"I love teapots."

"Well, choose one, and I'll donate it."

"Really?"

The woman went over to examine the teapots. She picked some of them up and set them down again, then said, "I love this blue Wedgewood one, but it's very expensive. What if I take the shamrock one for the auction?"

"You may choose either one."

"That's very generous, but let's stick with the shamrock one for your donation, and I'll buy the Wedgewood one. I just love it."

"That works for me!" I said as I happily wrapped them up.

Chapter 103

After a while, Randal and Judy arrived holding a birthday cake. "Happy birthday, Lily Girl," they sang out joyfully.

"What? How did you know?"

"You live in a small town, remember?" Judy laughed. "Marge baked this for you."

"Please thank her for me. Would you like a piece?"

"No, we have to get back to work," Randal replied. "I'll bet there's someone special you can share this with."

"Yeah, like Marc," Judy teased. "See you at class on Monday."

Off they went, wishing me a happy birthday. When I saw that the cake was chocolate, I realized that I didn't need anyone to share it with at all!

Minutes later, Susan and Gracie walked in. "Happy birthday, Lily!" they said in unison.

"Wow, thanks," I responded. "Who told you?"

"A little bird." Susan smiled. "We just brought you a little something to help make your day special."

Gracie handed me a gift bag, and I opened it to see

something red, of course. There was a pack of red fabric, a package of red rickrack, and a package of red buttons. It was a thoughtful selection that made me smile.

"It's from both of us," Gracie said.

"Thank you so much! You know I love seeing red."

They laughed at my silliness.

"So, are you seeing Marc tonight?" Gracie inquired.

"Yes. I've recalculated, and he is still in my life," I laughed.

"Well, enjoy your day. We're off to lunch at Augusta Winery. Do you want to join us?"

"Thanks, but I'll be leaving soon for my sister's house in the city," I explained.

"Sounds like a nice day!" Gracie said as they left.

Having friends drop by had been so nice. On my drive to Lynn's house, I reminded myself of how lucky I was. Even Carrie Mae had arranged to have a cupcake for me. When I arrived at Lynn's house, the first thing I got out of my car was the blackberry pie. She would never believe that I'd made it! When she answered the door and I held it proudly in my hands, her eyes grew wide in disbelief.

"Oh, Lily, you didn't have to bring anything. I ordered a birthday cake from the Missouri Baking Company for dinner."

"That's great, but I baked this for you."

"The pie lady really bakes?" she teased.

"I made two of them—one for you and one for Carrie Mae. Alex couldn't believe it!"

Lynn chuckled. "Come on in. Marc said he would be here around six, so you and I have some time to spend together before the festivities begin."

"Where's our chef?"

"He went out to get a few things at the grocery store. He should be back soon."

"Can I do anything to help? It's so nice of you to go to all of this trouble."

"You just leave the dinner to us. Would you like a drink?"

"That would be wonderful."

"I'm so glad that you decided to invite Marc," Lynn said.

"He seemed pleased to be invited."

Lynn and I always had much to talk about, and before long, she was refilling our drinks.

"Where's Carl?" I asked after a while. "Isn't he the cook for tonight?"

"All he really has to do is boil water for the lobster. I prepared the sides ahead of time."

When it was after six, Lynn nervously checked her watch again. Marc would be here soon, and the table wasn't even set.

"Maybe you'd better call Carl to see what the delay is. Marc will be here anytime," I said.

The doorbell rang, and I stood, expecting that it was Marc who had arrived. I was a bit perplexed at Carl's absence, but perhaps the traffic had gotten bad.

"That's probably him right now," Lynn assured me. "Would you mind answering the door for me while I check on something in the kitchen?"

"Sure," I agreed.

I opened the door, and loud voices yelled, "Surprise!" In front of me stood a crowd of people!

"What's going on?" I asked as my eyes landed on Laurie, who stood directly in front of me. How could this be?

"Happy birthday, Lily!" she said, stepping forward and

giving me a hug. "You weren't going to celebrate without me, were you?"

"Happy birthday, little sister," Loretta greeted me with a big smile on her face. Next to her stood Ellen.

"Oh my gosh! Ellen!" I gushed.

Out of the corner of my eye I saw Marc standing with Carl, enjoying every moment of my big surprise.

Chapter 104

"Lynn, come here!" I shouted. I turned around, and she had tears of joy in her eyes. "Alex! Bill! Richard!" I exclaimed. "This is too much!"

Marc stepped forward and put his arms around me.

"Did you know about this?" I asked Marc.

He nodded and smiled. "There for a while, I wasn't sure I was going to be invited to the party," he confessed.

I laughed, feeling rather sheepish.

"When you gave up on us being together, we had to do something," Laurie explained. "Lynn did everything she could to make this gathering happen, so you need to thank her."

In the back of my mind, I also surmised that Lynn had paid for everything.

"I'm sorry that Sarah and Lucy couldn't come, but Sarah couldn't afford to miss work," Loretta explained.

"Oh, I understand," I replied.

"I'm pleased that your family included me, Lily," Richard said with sincerity. "Alex has introduced me to everyone, and I want to personally thank you for all you've done for the magazine."

"She's pretty special," Alex said as he joined us. "By the way, she's also a good pie baker, Richard. I believe she brought one to share, so I hope to taste it."

I didn't know what to say. I looked at Lynn, who was watching me. "What about dinner?" I asked innocently.

"Don't worry about it. The caterer has just arrived, and we'll have plenty to eat. We're still having lobster, by the way."

"Seriously?" I asked in disbelief.

"I hope you like lobster rolls, because we ordered a lot of them," Lynn said, laughing.

Marc was rubbing his hands together like he couldn't wait. I watched the crowd scatter, but Marc remained by my side. "I think you were truly surprised!" he said with a grin.

"No question. To see Laurie standing at the door was shocking."

"I'm going to help Lynn and Carl with the food. You enjoy yourself!"

"How did you and Bill get off from work?" I asked Loretta as I joined her. Laurie was also nearby.

"It's a short weekend, but it's well worth it," she said. "Laurie flew with us. When we heard that Ellen could join us here, we knew we had to make it happen. We have a couple of days. Carl booked us at a charming hotel near here," Loretta continued. "I can't believe we're having lobster tonight. What a treat!"

The evening began to shape up quickly. Everyone chipped in to assemble the dinner. The buffet table was filled, and there were red-and-white balloons placed at the bar in the den. I heard that Alex had brought them. After the balloons were arranged, he could be found standing behind the bar, helping everyone get drinks.

The array of food was amazing. It appeared that most of the dishes came from The Hill. In the center of the food table was a large cake that said "Love for Laurie and Lily." It had red roses piped over white icing. I was glad that this celebration was for Laurie and me to share together as we always had.

"Lily, I hope you don't mind, but I invited Jenny to join us," Alex confided. "She can't make it until after seven. By the way, I'm anxious to taste that pie."

"I'm so glad you thought to invite her," I answered. "She'll love meeting everyone. It looks like it's going to be quite a party."

Carl tapped his glass to get everyone's attention. "Thank you for coming and making this a great surprise," he began. "Let's all raise our glasses to wish two great sisters, Laurie and Lily, very happy birthdays!"

Everyone stood and raised their glasses. Lynn and Loretta boisterously led everyone in song. Cheers erupted at the completion of the song, and then the crowd headed to the food table. I held back and just watched everyone.

"I'm not going to dig into any of this food unless you join me," Marc said, giving me a warm smile.

"Of course! I'm dying to try the lobster rolls," I replied.

With all the animated conversation throughout the meal, it was hard to really visit with anyone. Lots of photos were taken throughout our time together. I especially liked watching Carl and Lynn and Bill and Loretta enjoying themselves as couples. Marc and I also had a fabulous time together. Jenny arrived in time to eat, and Alex didn't waste any time introducing her to everyone.

Chapter 105

"Happy birthday!" Jenny said, greeting me with a hug. "How lucky you are to have these nice sisters. I envy you."

"I am lucky," I said, suddenly choking up. I swallowed hard and tried to regain my composure. "I'm so glad you could come!"

"Alex is so proud that you made that pie all by yourself!" she teased.

"Just so you know, Jenny, no one has tasted the pie yet," I warned.

We laughed.

Laurie and I cut the cake for everyone. It was delicious. Richard, Alex, and Jenny ate their cake and said they'd be on their way. It was the first sign that the party was coming to an end. True to form, the women gathered to clean things up. Carl turned on the Cardinals game in the den to check the score.

"I didn't tell him to do that," Marc teased. "I hope you'll spend the night at my place, but if not, I'm sure that you and your sisters will have lots to talk about."

"I want to be with you, Marc," I assured him. "I'll be seeing everyone at lunch tomorrow. Lynn has that planned on The Hill for all of us women."

"That's so nice. Just tell me when you're ready to leave. In the meantime, I'll join the fellas who are watching the game."

I smiled, kissed him on the cheek, and joined my sisters in the kitchen. They seemed to be talking all at once. It was a great photo opportunity. It was especially nice to see Ellen interacting with the group. It felt like we had been sharing events like this forever. I thought everyone was delighted to be away from home and in the company of family.

"You'll get your sister gift at lunch tomorrow, Lily," Loretta said, taking charge as always.

"Just having all of you here is the best present ever," I replied. "Where are we going for lunch?"

"The Hill, of course," Lynn answered. "Charlie Gitto's! Nothing but the best for my sisters!"

"I'm so excited," Ellen said, joining in. "Would you believe that I've never been to any of the restaurants on The Hill?"

That got a big reaction from everyone. Lynn had expensive taste because she could afford it, but I worried that she could put the others in a compromising position financially. At around eleven, Marc and I looked at each other. We knew it was time to go. Everyone else was fading as well. It was nice to say goodbye to my sisters knowing that I would see them again the next day.

Marc and I chuckled and relived some of the moments of the party on our way back to his place. When we got settled in his living room, he fixed me an amaretto on the rocks, knowing it was one of my favorite after-dinner drinks.

"I have a couple of things for you," Marc said as he put

two wrapped gifts in front of me. "One is more personal than the other."

"Well, thank you, sweetie!" I responded. I opened the larger package first. It was wrapped in white tissue and felt heavenly. It was a white sweater set. I held it up with total admiration. "This is gorgeous! It feels like cashmere. Is it?"

He nodded.

"I've never owned anything that was cashmere!"

"With fall and winter coming, I thought you might like it."

I gave him a little hug before I began to open the next gift. I opened a lovely box, and inside was a nine-by-twelve-inch piece of stained glass done in the Feathered Star quilt pattern. It was amazing.

"How perfect and beautiful!"

"Did you notice the chain? You can hang it in one of your windows."

"Yes! You spoil me, Marc! How can I ever thank you for all of this?"

"Hmm, let me count the many ways," he teased.

So far, it had been the perfect birthday!

Chapter 106

When I arrived at Lynn's the next day, the ladies were ready to go. Bill and Carl went to play golf, but Marc had to be in court.

"I didn't think Charlie Gitto's was open for lunch," I commented to Lynn.

"Well, they took my reservation, so let's get going!" she replied.

Lynn was nice enough to drive down my former street just for old time's sake. When we saw the Missouri Baking Company, Lynn promised that we would stop on the way home.

"I miss the area so much," I told them.

"I met Jenny last night," Ellen said. "She's really nice and seems to be happy living in that area as well."

"Yeah, what's the deal with Jenny and Alex?" Loretta asked. "I can't see him with anyone but you."

"Loretta!" I scolded.

"That didn't come out right," she said quickly.

When we got to the restaurant, we went from a bright

sunny day to the warm indoor coziness of the Italian décor. We decided to break our five o'clock cocktail rule and have a glass of wine. Our waiter knew he was in for quite a challenge when we took our time to order the wine and then struggled over what else we would order. Loretta insisted that we tell the waiter that we were celebrating two birthdays so we would get a free dessert.

As we were enjoying our dessert, Loretta informed us that lunch for Laurie and me was everyone's treat, but that they had one more gift they wanted us to have. I was overwhelmed. The celebration continued! Loretta handed us each a small wrapped box that appeared to be jewelry.

"You go first, Lily," Laurie insisted.

"Okay, but I need to tell you what Marc gave me," I said.

"Forget Marc!" Loretta said sternly. "This is about us."

I couldn't believe my eyes when I opened the box! It was a sterling silver charm bracelet.

"My goodness!" Laurie exclaimed.

"Ellen deserves the credit for it," Loretta explained. "She knew just the place to get this done."

"Go ahead and check out each charm," Loretta urged.

"There are so many!"

I first noticed the flower charm. It was a single lily bloom. That was me, I presumed. There was a painter's pallet representing Lynn, a quilt representing Ellen, and a flamingo representing Laurie, who had flamingos in her front yard. The last charm was a nurse's head representing Loretta.

"There are charms representing Sarah and Lucy too," Ellen informed me. "Then I had to add a wine bottle charm, just because."

Everyone chuckled.

"How personal and sweet," I said. "I can't thank you enough."

"Neither can I," Laurie said as she opened and admired her own gift.

The waiter had been very patient with us. When Lynn asked him to take a few minutes to explain that this was the restaurant where toasted ravioli was discovered, everyone listened intently.

"I'd never had toasted ravioli until last night at the party," Ellen confessed. "I love them."

More wine was poured for those who were not driving. I, on the other hand, reminded the others that I would be driving back to Augusta very soon. This group knew how to party! We finally left the restaurant and got back to Lynn's around four in the afternoon. I took a deep breath. I was trying to think how I was going to say goodbye to everyone. The sisters gathered in Lynn's kitchen for a group hug. Everyone began to shed a few tears.

"Well, I'm not going home until I taste my sister's pie. How about everyone else?" Loretta asked.

Lynn said she would make coffee. I was getting nervous. My sisters claimed that they were still full from lunch, but everyone seemed to want to have a bite of the pie. Lynn cut tiny slivers of pie, and I watched everyone's faces in nervous anticipation.

Chapter 107

"Oh, sister!" Loretta cried out. "You've got this down! The crust is just right!"

I looked at her in disbelief.

"Try it, Lily. It's delicious," Ellen said with her mouth full of pie.

"Congrats!" Lynn added. "Yum, yum, yum!"

"You are officially a pie girl!" Laurie announced.

I finally took a little bite and paid especially close attention to the crust. It was as good as store-bought, but I still wasn't quite sure that it was really awesome.

"Time for us to hit the road to the airport," Carl ordered as he entered the room.

We didn't want to hear that.

"We'll be there shortly," Lynn responded.

Loretta took my hand, I took Ellen's, Ellen took Laurie's, and Laurie took Lynn's. Lynn reached out for Loretta's hand, and our circle was complete. Loretta led us in prayer, saying, "May God bless and keep the Rosenthal family until we meet again." She looked up and proclaimed, "Love to you all!"

"We love you, too!" everyone affirmed.

When I looked at the others, tears were rolling down their cheeks. I followed them out to the car and tried to be brave as Lynn and I watched Ellen get in her car and the others get in Carl's SUV.

"It's you and me, babe," Lynn said with her arm around me, even though she knew I had to leave as well. I put my things in the car and thanked Lynn for making this weekend happen.

My drive back to Augusta was quite emotional. I kept looking at my bracelet and recalling the memories I'd made over the weekend. When I got to my happy yellow house, I had to return to the life I had created. I brought everything upstairs, then peeked at my mail. I had received a few more birthday cards. I threw myself across the bed, feeling emotionally drained. I was too tired to change clothes. I needed sleep now, no matter the time.

It didn't take long for me to drift off to sleep. I didn't wake up until ten o'clock the next morning. Since it was Sunday, I didn't have to open until noon. I checked my phone and saw that I had missed some text messages.

Loretta and Ellen had sent short messages saying that they had gotten home safely. Alex had sent a simple text asking for details of the remainder of the celebration, like always. His last line said he'd had a great time at the party with the friend of a lifetime. That was sweet.

I got dressed and made coffee. I took it to the front porch and sat in Rosie's rocker, which started to rock. She was with me. I smiled. Then, I couldn't believe my eyes as a pickup truck pulled up in front of the shop. It was Kitty! She was home! She jumped out and ran to me, giving me a big hug.

"Welcome home!" I greeted her. "I can't believe you're here!"

"I should have called, but Ray and I weren't sure when we would actually arrive. I can't thank you enough for keeping an eye on things for us."

"How about some coffee? Can you sit for a few minutes?"

She smiled. "Sure! I feel like we've been gone forever."

We went inside, and I poured her some coffee. We went to the back porch, where we could be comfortable.

"Did you bring back some great stuff to sell?"

"Yes, we did. We need to get the shop back open so we can sell some of it. I even missed the cottage."

"Well, Johann kept the flowers alive. Have you gotten any calls from anyone who may be interested in the cottage?"

Chapter 108

"Not really, but that's okay. I have mixed feelings now about whether to let it go or not."

"Sally is very interested in renting it. I don't think she could afford to buy it."

"Sally? That's interesting."

"You may just want to visit with her. She would love to live here in Augusta," I said.

"I need to clean it and do some painting. I've done nothing in years to update it."

"I love it just the way it is," I said.

"By the way, we heard about Carrie Mae. I'm going to see her this afternoon."

"Good. She keeps improving. Did you know that Snowshoes had a heart attack?"

"No! Is he doing okay? I guess Barney is filling in for him, then."

"He's stable, I hear," I replied.

"And you? Are you still seeing the baseball man?"

I laughed. "Yes, the last time I checked. My siblings came

to the city for my birthday, and he shared all of the festivities with us."

"Well, happy birthday!"

"Thanks! Now, I'll bet the real reason you're here is to pick up that wonderful birthday present that's been waiting here for you."

She smiled, and her expression looked expectant. "I can't believe that Ray really bought it for me. Is it all paid for?"

I nodded. "Let me run upstairs and get it for you." It took me a while to get it. The Baltimore Album quilt was truly a beauty, and no one deserved it more than Kitty.

"Thanks again. I can't believe that it's mine! Have you sold any others?"

"I actually have, believe it or not. It's a good thing I have a few rich friends."

She laughed. "It was hard to return home until I remembered that this quilt was waiting for me. I've never owned a quilt this valuable before. Should I be afraid to use it?"

"Not if you use common sense. Were you planning to put it on the wall or on a bed?"

"I want it in our guest room, which has a four-poster antique bed."

"Sounds nice. Just make sure there won't be any direct light shining on it and keep the room as dark as you can when you're not using it."

"Good advice. I brought back two red-and-white quilts from Lancaster. As a thank you for looking after the cottage, I'm happy to let one of them go to you."

"I can't let you do that. I was glad to keep an eye on the place," I protested.

"I need to get going. Stop by the shop when we finally get it open."

"I'll do that." I gave Kitty a hug, and off she went with one of the prize quilts from Butler's collection. It was a relief to see it gone.

As the day went on, I stitched on my block for the wine country quilt. Quilt class was the next day, and I wanted to have as much done as possible. I would ask each quilter there to sign their name so I could embroider it. After a while, Betty walked in, which always made me happy. She said she had just come back from seeing Carrie Mae.

"That woman is a fighter!" she reported, shaking her head in disbelief.

"That she is. Has her speech improved?"

"I think so. She keeps trying, which is half of it."

I filled Betty in on my wonderful birthday weekend, and she apologized for not remembering.

"Your gift to me was being there for Carrie Mae. Your friendship is so strong and beautiful."

Chapter 109

The next morning, I was more than ready to go to quilt class. I couldn't wait to tell everyone about my next block. I remembered to box up Carrie Mae's blackberry pie so I could drop it off after class. She would be shocked and delighted at the same time. When I arrived at the library, I walked in with Edna and Marilyn. Marilyn was carrying a birthday cake.

"It's Mom's birthday tomorrow. I thought it would be fun to help her celebrate today."

"Happy birthday, Edna!" I said. "I just had a birthday, too!"

Every member of the class showed up, and as soon as we got our coffee, Susan called us to order.

"Thanks go to Marilyn for bringing the cake today," Susan began. "We all wish you many more birthdays to come, Edna!"

"I will be eighty-eight years old tomorrow!" Edna announced proudly.

"You are one remarkable lady," Susan responded. "What's

your secret to getting older?"

"My quilting," Edna said confidently. "Of course, Marilyn keeps me on my toes."

"Okay, ladies, it's time to see your latest block," Susan continued. "Is anyone doing the extra block for the library?" Everyone shook their heads. "I understand," Susan said. "I think what we'll do instead is just display all the blocks here in the library for a while for the public to see during the Harvest Festival. Is that okay with everyone?"

Heads nodded in agreement.

Edna was the first to show her beautiful quilt block, which depicted Augusta's Christmas Walk. The snow scene of Walnut Street was amazing. Some of the others who showed their blocks had not yet completed them. When we started talking about what others were planning, I got to tell them about my library block idea. They gladly signed their names on my block when I passed it around.

"What a great idea, Lily!" Susan said.

"This class has meant so much to me, Susan," I confessed. "Thanks for inviting me. Getting to know each one of you has made my transition here so much more pleasant."

"You're sweet to say that," Susan responded. "You've brought joy and friendship to us as well."

When Heidi shared that her next block would be of the Biker Bar in Defiance, we all got a good chuckle. She felt that the busy curve in Defiance would be recognized by many.

Before we got to enjoy the birthday cake, Susan announced that there would be no class the next week because she would be on vacation.

"That's good," Marilyn responded. "Mom and I have so much gardening and canning to do."

"Actually, it gives us more time to work on our blocks," Heidi noted.

"Edna is going to show her needle-turn appliqué method to those who want to hang around," Susan announced. "Thanks for doing that, Edna. Also, thanks for sharing your German chocolate cake with us."

Edna blushed and smiled.

I sat down at the end of the table with Judy and Heidi and was ready to eat a slice of cake when my cell phone rang.

"Lily, it's Kitty."

"Hi, Kitty. Sorry, I didn't recognize your number."

"Can you do me a favor and come by the cottage sometime today? I'm here doing some cleaning."

"Sure! I'll be leaving quilt class soon and then plan to deliver something to Carrie Mae. Could I come by after that?"

"Oh, I'm sorry to disturb you during your class. Just come by when you can."

"No problem. I'll see you soon!"

"Were you talking to Kitty?" Judy inquired. "Are she and Ray back?"

"Yes, they got back yesterday," I answered.

"Wow! Don't they usually call first?" she asked.

"I thought they would, but their plans changed along the way, I think," I explained. "They had an amazing trip, from what I hear. Kitty's at the cottage today giving it a good cleaning."

"Cleaning?" Judy asked. "Did they find a buyer?"

"No, I think they may be thinking about keeping it," I explained. "I need to get going. See you later!"

Chapter 110

I walked into Carrie Mae's shop with my pie. Korine was busy dusting shelves since there were no customers.

"How is our lady of leisure today?" I joked.

"She's good! She's just had a little visit from Ruth Ann, so I think she's up for visitors. You have a pie in your hand, do you?"

"Remember? I'm the pie lady," I reminded her with a chuckle. "I baked it myself using some of Johann's fresh blackberries. I'm sure she'll share it with you."

"She won't believe it."

I laughed and headed upstairs to find Carrie Mae holding a book with both hands when I knocked at her open door. It appeared that someone had been cleaning the upstairs area since my last visit. "Blackberry pie, Carrie Mae!" I said, holding it proudly.

"Oh, honey, it looks delicious! I'll have Korine make us

some tea."

"Not for me, thanks. I just came from quilt class, where I had birthday cake. Can you believe that Edna is turning eighty-eight tomorrow?"

"Lordy! She's older than I thought!"

"I see you're using your right hand a little bit."

She smiled proudly.

"Now wait until I tell you all about my lobster birthday dinner." It took about half an hour, but Carrie Mae relished every detail as if she were there. When Korine came up to remind her to take some medicine, I decided it was time to go. Carrie Mae gave Korine the pie and told her to help herself.

"Thank you for the pie," Carrie Mae said. "I love you."

I wanted to squeeze her. "Oh, Carrie Mae, I love you, too! You don't know how much you've changed my life for the better."

Her eyes glistened with tears. We hugged each other as if it would be the last time. I was so grateful that God was healing her and making her stronger every day.

I left the store feeling such emotion, but now had to focus on what Kitty had in mind for me to do. I decided to leave my car parked where it was and walk down the hill to the Cottage Guest House. "Hello!" I shouted as I entered the little front yard.

"I'm in here!" Kitty responded.

I had to giggle when I saw her with a scarf wrapped around her head. "Look at you! You look like Rosie the Riveter!"

She laughed. "I thought that, too. One thing leads to another when you start cleaning, and I didn't realize how I had neglected the place."

"So, what can I do for you?"

"Do you know anything about the quilt in this bag? I found it in the closet."

I couldn't believe my eyes. There was Butler's missing crazy quilt! "Oh my goodness! That's the missing quilt that belongs to Butler! I've racked my brain trying to figure out how that quilt had been stolen from me. I keep the cabinet locked all the time."

"So what's it doing here?"

"I have no idea. The only two people who have been inside here have been Judy and me. When I went out of town, Judy checked on your place for me."

"No one else?"

I shook my head. "Did you leave Johann a key since he was watering the flowers?" I asked.

"No. You were the only one with a key."

"I'll check with Judy right away. I can't imagine that she would know anything more about it than I do."

"Well, did you notice anything different when you checked here last time?"

Chapter III

"Each day, things would be essentially the same. When it got too warm, I turned on the air conditioner. I have to say, however, that the last time I was here, something seemed different, but I can't for the life of me tell you what it was. I am so pleased that you're back and have found this. I had no reason to look in your closets!"

We carefully folded the quilt as Kitty gushed over its beauty. I was so thrilled to have the quilt back that it was hard to concentrate on how it got in the cottage.

"If you or Judy didn't put the quilt here, then I have a problem. That would mean that someone else has access to this place."

"I see. Perhaps Johann can give us a clue or two."

"I'll ask him," Kitty said.

"Do you want me to go with you?"

She nodded, so I left the quilt at the cottage as we walked over to Johann's. Johann was about to get in his truck when he saw us walking towards him.

"Welcome back, Kitty!" he greeted her. "It looks like

you're ready to go to work. I just closed the store. Did you need something?"

"Oh, no," Kitty responded. "I wanted to thank you for watering the flowers. I also need to ask you a few questions. Did you see anyone besides Judy and Lily go inside the cottage while I was gone?"

"Can't say that I did," he said, scratching his head. "I saw folks looking at it from the outside every now and then."

"I just had Judy come a couple of times to check while I was out of town," I offered.

"Well, she's been there more than that," he said, sounding certain. "She was just over there last week."

"She was?" I questioned. "Did she go inside?"

He nodded.

Kitty and I looked at each other.

"Thanks, Johann," Kitty said.

We said goodbye and let Johann get on with his evening. My stomach was churning. How had Judy been able to come back and get inside the cottage? Had she had a key made? Why would she do that? I remained silent, trying to process it all. We returned to the cottage and walked inside.

"Are you thinking what I'm thinking?" Kitty asked, giving me an even gaze.

I sat down on the bed. "Why would Judy want to come in here? If she stole the quilt from me, why is it here?" I wondered aloud. "I trusted her with my whole shop!"

"I don't know her as well as you do, but if she's guilty, Randal certainly needs to know."

I nodded in agreement.

"I still can't believe this," I said quietly, feeling completely confounded.

"I'll have the locks changed tomorrow, but I think you need to have a conversation with her," Kitty advised.

"I am so, so sorry, Kitty. I don't know what's going on, but I'll find out. I really feel responsible. I'll go right now and let you know right away what Judy has to say." I took the quilt and walked back to my car, feeling completely bewildered. I drove home, and once inside, couldn't put that quilt in the cabinet fast enough! I wanted to tell Butler right away, but I had to get this straightened out first.

Where was Judy now? I knew that she was off on Mondays because that was how she was able to attend quilt class. I needed to find her. I certainly didn't want to ask her about any of this over the phone. I called the library to make sure she wasn't still there. The volunteer who answered said that everyone from quilt class had departed. Next, I decided to see if Judy was at Kate's Coffee, where she worked part time. I made the call, and when a man's voice answered, I said, "Hey, Randal. It's Lily."

"What's up?"

"Say, is Judy there?"

"Yeah, I think she's in the kitchen shooting the breeze with Marge. I'll get her."

"No, no, I don't want to talk to her. I just wanted to know if she was there. I'll be there shortly, Randal, but I need to talk to her in private. Can we use your office?"

"Well, I guess. This sounds serious. What's up?"

"I'll let you know later. Don't let her leave, okay?"

"Okay."

Chapter 112

I didn't waste a moment. I locked the door and jumped in my car. I also asked God for guidance in this horrible situation. I certainly didn't want to accuse a friend of anything if she turned out to be innocent. Randal said hello when I came in and then went into the kitchen to tell Judy that I was there to see her.

"Hey, Lily," Judy said. "What's up? Did I leave something behind at class?"

"No. I came to check with you about something," I stated.

She looked at Randal and then at me.

"Is there a private place where we can talk?" I asked Randal.

"Just use my office, if you want," he offered.

I thought I saw a concerned look cross Judy's face. When I closed the door, she stared at me.

"What in the world is going on?" she asked quickly.

"I just left Kitty at the guest house, where she found a quilt in a plastic bag in the closet. When you checked on the guest house, did you notice anything that would explain that?"

"No," she said, looking pale.

"When did you stop there last?"

"I don't know. Whenever you were gone," she answered, frowning.

I sighed. "Johann said you've been by there quite frequently. Did you have a key made?"

"No! Why would I do that?" Judy answered quickly.

"To hide a quilt that you took from me, perhaps?"

"You think that I stole a quilt from you?" she asked, her eyes wide as she gave me an even stare.

"Judy, I'm sick about this. How could you steal from me when I trusted you?"

"That is a pretty atrocious accusation from someone I thought was my friend," she shot back.

"Yes, it is! Please tell me that I'm wrong and that you would never do such a thing!"

She turned and looked away.

"Please tell me!" I pleaded.

"Okay, look. I was just borrowing it. I had no intention of keeping it. I planned to return it when I had the opportunity. It's no big deal. You didn't even miss it. You have the quilt back now, so just let it go," Judy said haughtily.

"No big deal! Do you have any idea what I've been going through, not to mention Butler, the owner of the quilt? Do you know how serious this is? I completely trusted you with my business and considered you a friend."

She started to cry.

"Your tears are not going to fix this. I can't believe it!" I opened the door while she cried quietly, and then I called for Randal.

"Hey, what's going on in here?" he asked, entering the room. "We have a couple of customers out there, and they can hear you."

"Judy stole a very expensive quilt from me and hid it at Kitty's cottage," I stated. My voice was trembling.

"Oh, now, Lily!" Randal replied. "Judy, is she making any sense?"

Judy continued crying and then choked out, "Please, Lily, I didn't mean to hurt you. You've got this all wrong. I'm so sorry. I really did want to return it." She was sobbing.

"Judy, look at me," Randal said in a stern tone. "Have you stolen from us?"

"No, no, I would never do that," she claimed. "You all are like family."

"Then why would you steal from me?" I questioned, hearing my own exasperation as I pressed her further.

Judy looked stricken. Then she blurted out, "Because you had such success selling the quilts that I had consigned at your shop before. I don't have a full-time job and I needed the money. I didn't think you would miss one of those quilts since you kept them locked up and didn't count them regularly. I took one to try to sell somewhere else to make a lot of money at once. I knew that if you called the police and told them I had been the only person with access to those quilts besides you, they would search my house. So I decided to put it in the closet of the cottage until I could find a buyer."

My eyes were wide at this point, and I could tell from Randal's expression that he was shocked as well.

Once the words began tumbling out of Judy, they continued. "Then I used the key I had for your shop to sneak in every now and then, disable the alarm system, and turn on the lights in the quilt room. I'd set the alarm again and then leave. I knew that you had talked about your ghosts, and I felt that if you believed Doc or Rosie had taken the quilt, then you wouldn't call the police at all!"

Judy paused and looked from me to Randal, trying to read our expressions. We remained silent.

Judy then took a deep breath and said, "In the end, I kept checking the cottage to see if it was still there, but I couldn't go through with the plan of selling the quilt. I decided to return it to your shop, but then Kitty returned unexpectedly, and I didn't have a chance to put it back with the other quilts."

I could only stare at Judy. I couldn't believe what I had just heard! In disgust, I decided to leave her with Randal. As I was leaving, I could see that Marge had put a closed sign on the door and thought she'd likely overhead the conversation.

"Lily, did she admit it?" Marge asked, following me to the door.

I nodded. "She made a duplicate of the cottage key and hid the quilt there. That quilt is worth over ten thousand dollars! I can't take this lightly."

"My word!" Marge said in shock. "What would make her do such a thing?"

"She said she needed money. I'd better get back to Kitty to see how she wants to handle this."

Chapter 113

Kitty and Ray were relaxing on their front porch when I arrived. Kitty could tell that I was upset. I sat down and started to explain Judy's version of what had happened. They listened intently and didn't interrupt. I could tell that Ray had an opinion that he wanted to express.

"Lily, without question, it's a bizarre situation. I'm sure she'll never work for you again, but try to look at the bigger picture."

"I'm trying!" I replied.

"She did something really foolish," he began. "I doubt if she even thought about how all of it would work out. The good news is that you got your quilt back and it isn't damaged. If you press charges, the story will shed a bad light on Judy, Kate's Coffee, The Cottage Guest House, and Lily Girl's Quilts and Antiques. Is it worth it?"

I paused and shook my head. "I just can't believe she did this to me."

"People just do stupid things, and it's sometimes to the folks they love," he said slowly, as if speaking from experience. "I didn't always have the nicest and most honest people working for me, but I figured that if I gave them a break—depending on the situation, of course—then we both won."

"Ray, I didn't know you were that sort," Kitty teased.

"Thanks, Ray," I responded. I thought for a moment and sighed deeply. "I'm going to take your advice." We chatted for a bit longer before I decided to head back to Kate's Coffee. The door was locked, but Marge saw me and let me in.

"Is Judy still here?" I inquired.

"Yes, she was so upset that I was reluctant to let her go home, so I put her to work in the kitchen. I'll get her."

Judy looked as white as a ghost when she came out to see me. Marge quickly disappeared.

"What did Kitty say?" she asked.

I took a deep breath. "Nothing like this has ever happened to me before," I informed her. "Losing that quilt was upsetting and painful, but even more painful is finding out that my friend betrayed me when I had trusted her personally with my business."

"I know, I know. I can't tell you how bad I feel."

"I'm glad to have the quilt back for Butler's sake." I paused. "I guess we both need to move on and learn from this. I can't really help you. You have to answer to the Almighty on this one."

She looked away and then lowered her head. I didn't give her a chance to respond. I walked out, hoping that I would eventually feel the forgiveness that I had just extended to her. I felt that I had expressed kindness to her, but my feelings of hurt and disappointment would likely remain with me for a while. When I got back to the house, I took a deep breath, hoping I had done the Christian thing.

I really wanted to talk to Carrie Mae, but she didn't need this kind of drama right now. What would I tell Butler? Would he be as forgiving as I had been? I glanced at my phone and saw that I had a text from Alex.

. . .Confession: I said the L-word to Jenny.

. . .WHAT???

. . .I know! I'm hooked!

. . .Seriously?

. . .If we make it until Christmas, yes... I'm giving her a ring!

. . .OMG! I'm so happy for you.

. . .Are you serious or joking?

. . .Alex! I'm NOT joking!

. . .You are the best friend ever. Love you!

I didn't make any further replies to his text. I looked at the exchange between us and blinked. Why was it so difficult to be happy for someone else when you were feeling down? Was I happy for him? Would it change our friendship? I sure didn't want to lose another friend. I felt I needed to talk to someone and thought of Holly, who had been my best friend for the longest time.

"You called me just as I was heading out," she said,

sounding out of breath.

"I just need to talk. Do you have a minute?"

"Sure! I've wanted to call you, too. I have some exciting news."

"What?"

"I'm putting the house up for sale!"

"No! I can't believe it!"

"I'm looking at condos. I'm finally ready for a different lifestyle. There's so much upkeep with this house, and I'm not home much anymore."

"It makes sense, but it's a beautiful house."

"It's a house, not a home. It has too many unhappy memories for me. I thought I could fix it by changing the wallpaper and doing some painting, but it hasn't worked. I'm so excited about my decision. My next home will be my very own place. I have a good realtor, so I'll likely find just the right thing."

"I'm so happy for you."

"I'm sorry for interrupting you. What did you call about?"

I could hear in her voice how happy she was about her decision to move. She had endured years of suffering at the hands of her overbearing husband until he passed. I didn't have the heart to burden her with this recent business with Judy. Instead, I replied, "Oh, nothing, really. Can we have lunch soon? You know—like we used to?"

"I'd love that. I miss our lunches."

"Great! Happy condo hunting. I love you!"

"I love you, too!"

Chapter 114

As the day ended, I had to admit to myself that it was a bit difficult to be happy for Holly when I felt like I had just lost Alex as my best friend. As he got closer to Jenny, our relationship would necessarily change, and that was simply a fact. I made myself remember Ray's words from earlier. I had to look at the bigger picture. The good news was that the missing quilt was no longer missing! There was just one more step to making this nightmare disappear. I needed to call Butler. I took a deep breath.

"Butler, it's Lily! Am I calling too late?"

He laughed at my question. "For someone who rarely sleeps, no."

"Good! I'm calling to tell you that the crazy quilt has been found."

"Was it stolen?"

I paused. "Butler, I regret to tell you that a friend who was filling in for me at the shop took the quilt. In the end, she said she had hoped to return it before I discovered it was missing. That's the nice way of putting it, anyway. I'm still in shock. I'm also feeling a lot of disappointment regarding her actions."

"I see."

"Someone else found the quilt, and not knowing how it had gotten into her possession, had the presence of mind to ask me about it. As we investigated the matter, we traced it back to the person who took it."

"Hmmm," he replied slowly.

"She'd obviously had a huge lapse in judgment, and even worse, I'm embarrassed to tell you that I used poor judgment in allowing her to work in the shop. Honestly, I considered her a trustworthy friend. I had no reason to believe otherwise."

"Being in business isn't easy. We try to use our best judgment to make the best decisions. Remember, I had to swallow a similar disappointment as well when my own nephew stole from me. You must forget the bad and try to remember all the good times."

Hearing his thoughtful response caused me to breathe a sigh of relief. "Thanks for understanding, Butler. You're a wonderful friend."

"Friends forever, I hope," he said softly before we hung up.

Feeling like a weight had been lifted from me, I got on my laptop to see if there had been any word from my siblings. I needed my family, even if I had to open my computer to hear from them.

Laurie had been the first to email. She thanked us for the birthday celebration and said she loved the afghan I had sent her. She said it had been a delightful surprise waiting for her when she'd arrived home. She also declared that the charm bracelet was never coming off, as she truly loved it.

Loretta said that she and Bill had had a marvelous time and that she was so glad they had taken the time to gather with family. I'd been hoping that she would give an update on Sarah and Lance, but perhaps this Christmas would be the time when we'd hear bigger news.

Ellen was delighted to be a part of the festivities and commented about how funny we all were when we got together.

There was no response from Lynn, but I replied that it was the best birthday ever, thanks to her. I thanked everyone once again for the clever charm bracelet. It was the best keepsake ever because it showed how different we all were, and yet that we all came from the same silver ring of the Rosenthal family. I closed the laptop with a smile and felt my contentment returning. My family was home safe and sound, doing what they did in their daily lives. I noticed that I had gotten a text from Karen while I was chatting with my siblings.

. . .The Dinner Detectives will meet at Carrie Mae's on Sunday. Carrie Mae agreed. I'm bringing dinner. Betty will bring drinks. Lily, you bring pie, but leave Doc and Rosie at home. We're meeting at six o'clock sharp.

. . .I'll be there!

I smiled. We were back on track. I could report to the Dinner Detectives that all was well. Doc had been significantly silent since the fire, and Rosie would always be my protector, no matter what. Feeling so much better and wide awake, I decided to write my next article. It was due soon. Still thinking about Judy leaving the quilt at the guest house, I thought I could send a message to my readers about the risks as well as the rewards of leaving a quilt behind. I could call it "The Quilt Left Behind."

I seemed to have been the recipient of many quilts left

behind. I wouldn't have met Jenny if Bertie hadn't left a quilt behind with my name on it. As a result of our new friendship, Alex and Jenny were happily getting to know one another.

Little had Aunt Mary known I would end up owning a quilt she'd left behind. It hadn't been meant for me, I was sure, but I was happy to own something from an aunt that I'd loved.

Giving quilt advice to folks like Marc's friend Bill Larson and the truck driver who was a collector of quilts was part of my purpose. The worn quilt left in the guest house by a visitor had ended up making a young girl very happy. Old fabrics left behind in barn rafters had brought amazing joy to people generations later.

"Perhaps there should be orphanages for unwanted quilts! Quilt owners don't often live up to the inherited responsibilities of properly caring for something that was created with so much love and attention to detail. In reality, some people feel an obligation to deal with quilts left behind and some do not. Quilts left behind should be properly cared for and given the opportunity to be adopted by someone who will cherish them.

"Quilts do not often get mentioned in wills and included in estate plans, but for those who leave quilts behind, there are other ways to let their wishes be known. Nothing would be better than expressing one's desires personally or attaching a note, sewn or pinned to each quilt. Some attach a personal letter to their wills, letting others know how to distribute their quilts. It is a comforting thought to know that one's precious quilts will live on with beloved people when they are left behind. Thanks once again for following 'Living with Lily Girl!'"

I pressed send—and off it went to Richard!

Afterword

For the third time, I have to say goodbye to a series. I will truly miss my friends in Missouri's Wine Country. Lily Rosenthal represented much of who I am as a woman, retailer, writer, appraiser, and collector of red-and-white quilts. She, too, was the youngest of five siblings, and we shared some of the same experiences.

To my friends in Augusta, thank you for giving me personalities like Carrie Mae Wilson, someone I truly admired and respected. I wish she could know how her memory lives on in a novel series. Inspiration—from the beautiful countryside and the great wines produced by the many wineries—was certainly a bonus as I wrote about this exceptional area of the country.

To my dedicated readers, thank you from the bottom of my heart for following me on another journey. I knew you were there, and that always gave me joy and encouragement. I'm counting on you to join me in my next adventure, God willing!

Ann Hazelwood

ANN HAZELWOOD

The Fifth and Final Novel in the
Wine Country Quilts Series

the

QUILT

Left

Behind

A missing quilt
sparks drama in Augusta…

When Lily Rosenthal helps a friend sell some very
expensive quilts, she is determined to keep them
safely under lock and key. When one goes missing, not
even the Dinner Detectives can figure out the culprit.

Dreams come true in surprising ways—and quilts once
left behind become new sources of joy in the fifth and
final novel in the Wine Country Quilts series.

Proudly printed
in the
UNITED
STATES OF
AMERICA

Ann Hazelwood is a former shop owner and native of
St. Charles, Missouri. She adores quilting and is a certified
quilt appraiser. Ann, who is passionate about writing, is also
the author of the 7-book Colebridge Community series and
the 5-book East Perry County series of quilt novels.

AMERICAN QUILTER'S SOCIETY
FICTION SERIES

ISBN: 978-1-68339-119-7

51495

9 781683 391197

AQS #13854   US$14.95